GOPTO

Duane N. Burghard

Copyright © 2015 Duane N. Burghard

All rights reserved.

ISBN: **1514161818**
ISBN-13: **978-1514161814**

First Edition. Version 1.03

This book is dedicated to my loving and wonderful wife, Mara, and to our girls; Taylor, Jordan, Kristina and Alexandra.

AND

To every young man and woman in the United States Armed Forces standing watch tonight, thank you.

CONTENTS

	Acknowledgments	i
	Prologue: SPACEWALK	1
1	UK142356	5
2	IMPACT	14
3	ALONE	26
4	CONTAINMENT	29
5	THANK YOU FOR YOUR COOPERATION	36
6	THE CHAINS OF COMMAND	38
7	OFFBASE	45
8	ROADBLOCK	47
9	BONITO LAKE	51
10	COMPLICATIONS	61
11	FAMILY	64
12	SPECIES 14	68
13	BIOSEC INC.	81
14	B-WING	89
15	CUSTODY	93
16	CONTACT	100
17	EMERGENCE	119
18	POWERPLAY	138

19	THE ASSIGNMENT	145
20	LOADING UP	148
21	HIJACK!	159
22	ON THE ROAD	168
23	KLANNA, HIFE DU NEJA	181
24	HIDING	195
25	WHERE'S THE TRUCK?	201
26	RESCUE	208
27	ONE MORE BLUFF	212
28	RACE TO BONITO	223
29	INTERFERENCE	227
30	REPAIRS	231
31	IT'S ABOUT TIME	238
32	JUMP!	243
33	THAT WAS *NOT* THE SAFETY	253
34	AFTER ACTION REPORT	259
	Epilogue: COME WITH ME	271
	Map of Bonito Lake	279
	BONUS! PREVIEW OF ADA	280
	AUTHOR'S REMARKS	297
	ABOUT THE AUTHOR	302

ACKNOWLEDGMENTS

The first and most important person I have to thank is, not surprisingly, my wife Mara. Mara has been living with me and the characters and stories that inhabit my head for decades. You are reading this book today because she literally forced me to take myself seriously as a writer. I am deeply grateful for her love, support and assistance. Webster defines the word muse as "a source of inspiration." For more than 30 years now, she has been that and much more.

Right behind Mara I need to thank my girls; Taylor, Jordan, Kristina, and Alexandra, for their love and support. Taylor and Jordan deserve a special nod as they were "in house" as I wrote this book and thus had to deal with "crazy Dad" as I faced the challenges of switching careers. Finally, Jordan, who is currently 12 and an aspiring writer herself, deserves extra special recognition. She was one of the first people to go tearing through the final draft of this book and, in that process, found more typos and minor errors than literally every other test reader and editor combined.

Next, I want to thank all of my test readers and editors (the vast majority of whom are family members and/or Facebook friends) as well as other friends and family who encouraged me.

Finally, I need to thank YOU. The truth is that I have always been a writer. For the vast bulk of my life I made my living as a businessman, but writing and telling stories has always been the true calling of my soul. In buying and reading this book, you are making my dream a reality. Thank you

PROLOGUE: SPACEWALK

Time: 1100 Greenwich Mean Time, October 24, 2019
Location: International Space Station

Astronaut Peter Lessing struggled to focus on his mission as he made the final preparations for his first space walk, but he was irritated, frustrated, and tired. Before arriving at the International Space Station (ISS) just three weeks ago, he had trained extensively at NASA's Neutral Buoyancy Laboratory in Houston. He felt well prepared for several, specific missions involving space walks. But not this one.

He remembered the moment when they discovered the problem like it was yesterday. Of course, that was because it *was* yesterday, but as he hadn't slept since that moment, about 28 hours ago (despite having been ordered to do so), for Peter it was just one very long day. The problem began with a diagnostic report on the motor near the Solar Alpha Rotary Joint (SARJ). The SARJ is the mechanism that makes sure the solar panels are facing the sun at the proper angle. The report indicated that the motor was functioning, but it was taking far more power than it should and the solar panels weren't turning properly. Because one of the panels on the other array had been down for months due to a tear, unless the problem was fixed quickly, there might not be enough power to run the station.

Peter was an engineer. His primary mission aboard the ISS involved materials research, including some fascinating work on a polymer based hydrogel. He knew comparatively very little about the power systems on board the ISS, but he knew enough to know that this was a serious problem. He had spent the vast bulk of the last 28 hours pouring over the technical schematics of the SARJ and discussing the various possible causes and solutions with engineers at both Mission Control and Lockheed (several of whom he had woken up in the middle of the night to discuss the issue). He learned that there had been a problem with the other SARJ in 2007. That problem had been caused by metal shavings which had gotten caught in the motor itself. The prevailing opinion was that something similar had happened now, but there was no way to be sure, so Peter asked his ISS crewmate, Cosmonaut Dimitri Rodchenko, to load every tool he could possibly need into the tool bag before the spacewalk.

When the moment came and Peter floated through the airlock for the first time, he was momentarily overwhelmed. He thought that his body and mind had already experienced the maximum possible mix of fear and excitement during a near miss incident with a piece of space junk on his journey up to the ISS. He was wrong. He had heard other astronauts talk about how different and amazing it was to be outside the station, but to actually step out into the vast, black space ... alone ... it was unlike anything that anyone who hadn't done it could imagine.

After taking a moment to acclimate as best he could to the vastness of his environment, he activated the jetpack controls on his suit and rotated around to face the station. As expected, he immediately saw both his tool bag and the tether floating towards and around him. He secured the tool bag to his right hip and began making his away along the station. When he reached the SARJ, he detached the tool bag from his hip. It was still connected to the tether, but it floated next to him so he could get at its contents more easily. He carefully unzipped the bag and reached for the tools he needed to begin removing the thermal covers. The tools were secured to the inside of the bag by strips of Velcro that had been glued to the tools (a measure taken following a costly lesson in 2008 when an entire bag of tools was lost in space). As instructed, Dimitri had packed the bag with pretty much every tool Peter could possibly need, but it wasn't at all organized and Peter had to go hunting for each one. As he looked around for one particular tool, he again found himself feeling stressed and irritated by having such an important job thrust on him so quickly. When he finally found the tool he needed, his annoyance got the better of him and he yanked it free. As the tool came out, the edge of it caught the Velcro of a large, A4 socket wrench and pulled it almost entirely free. There was no sound, of course, and Peter didn't notice.

He began removing the thermal cover. There was more resistance than he anticipated when he pulled on it. His legs swung away from the station and hit the tool bag with more than enough force to dislodge the socket wrench and send it silently flying out into space. Peter felt his feet touch the bag and turned to look, but the tool was already in the shadow of the station. Peter saw nothing and quickly returned his attention to the thermal panel.

The work was exhausting, but panel-by-panel, system-by-system, Peter checked every single possible cause. When he finally made his way to the second Rotary Joint Motor Controller (RJMC #2), the cause of the power drain was immediately obvious (literally a loose wire) and the fix was mercifully very simple. Nearly six hours after venturing out, Peter returned to the space station. He had now been up for about 34 hours straight. He put away his spacesuit and would have inspected and unpacked the tool bag, but he was tired and he knew that the tools would be needed again in just a few days when his first *planned* space walk was scheduled, so he decided to just hang the bag on the bulkhead and go to bed. It would be almost three months before they noticed that the tool was missing, and by then they simply assumed it was somewhere on board the station and would turn up eventually.

But it didn't.

By that night, the A4 socket wrench was silently drifting off into its own orbit, circling the Earth at about 20,000 miles per hour. But unlike the tools that were lost in 2008 (which harmlessly burned up in the atmosphere as they fell to Earth a year later), this wrench was tumbling towards a very different fate.

Peter Lessing was completely unaware of the pivotal role he had just played in altering the course of human history. He strapped himself into his bed and fell asleep almost instantly.

1 UK142356

Time: 1:14 a.m. MDST, March 22, 2025
Location: Project NEO (Near Earth Orbit) Tracking station, Kirtland AFB, Albuquerque, New Mexico

Air Force 2nd Lt. Andy Newton was frustrated and bored. Like many recently commissioned officers, the realities of life in the military were just not mixing well with what his expectations had been. He had only been doing his job for a few months, but already he was feeling disillusioned. He thought about the images from the TV commercials that had helped sell him on the idea of joining ROTC five years ago. He didn't question the noble sentiments he'd had (and still had) about serving his country, but he did feel like he was, at least to some degree, the victim of false advertising.

Andy wasn't a pilot and he didn't go to the Academy. He also wasn't a brain surgeon, lawyer or engineer. He was a smart, reasonably good looking young man in good physical shape, but at the end of the day, the Air Force saw him as just an above average biology major with a minor in English lit from the University of Illinois. And the rather cold, hard reality was that the jobs that he had seen on those TV commercials just didn't go to people like him.

Of course, Andy also knew that there were worse jobs than his, and a LOT of them. Still, he was more than occasionally annoyed that his detailer had made this job sound so interesting and important. "Cutting edge" he had said. "Safeguarding the planet itself," he had said. The reality had turned out to be so different. Andy's job didn't require a fraction of the brainpower he had, or any of the knowledge he'd just spent years of hard work acquiring. It was, in fact, about as brain dead a job as he could imagine. It was frustrating to think that he had suffered through four years of college and then another six months of "specialized" training so that he could basically babysit a radar. He was certain that his job could be done just as effectively by any high school dropout Airman (not surprisingly, the Airmen, dropouts or not, all agreed). If this was the height of intellectual challenge and excitement that the Air Force had to offer him, then it was going to be a very, VERY long four years.

But it wasn't just the job that was annoying Andy at the moment. No one seemed to have any respect for him or what he did either. Many, if not most of the enlisted personnel saw Andy as irrelevant, unnecessary, inexperienced and overpaid. And most of the senior officers were far too busy to answer any questions or help. They would just point him to a desk and expect him to instantly know everything about stuff he'd never done before. And, of course, most importantly, they wanted him to stay quiet and out of their way.

The situation sounded grim when he lined it all up like that, but Andy knew that it really wasn't that bad at all. Unlike several of his friends, his college education had been mostly free. And he had a professional job, a job that wasn't difficult, and one where he was largely ignored and left alone (which absolutely *did* have its advantages). Overall, Andy didn't have much to complain about, but he knew that his talents and abilities were going largely unused where he was and that, eventually, that would be bad for him.

Andy worked for "Project NEO," which is short for "Near Earth Orbit." By the 2020s, mankind was getting serious about space again. The International Space Station had a permanent population of over a dozen people, and construction had finally begun on a new and much larger station. Innovations in rocket technology and changes in regulations were transforming space as well. Any backyard rocket enthusiast with two brain cells and a couple thousand dollars could reach orbit now. As a result, the number of satellites was exploding and, with it, the amount of space junk circling the Earth at high speed. The situation quickly reached a point where it became critically important to catalog and track every piece. Andy had to admit that his job was important in that, if a satellite or spacecraft hit a piece of space junk, the results were usually disastrous and costly.

Project NEO had been part of the Air Force's proposed budget for many years, but it wasn't until a VERY near miss by an Orion space capsule in 2019 that funding was finally approved and the program went online. Most of the command and control systems for the program were centralized at NORAD, but the Air Force initially wanted human beings watching the systems at their various monitoring stations as well. By 2025, however, it had become clear that these jobs were largely unnecessary ... but having them as part of the program increased the budget allocation, so no one in the Air Force really wanted them to go away either. The end result was that the jobs were now delegated (and relegated) to junior officers like Andy.

It was just after 1am on Saturday morning. Andy was on the "midwatch" (midnight to 4:00 a.m.). The midwatch was disproportionately assigned to junior officers, but Andy had quickly learned to not complain because, at night, there was no one else in his building and therefore no one to give him any shit about reading or playing games while he was on watch. "If this job is going to kill half my brain cells," he thought, "at least I can decide how they die." His job was to literally just sit there and watch the computers (which also, for the most part, just sat there). Every now and then, the system he was monitoring would "tag" a target that the computer didn't recognize. The computers at his monitoring station were linked to a central database at NORAD. The database contained all the data they had on every known piece of equipment, debris and space junk in orbit. When the computer tagged a target, an alarm would go off, and the computer monitor at his desk would flash out a bunch of numbers. Andy would then record the data in a log file that went to Project NEO's Master Control Center (also at NORAD). Most of these unknowns would eventually be classified into one of three categories. The first category was unregistered satellites, a problem that was becoming increasingly common. The second and most common category was falling debris, also known as "space junk." The third category was meteorites. In the three months since he'd arrived at Kirtland AFB, Andy had been responsible for helping identify twelve "unknowns", all but one of which eventually fell into the "space junk" category. The remaining item was a class 4 meteorite, which actually turned out to be Earthbound, but by the time it reached the Earth, the largest chunk left was about the size of a baseball, and it splashed down harmlessly in a remote part of the Gulf of Mexico.

Andy had just finished downloading a new Civilization game on his now aging Galaxy x15 phone. He was just about to try it out when the radar's master alarm went off. He was annoyed by the poor timing, but he dutifully tossed the phone on the desk, took his feet down and swung around to look at the screen. He pulled up the logbook app on the computer's screen, noted the time (1:17 a.m.) and began copying down the target number and relative coordinates. But when he looked again at the target data, something impossible happened. The target's descent trajectory and speed had changed. Andy blamed his eyes and/or the software and started copying the numbers again. He looked back. They changed again. "What the hell?" he thought, "that's impossible." Then he frowned. "It's an exercise," he thought, "great." He reached over and picked up the red phone that was connected to Project NEO's Master Control Center at NORAD.

"NORAD NEO Control, this is Major Anderson, go." It was Major Tom Anderson. Andy had met him at the training school for this job. He was a very no nonsense, "AJ squared away" type.

"Yes sir, this is Lieutenant Andrew Newton down at Kirtland," he said, trying to sound more professional than he felt.

"Go ahead Lieutenant," the Major fired back.

"Uhh, sir, I'm having a ... uhh, issue, with a contact. Are we running a surprise exercise this evening?" Andy asked.

Now it was Major Anderson's turn to pause, "Uhhh, I don't think so Mr. Newton, why? Whaddaya got?" he replied. Major Anderson sounded like he was in a reasonably good mood this evening. His tone of voice indicated that he was more perplexed and bemused than annoyed by the call.

"Well sir," Andy replied, "the computer here just tagged a bogey and, well, the inbound coordinates are ... "

"Are what Lieutenant?" Major Anderson was clearly losing patience quickly.

"Well sir," Andy replied, "it appears that the inbound has ... changed trajectory and rate of descent sir ... twice, sir."

Now the Major sounded annoyed. "Well I doubt that Lieutenant," he said dryly, but then seemed to go into his "teacher" mode that Andy remembered from the school. "Buuuut, there are a couple of things that might make it look like that. We'll figure it out, standby." The Major was clearly typing something and there was a pause. "Give me the control number for the bogey please."

"Yes sir, the computer tagged it as UK142356," Andy replied.

"UK142356, roger that, stand by," said the Major as he put Andy on hold. Andy knew the Major didn't believe him, figured he was just some stupid kid who didn't know how to do his job. Several moments passed while Major Anderson pulled up the data on the contact at NORAD. He had access to all sorts of things there that Andy didn't. Andy was sure they'd figure it out in a couple of moments and he could get back to his game. But when the Major took him off hold, his voice was abrupt and, if Andy didn't know better, he would have sworn he sounded, stressed. "Lieutenant Newton," he said, "I have confirmed that you are the proud target of an unannounced exercise this evening."

Andy was relieved. "I thought so sir, thank you. Shall I proceed with path and trajectory analysis?"

"Negative Mr. Newton," replied the Major, "this exercise was actually not intended for you, which is, uhh, why I didn't know about it. It's a computer foul up from here."

"A computer foul up?" Andy thought, "at NORAD?" *That* certainly didn't happen very often. Andy didn't know Major Anderson that well, but a little voice deep in his head was suddenly shouting "bullshit!" Andy ignored the little voice and asked, "Is there anything more you want me to do?"

"Nothing," the Major said flatly. "In fact, to clear the drill, we're going to take control of your computer here and reset things. You should be back up in a few minutes."

Now that was definitely odd, but Andy just said "Great, thank you sir."

The Major hung up. Andy's brow furrowed almost involuntarily. He wanted to go back to playing his game, but something about his conversation with the Major was really bothering him. If it was an exercise, how come the Major didn't know about it at first? "And why would NORAD go to the trouble of taking control of my computer?" he thought. "Why not just have me do it?" *That* was the real problem, wasn't it? Why would a Major offer to do some 2nd Lt's job for him? The whole thing was just too odd. Andy shook his head and let out a slight chuckle as he thought about the irony of the situation. He had *wanted* to ignore it, forget about it and let it go, but now that he had been *told* to do so ... he couldn't.

The more he thought about the situation, the more he found himself becoming genuinely suspicious of what he had just been told. He knew that the "right" thing to do was to just shut up and do what he was told, but *something* wasn't right, and because it wasn't right, Andy felt something he'd never felt about his job before; curiosity.

Andy sometimes felt like the military was almost intentionally trying to drive every bit of intellectual curiosity and independent thought from his mind. But they also said that they didn't want automatons in their officer corps. They said that they wanted creative, critical thinkers who could think outside the box. Andy smiled. For better or worse, he thought, they were about to get what they said they wanted.

He spun around, looked at the computer screen and quickly memorized the coordinates. A moment later, the screen went blank. Andy knew that he would be in *serious* trouble if anyone knew what he was about to do.

Project NEO's tracking system was based on the old phased array radars of the late 20th century (creating a high definition, three dimensional image of the target). The systems were supposed to be inextricably linked to the computers at NORAD, but from his training, Andy knew that wasn't entirely true. In fact, the entire system could be taken offline and placed into a diagnostic, "stand alone" mode. This procedure was used for testing, maintenance, upgrades, that sort of thing. Andy had even performed the procedure once to install a firmware upgrade. While in "stand alone" mode, no data would be recorded or transmitted, but the system could be set up to otherwise function completely normally. There was even a recent copy of the NEO database on the system as a failsafe backup.

Of course, NORAD would be able to see that the station was offline, but the system was designed to ignore short-term outages of data (to allow for Internet hiccups etc.), so if it were only offline for a few minutes, they'd only know if they specifically looked, and even then they'd likely just dismiss it.

Andy knew he had to work fast. The system was still powered down, which would make it far easier to look like he hadn't done anything. He set the timer on his phone to 5 minutes. He went to the network panel and carefully removed the wires connecting his system to the network. He ran across the hall to the utility closet and flipped the breaker for his office, cutting the power. He then went back to his office and switched the NEO system to diagnostic mode. Then he returned to the closet and flipped the breaker back on.

It took the computers a seemingly endless amount of time to come back up (nearly an entire minute). Andy began to sweat. Beep! "Bingo!" Andy said aloud, and he began typing in instructions to manually adjust the tracking system using the coordinate area he had memorized moments before (even if he were just close, he could manually move the radar around). Outside, the giant tracking system responded.

Nothing. Andy adjusted the angle so that it would follow the last known track. Still nothing. He moved it again. "Woot!" The target alarm sounded. There it was! The hair on the back of his neck stood straight up and he sucked air through his nose. "Holy shit," he said. He ran the trajectory analysis program immediately. The response sent chills through his entire body.

"Trajectory analysis indicates controlled approach. Surface Impact Imminent. Alert NORAD ASAP. Code 17." it read.

His heart was now pounding. Andy knew he had only seconds left so he quickly asked the software to compute the approximate impact area. He couldn't believe the answer. "My God," was all he could whisper. He would have sat there in pure shock for who knows how long, but his phone's alarm went off, nearly causing him to jump out of his chair and raising his heart rate still higher. At near panic speed, he raced to perform all the steps he'd just gone through in reverse order. The moment he plugged the network back in, NORAD began receiving data again. He checked the computer. There was no outage alarm. He'd done it! He blew every bit of air from his lungs through his barely open lips.

With the system back to normal, he immediately called up all the logs for his current watch. He stared at the screen. Very slowly and softly he said "wow." All the data related to UK142356 (including every entry he had made) was gone. He slumped back in his chair stared at the screen, and tried hard to absorb what had just happened.

At NORAD, Major Anderson was shouting orders to several people at once. Then he stood up, turned around, and shouted up to the duty officer, "I need General Bradley sir! NEOCON is tracking an inbound bogey; trajectory path indicates controlled Earth impact. I say again *controlled* impact. NEOCON estimates point of impact to be (he turned back to his computer for a moment) ... Jesus, southeast New Mexico sir! I have confirmed that this is NOT a drill sir. I say again this is NOT a drill. Confidence is high. Sir NEOCON recommends executing OPSEC procedure 17 Alpha."

2 IMPACT

Time: Tarful 084559 (12:03 a.m. MDST, March 22, 2025)
Location: High orbit over Linto 1 (Kepler 22b)

Neja smiled to herself as she began wrapping up her final report on the planet below. She was smiling because, even though she wasn't facing him, she could feel that Taynar was already looking at her impatiently. Before joining the Space Exploration Corps several years ago, Neja had been an accomplished biologist on Japella, but she found this work far more interesting and rewarding. In her short time in the Corps, she had already completed dozens of planetary surveys like this one. As planets went, her current subject, Linto 1, was pretty mundane. Its primary inhabitants were impressively hardy (which, of course, they needed to be in order to survive the planet's extreme temperature variations). But they also required a microscope to observe and weren't especially interesting, unless you were someone like Neja.

Taynar was, in fact, staring at the back of Neja's head, but in fairness to him, he was doing it as politely as he could. He was bored out of his mind and getting decidedly anxious to leave and head towards their next destination. He didn't have anything against the study of microscopic critters swimming around in primordial goo. But Taynar wasn't a biologist; he was an anthropologist who specialized in the study of higher intelligence species. To him, mindless swimming amoebas were simply no match for observing intelligent life, and their next stop, Septar 3, was home to one of the most interesting, intelligent species in the known galaxy. The Japel had been watching Septar 3 for just over 50 of the planet's orbits around its star, and the pace at which its dominant species was progressing was staggering. One of the most interesting developments to observe was an impressive, global, digital data communications network ... they called it the Internet. He was very excited to see how they were getting along. He stared over towards Neja again. Finally, she turned and looked back at him. As she saw his face, she smiled a little and shook her head slightly. "He's right," she thought, "this is work I can finish after the jump, we should go." She saved her work in place and began the preparations.

There was a lot less for Taynar to do when preparing for a jump, so he was done significantly before Neja. He suspected that Neja was taking longer than necessary with her preparations because she and the Mortub were mentally "chatting" about her work on the planet below. Their relationship sometimes made Taynar feel a little like an outsider, but it didn't really bother him. In fact, Taynar often thought about the incredible luck that both species had in discovering each other. He also enjoyed talking to Neja from time to time about her connection to the Mortub (male Japel were, in general, often fascinated because, of course, they couldn't bond). It was a little odd to him that his ability to explore the galaxy was entirely dependent on this rather strange relationship between them. Of course, he knew that it was hardly the first time an intelligent species ended up dependent on a technology that it didn't quite understand or control. Heck, the galaxy seemed filled with examples of that sort of thing. In fact, Septar 3 was a perfect example of a species that was rather constantly battling to understand, control or at least come to terms with its own technology.

It took nearly an hour, but finally Neja announced that everything was ready. The calculations were perfect, and the jump, like all others before it in Taynar's life, was flawless. They reappeared in space exactly where they wanted to be: in orbit above Septar 3, the third planet from a rather ordinary yellow star.

Everything went exactly as planned ... for about three seconds ... and then a missing NASA A4 socket wrench, traveling at over 20,000 miles per hour, went tearing through the side of their ship.

There was no warning, no way to know what happened and no time to react. In less than a second, the heat from the friction of the impact had combined with the atmosphere inside the hull to set off the first explosion. The blast progressively ripped through the port engine of the ship, instantly disabling it and tearing part of the ship's outer hull like wet paper. On the bridge there was instant confusion and chaos. For several seconds, events progressed at a pace too rapid for either of them to mentally process what was happening (other than the painfully obvious fact that something had just gone horribly wrong). As with most intelligent beings, Japel brains are equipped with coping mechanisms for sudden threat or disaster, and within seconds both of them began frantically looking at their control panels, trying to determine what was wrong and how to fix it. Sparks were flying, there was smoke, alarms were going off, and suddenly there was a whooshing sound. Oxygen. Absolute horror gripped both of them as they realized what the sound meant. They were in survival mode now, acting on a kind of mental autopilot. Taynar's role completely changed. The ship could continue on without him, but without Neja or the Mortub (whose condition was unknown) they were all certainly dead. He looked at the airlock controls in front of him. They were all offline. He unclipped his safety harness and ran for the passageway leading down to the engine room. When he reached the engine room he went right to the much smaller passageway leading to the port engine. The heat was unbearable and the sound was deafening. He could see that the bulkhead had partially buckled and partially melted, there was no way to seal it from space. Worse, if the heat reached the main engine room, the ship would most likely explode (and even if it didn't actually explode, they'd all be just as dead). Taynar had to think and act quickly. He turned around and looked back up the passageway. There were three emergency doors. Without hesitation, he activated the middle one, cutting himself off from the rest of the ship. Neja heard the emergency door alarm. Taynar's decision would preserve the remaining atmosphere (assuming she could get the several small fires on the bridge under control) but it would cut him off without any oxygen. He would be dead in less than a minute. She shouted for him, but the door had closed. She pulled up the camera for the compartment he was in on one of her displays. "What is he doing?!" she thought, but just as quickly she knew; he was trying to starve the fire. She could see him activating the third emergency door, which would seal him in. "He could have done all of that from the bridge," she thought, but then she looked over at his station and saw only red lights on the panel controlling the emergency doors. As the emergency airlock door on the other side of Taynar closed, he looked up at the camera and began gesturing to Neja. She knew what his plan was immediately. The cold and the vacuum of space was as deadly to the Japel as it was to humans, but like humans, the Japel could also survive a momentary exposure to it, certainly for more time than would be needed to put the fire out. Taynar wasn't trying to sacrifice himself to save the ship. He intended to survive too. All Neja had to do was to close the next door forward, equalize the pressure, open the door to Taynar, he would get through, they could close that door again, repressurize and the main fire would be out and they could try to regain control. Neja looked at her camera and signaled that she understood, but when she looked back at him the panel on the bulkhead exploded in his face, and her screen went black. Neja screamed.

Neja leapt from her station and ran down to the airlock immediately forward of where Taynar was. The panel to control the airlocks on either side of each compartment was in the middle of that compartment. She reached the panel and closed the door. When it sealed, she took a deep breath and then set the compartment to decompress. She felt the air rush out, which made her body feel like a balloon, a balloon under intense pressure. Her eyes ached instantly, her fingers felt like they were going to explode. She activated the airlock that was separating her from Taynar. As the airlock opened the blurring in her vision became worse and she was instantly freezing cold. Her skin felt like there were millions of tiny needles all painfully sticking her at once. She looked down the passageway. Even with blurred vision she could see the charred wreckage of the area. But there was no fire.

Taynar's plan had worked. There was almost no light, and the artificial gravity in the deck plates was beginning to lose cohesion. She spotted Taynar on the deck and moved toward him as quickly as she could. She'd never be able to lift him, she thought, but she could drag him. Her lungs began to burn, and she could feel a very uncomfortable burbling sensation growing in her throat. She knew she would die if she couldn't move faster, but the intense cold of space and the pain from every part of her body was holding her back. Each step was like pushing a boulder uphill.

From the instant of the explosion, Neja and the Mortub were in constant, telepathic contact. Neja was transmitting everything she was seeing, hearing and feeling, and the Mortub was doing all it could to assist her in both solving problems and helping her stay calm and focused. But she didn't need calm right now. Right now, what she needed was courage, strength and raw determination. Throughout their history, Mortubs had rarely needed animal courage, but their collective experiences with the Japel had taught them about the need for such things in the physical world. So, knowing that she was in imminent danger, the Mortub concentrated on helping Neja's body generate the equivalent of a short, extreme burst of adrenaline.

For a moment, Neja's head cleared just enough for her to finish dragging Taynar past the line into the next compartment. She let go of him. Nearly blind and exhausted, she staggered to the panel, set the door to close and the compartment they were in to repressurize. She slumped to the floor and lost consciousness just as she heard the loud rushing sound of oxygen entering the space.

She was only unconscious for a matter or seconds before the sounds of alarms and the smell of the smoke brought her back to reality. As she came to, her body felt like it weighed a thousand pounds, and her head was pounding. As her vision cleared, she looked over to Taynar. Amazingly, it appeared that he might actually still be alive, but he was definitely unconscious and had a serious head wound. The cold of space had flash frozen the blood, coagulating it along the cut in his forehead, but she knew that wouldn't last. She forced herself to stand and walk over to him.

She bent down, slid her arms under his and began dragging him towards the Bridge. The Bridge was equipped with an emergency medical station, including a table that folded down from the bulkhead. With great effort, she got him back to the Bridge and on to the table. She strapped him down to it, slipped an oxygen mask over his mouth and activated the table's control system. She felt a momentary burst of relief when the panel over the table flashed to life. The emergency medical system had a small, independent power supply, but there had been no guarantee until that moment that it wasn't damaged too. Taynar was indeed alive, barely. His pulse was weak and faint, but he had survived. Neja exhaled.

Taynar needed serious medical attention, more than she was capable of giving him. She started to do what she could to seal the now thawing (and seeping) head wound. As she placed a bandage on his head, the ship began shaking. Neja spun her head around to look at her station on the bridge. The main display was flashing a warning; the ship was entering the planet's atmosphere. They were crashing.

Neja dove towards her chair and strapped in. She tried to gain control of the ship's descent, but with one engine destroyed and half the ship's systems either offline or damaged, it was almost impossible. Clearly, whatever they had hit had damaged the main power systems. If the ship had been stable enough to complete even one orbit before entering the atmosphere, Neja probably could have gotten main power back online and perhaps even saved the ship, but not now. And that meant the unthinkable.

Like most advanced, space faring species, the Japel had very serious laws about not interfering with the natural evolution of life on the worlds they observed. The first and most important of those laws included avoiding, at all costs, contact or even detection by the inhabitants of the planet being observed. Neja knew that the dominant species on the planet below was already more than capable of detecting a crashing space ship (in fact, with their shields down, they might have already been detected). Worse, she knew that even if the ship broke apart (and it might not), significant pieces of the ship would survive planetfall. Her thoughts were already way beyond the life and career that she had aspired to only minutes before; all of that was over now, even if they somehow, miraculously survived. Right now, Neja was focused on the incalculable damage they represented to the planet below. And the danger went far beyond what the discovery of their ship would represent to the planet's history and culture. The ship was carrying biological samples from half a dozen planets already. Any one of those samples might end up causing a nearly countless number of biospheric contaminations that could be deadly to some or all of the life on this world. Those samples would have to be destroyed now. Fortunately, her training as a biologist, her own moral code, and her dedication and sense of responsibility to both the world below and the Space Corps were now firmly driving her conscious mind to action. She proceeded without any thought for her research or her work. She called up and immediately executed the command to incinerate the biological samples, but the system controlling the destruct sequence failed. A moment later, the screen went black.

Through Neja, the Mortub was aware of everything going on. But as the events progressed, it began to feel a genuine sense that its life might be about to end. Its reaction was more curiosity and sadness than fear, but without its help to keep her mind under control, a sense of hopelessness and despair suddenly flooded into Neja's consciousness. The Mortub knew that they both needed a reason to hope. They needed a plan, no matter how unlikely it was to succeed.

Neja's mind was now racing faster than at any time in her life. Her training told her that she had very few options left. The final option, to initiate the self-destruct and kill them all, was rapidly becoming the only choice remaining. It was this realization that caused an odd shift in Neja's consciousness. Something inside her, something far deeper than all that training, fought to the surface and argued to survive. The ship might survive a crash landing, she thought, and if it did, and if enough of it were still airtight, and if the main computer could be brought back on line, and if main power could be restored, then she (with the Mortub's help) could initiate a jump from the planet's surface and jump home to the emergency rescue point in orbit around the Japel home world, where there was a chance to be rescued. And even if they couldn't do all that, in theory they could still activate the self-destruct sequence from the ground, and all the planet's residents would find would be evidence of what they would assume was a fallen meteor. Finally, with the bio-samples still in tact, she had an ethical reason to try to stay alive as well (to ensure they were not allowed to contaminate the biosphere of this world).

None of her options were good ones, but Neja was rationalizing now. Ultimately, she decided that she was unwilling to be responsible for the death of either Taynar or her Mortub without exhausting what she felt was every possible chance for life. Her desire to survive overcame her training, so she focused on trying to land the ship.

It wouldn't be easy. She was piloting what was essentially a falling rock. Worse, the outer hull on the port side of the ship was seriously compromised. The intense heat of entering the atmosphere could cause the port engine, or a large section of the ship itself, to simply tear away. If that happened it would destroy what limited aerodynamic stability remained and seal their fate. Neja focused her attention on restoring control to as much of the engines as possible. As the controls for the stabilizers flashed on and offline, the ship would lurch one way and then the other. Each time they came online she tried to orient the ship on its side, keeping the port side away from the most intense heat of entry. For several minutes Neja feared the ship would simply come apart and disintegrate, but she was calmed by the fact that the Mortub continued to insist that it would not (an insistence that was not based on hope but rather on its having built a perfect mathematical model of their situation running it through several tests to determine the most likely set of outcomes). Still, Neja was uncertain. But just as she was about to start the self-destruct sequence, one of the heat sensor alarms went out. And then another. And then another. The Mortub was right. The ship began to shake less. Within moments it became much quieter.

They had made it through entry and were inside the atmosphere. The outer hull temperature began cooling rapidly. In moments, the glow around the ship completely faded. Miraculously, they had made it this far. Now it was all about the landing. Neja knew that this moment of relative calm was going to be brief. As the ship continued to descend, the atmosphere would get progressively thicker and the ride would again get very bumpy. To protect the ship against the loss of both main and auxiliary power, the ship had several small, battery based, emergency power supplies that were located near key systems to provide temporary power. Neja's computer was now using one of those battery backups, but the power remaining was being used up rapidly. Still, she was able to call up the Emergency Landing Navigation System and ask it to chart any potential landing sites. Fortunately the Japel had surveyed this planet many times before, so the computer had detailed data to work with and, within moments, it came back with three options. It was an easy choice. All of the landing options were in a relatively unpopulated, desert region on a landmass that was home to one of the planet's major cultural groups. But one in particular was in a high and even more remote area. It appeared almost completely unpopulated, and most importantly there was a small body of water. The conditions in that area of the planet were cold and extremely dry, which made it especially hostile to both her and the Mortub, but IF they were going to survive the landing and be able to make repairs and attempt a jump, this location was clearly best chance to make that happen ... and if she was wrong, they were dead anyway. She programmed in the landing site and hoped the ship had enough power to make it.

The ship wasn't really designed for "in atmosphere" flight. It had to be capable of it in case of an emergency, but what Neja was having to do now was never considered desirable or, for that matter, likely. As the ship descended, Neja fought to protect the port side of the ship and keep it on course. It wasn't easy. The ship lurched and jerked unpredictably as it sped across the night sky. After one particularly violent bump in the air, Neja's head involuntarily swung enough to catch a view of Taynar on the emergency table. His head was bleeding again, and the panel above him had numerous warnings, but there was nothing she could do about that now. The Mortub was doing everything it could to help keep her calm. When it came to short distance navigation or actually landing the ship under these circumstances, there wasn't anything else it could do anyway.

Neja called up the visual display. They were close to the landing site now. She allowed the ship to roll left slightly and decided it was best to try to land the ship on its belly on the body of water. She could see the lights of several small cities in the area. "It's fortunate that it's the middle of the night," she thought. With no lights on and almost no glow, it was unlikely that anyone would see the ship, and if they did they'd think it was just a meteor.

Finally, she saw it. It was a very small body of water, but if there was enough power left for the retro jets to fire at just the right moment, this might actually work. She reassured herself that she had chosen the right landing site. If they could safely land, she thought, this site surely gave them the best chance of both surviving and remaining undetected. She looked at the screen and asked the Mortub if they could make it. It did the math in less than a second, "yes," it replied.

The last minute seemed to last forever. Neja couldn't move from her station. The navigation of the ship took all of her attention and strength. As she lined the ship up for its "final" and only approach, she continued trading altitude for air speed. She leveled off just as the computer started firing the small landing jets. At least half of them fired, but several didn't. There was no time now to figure out whether or not they had slowed the ship down enough. Their first point of impact *would* be on the water though, just a few feet off the west shore. Neja mentally braced for impact.

Skip! They bounced hard once, and as they rose off the water Neja felt the forward retro jets fire hard. The ship lost a lot of airspeed, and with it a lot of control. There was nothing to do now but hold on. Skip! A second bounce, but much smaller this time. As the ship came down for its third bounce it was clear they weren't going to slow down enough. The ship was going to skid and then smash into a hillside on the southeast shore of the lake, just west of a dam. The next impact would be the last. Neja had just enough time to think that she had made the wrong decision. She had been foolish to hope to survive such a landing. She should have initiated the self-destruct when she had the chance.

The ship slammed violently into the ground on the south shore of the lake. The stress nearly tore the port engine off the ship and the bottom of the hull buckled under the force of the impact. The skin of the ship dug deep into the ground on the shoreline. But none of that mattered. The buckling of the lower hull caused one of the small support rods under the deck plates to sheer off and launch through the deck like a missile. It struck the back of Neja's chair, traveled through it and pierced her body just below her lowest rib on the right side. It went just far enough for Neja to see the other end come out of her chest.

Neja's world went spinning. Sensations of intense heat and cold and panic overwhelmed her. She tried to scream but surprisingly little sound came out of her mouth.

They had landed, but Neja had only moments to live and she knew it. There was no hope now. She looked over at Taynar. He was dead. There was nothing to do but destroy the ship. But what about the Mortub? All of her training told her to destroy the ship and him with them. But her training never included believing anything like this would ever happen, and now that she was in the moment, the totality of the mental, emotional and physical bonds she felt for it were overwhelming. Unlike Taynar, it was still alive. Unlike her, it would survive the crash. In Neja's mind there was a difference between destroying the ship and killing all of them when she thought there was no hope and just flat out killing a survivor. "We're by a lake," she thought. The area was deserted. There was a good chance he might survive until a rescue ship came (she had no way of knowing that the automated distress message was never sent). "I can't kill you," she thought, as tears came to her eyes. She decided to put his life in his hands. She opened the lower port airlock (it was the only one to respond). With her last moments of motor control she forced her hands to the ship's self-destruct sequence. She set it for 15 minutes. That would be time enough for him to get clear if he wanted. "You're free," she thought to him, "go."

"It's alright," she felt it respond. "I will save you," it said.

Neja knew that was impossible, but she felt comforted by his words and focused on opening every door in her mind to him. The Mortub seemed to flood into her mind with a force and power and depth far greater than ever before. She spent her last moments engulfed in a sensation of peace and calm and contentment she had never known before. "Goodbye Gopto," she thought, "I ..." and she was gone.

Moments later, the power unit controlling the self-destruct sequence failed, and the screen went black. There was a manual override switch with its own emergency power source right next to the panel. All she had to do to resume the self-destruct sequence was push the button, but Neja was already dead.

3 ALONE

Time: 1:42 a.m. MDST, March 22, 2025
Location: Bonito Lake, New Mexico (approximately 11 miles Southeast of Carrizozo)

The world was dark, cold and eerily quiet, and for the first time in his life, Gopto was completely alone. He could no longer hear his Twellock (Neja), and knew that meant she was dead. He calculated a 95.7% chance that he too would be dead in a matter of minutes. He knew that allowing himself to be destroyed with the ship was the right thing to do, but Neja had wanted him to live. She would have argued that even the very small chance that a rescue ship might come in time made it worth the effort to try. He knew from her last thoughts that there was a lake just outside the ship. The air on this planet would be very cold and thin, but survival was possible. Trying to survive was what she wanted him to do, and for reasons he couldn't quite explain to himself at that moment, those last wishes were very important to him. Finally, he decided that he also owed it to the Mortub collective to at least attempt to survive so that he could add what was certainly a unique and new experience to their collective consciousness.

Unlike his Japel crewmates, Gopto had survived the crash in relatively good condition. Evolution had placed the Mortubs' giant brains in the center of their bodies, surrounded by several layers of protective fatty tissue. He had sustained one significant laceration to his outer skin, but even that would heal on its own in time. He disconnected himself from the ship's systems, pulled himself free from his safety harnesses (which wasn't difficult as they had been badly damaged during the crash) and proceeded out of the ship. As he scooted down the corridor towards the escape hatch, he reviewed Neja's last moments. Was there something more that he could have or should have done? He had done his best to help her through the confusion and the panic, but the focus on survival and the emergency landing itself, that was all Neja. She had absolutely saved his life. And now she was gone. All that he knew of her was, of course, also part of him, but he was still experiencing something unfamiliar when he thought about the fact that he would never again have a new, living interaction with her. He knew that other Mortubs sometimes experienced this sensation when a joining was permanently broken, but faced with it himself, he was ... confused. He felt a sense of something missing, something lost. "Could this be grief?" he wondered.

As he reached the hatch and slid out of the ship onto the surface of the planet, he was suddenly shocked back into dealing with his own predicament. He was now the sole survivor of a ship that had crash-landed on an alien planet, and he had very little ability to do anything for himself. The surface was cold, hard and uncomfortable, but mostly he felt the cold. It was colder than anything he had ever known. As he made his way out of the ship and onto the surface of this alien world, the rocks he moved over scratched at his outer skin. There was barely enough oxygen outside to keep him alive, but he kept moving, knowing that, in only a few more minutes, the ship would be vaporized. He sensed the water and proceeded towards it. The hard rocky ground continued tearing at his outer skin in a most uncomfortable way. He moved as quickly as he could along the shore of the lake. Every now and then some of his skin would come into contact with the water on the shoreline. It too was colder than anything he had ever experienced, but it was water and he would certainly need it eventually. It was also so shockingly cold that it helped keep him conscious. He sensed some vegetation near him and immediately reached out with a tendril to grab it. He contemplated the risks of eating it. If he ate it and it was poisonous to him, he was dead, but if he didn't eat, he was also dead. He decided that it made sense to try it. It tasted terrible, but it was not poisonous, and it gave him a tiny bit more energy to proceed. He stopped when he determined that he should be far enough from the ship to avoid being caught in the self-destruct wave. "I'll wait here," he thought, "and if a rescue ship doesn't come before I sense that I'm about to lose consciousness or if I sense any aliens, I'll simply enter the water and drown myself in the lake."

The problem, of course, was that Gopto didn't have any experience with losing consciousness, and certainly had no experience with hypoxia. The fact was that he was already losing consciousness and didn't know it … and by the time he did know it, he lacked the strength to move. And so there he sat, on the shore of an icy lake, on a dry, barren, dark, cold world. And he was totally, completely, utterly, alone.

Without help, he would be dead in a matter of hours.

4 CONTAINMENT

Time: 2:12 a.m. MDST, March 22, 2025
Location: NORAD (Inside Cheyenne Mountain) Colorado.

Major Tom Anderson stepped away from the urinal and zipped up his pants. He walked over to the sink to wash his hands and splash his face with water. As he looked at his reflection he thought about the last hour of his life. For the last couple of years and until just an hour ago, working on Project NEO had been a quiet and refreshingly dull job, one that he had hoped would carry him the rest of the way to Lieutenant Colonel without incident. And now, suddenly and without warning, the fate of his entire career was on the line with every single move he was making. If he could make the right moves, say the right things and make the right decisions in the next few hours, his career could be made ... and if he blew it, he could be the Officer In Charge of dogsled maintenance at the radar outpost in Adak by next week. The situation made part of him feel as jacked up and excited as a little boy on Christmas morning. The other part of him was scared out of his mind.

He walked out of the Men's room and quickly towards the MacArthur Briefing Room. As he entered he immediately noticed that the General had not yet arrived. There were several other officers and senior enlisted people present. All of them were gathered around the giant table/display in the center of the room. Everyone in the room knew that Tom was the man under the giant microscope, and they were there to help. The most challenging of circumstances often brought out the very best in people, and Tom was incredibly impressed by the speed at which the people in the room had been able to get a grip on such an incredible situation. These people had earned the right to be at NORAD just as he had; they were *very* good, and they were proving it tonight.

General Mitch Bradley was one of the most competent officers in the entire United States military. Tall, muscular and still rugged looking, he had neither the time nor tolerance for bullshit or incompetence, but he was also known for being genuine, smart, fair and even friendly once he got to know you. He inspired respect and loyalty from everyone who served with him. He entered the room at top speed and managed to loudly say, "As you were" before anyone could even react to his presence. He looked at Tom and said, "OK, let's have it Major, where are we?"

Tom looked down at the table, which was currently displaying a giant map of New Mexico. "Well sir," he began, "we believe the object is at or very near here sir." He pointed to a spot on the map.

"And that is...?" the General asked.

"A place called Bonito Lake, General," Tom continued. "The lake is the main water supply for the city of Alamogordo. There's a dam here, and a water supply system that runs from here, along here down to the city."

General Bradley looked around the room, then looked down and quickly blew air through his nose, smiling and suppressing a half laugh as he considered irony of the situation. "New Mexico," was all he said.

"Yes sir," Tom replied.

The General shook his head slightly, obviously still at least slightly amused, "almost like they're aiming for the damn place."

"Yes sir," Tom replied, and then paused before saying, "it's funny you would use those exact words sir." The General looked at him, clearly waiting for him to elaborate. "Well, because, as it happens, there's a pretty strong possibility that the object *didn't*, in fact, crash into this location but may have actually ... landed ... sir."

The room was silent. Everyone waited for the General's reaction. His face became very serious. "Landed?" he asked.

"Umm, yes sir," Tom said a little nervously. "Sir, obviously we don't know for sure, but just before we lost contact with the object, it appeared to be..."

"It appeared to be what Major?" the General asked somewhat impatiently, "spit it out."

"It appeared to be braking sir," Tom said honestly.

"Braking?" the General said, "you mean..."

"Slowing down," Tom said, "yes sir."

"That means..." the General started.

"Yes sir," Tom agreed, then inhaled, "the data implies that something, or someone, was at least attempting to control the object as it came down."

The room was silent for several seconds. All eyes were on the General. No one knew what he would say. He stared at Tom for several seconds, and then he said, "are we talking about little green men here Major?"

"Well sir," Tom replied carefully, "at this point that theory has been advanced, and frankly we think it should be seriously considered sir."

"I assume everyone in this room has UTS clearance," the General said quickly.

"Yes sir," Tom replied.

The General paused and then sucked in a breath through his nose, exhaled loudly through his lips, tipped his head slightly and said, "You know, one of these days, one of these damn things is gonna set down right in the middle of Times Square or something and we're gonna have a hell of a mess." Then he paused. "Fortunately, that day is not today. All right, well, everyone here has clearance on this topic, so we all know this is pretty uncommon, but we also all know that it has happened before. And if this is what you think it is, that means..."

"That we won't have ultimate jurisdiction or responsibility, yes sir," Tom said.

"OK," said the General, "so where are we with Colonel E.T. and our friends at UNCLE then?"

"Already in the air sir," Tom replied. The General looked at Tom, raised his eyebrow and gave him a look of disbelief. Tom shrugged, "apparently they're that good sir."

The General smiled, "yes ... she is," he said. "How long?"

"They should be onsite in less than two hours General," answered Major Rob Thomas, who was in charge of monitoring the ATC for the operation.

"They're going to land out here sir," Major Thomas continued, "at the Oscura Auxiliary landing field. It was just resurfaced and expanded two years ago and we figure they can get in and out of there without being spotted or drawing any attention to themselves."

"What are we doing to help until they get there?" the General asked. "Where are we with the State Police?"

Captain Beth Jordan spoke up, "they've already been alerted sir, and the National Guard. The State Police are en route and setting up a perimeter as we speak."

"Cover story?" asked the General.

"Top secret intel satellite," answered Lt. Commander Mike Todd, the lone Navy officer in the room. He was the senior Public Affairs officer for NORAD. "We figured it was plausible and would explain all the attention and security we're about to shower on the area."

"And when the Mayor of Alamogordo and/or the Governor of New Mexico call us to ask us about their water supply and what the hell we're doing up there?" the General said.

"I've already spoken to both sir," Commander Todd continued, "I've assured them that we don't believe there's any danger but that as a precaution we must insist on complete control of the area until we recover our equipment."

"They buy it?" the General asked.

"I believe so sir," the Commander replied.

"OK," the General said. He looked back at Tom. "Leak points?"

"Very few potentials that we're aware of sir," Tom replied. He returned everyone's attention to the map by looking down at it and pointing. "The area has a number of campgrounds that are used for recreation in the summer. Fortunately for us, access is seasonal and they're not open now. There is a very small group of people who live down the side of the hill here. We won't know if we have any issues there until we've got boots on the ground, but unless someone was awake and watching, it would be difficult to determine that any impact, if they felt one at all, was anything other than an Earthquake or something like that. Unless someone can visual the actual landing site from where they are, and because of the location we don't think they can ... well, I don't think there's a problem ... but obviously we'll stay on that sir."

"Good," the General said, "others?"

"The inbound was initially tracked by a 2nd Lt down at Kirtland," Tom said, "but we told the kid it was a drill..."

"And?" the General said.

"He seemed to buy it," Tom replied. "We reset his system, deleted the data, I think it's all right."

"OK," said the General, who seemed satisfied with everything he heard. "Good work. Now, just so we're all clear, as soon as the UNCLE people arrive and assume control, this is going to be *their* show and our role switches to supporting them and giving them whatever assistance they require. Is that clear?" Everyone nodded, but no one moved. "Anything else?"

"Yes sir, there is one other thing sir," Tom said slowly and carefully. The General looked at him, waiting. "It's Holloman sir."

"Holloman?" said the General.

"Yes sir," continued Tom. "We lucked out in that the folks at the VLA in New Mexico were doing maintenance tonight, and there's no evidence that they or any other civilian observatory tracked the inbound ... but Holloman did ... and they'll certainly see the UNCLE people on approach to Oscura." Tom paused again.

"And?" the General said.

"And," Tom said nervously, "the base is commanded by General Colin Bradley sir."

"I'm aware that the base is commanded by my brother Major, what's your point?" the General asked pointedly.

Tom felt himself sweat a little. He knew that, at that moment, everyone in the room was glad that they weren't him. "Well sir," Tom said slowly, "your brother is ... well, he's obviously known for ... that is to say..."

"Major," the General said in a slightly exasperated but also understanding tone, "you're never going to make Lieutenant Colonel if you can't look me in the eye and tell me that my brother has a reputation for being a mean spirited, power drunk, loose cannon, asshole."

The room enjoyed a slight round of nervous laughter, but rather than be embarrassed by the General's comment, Tom suddenly felt stronger, smiled, laughed slightly and said, "yes sir, well, the concern is that, he may ... interfere ... sir."

"I see," said the General. "Well, let's see what we can do to keep him ... uninvolved."

"Yes sir," said Tom.

The General looked down, paused and again took a deep breath, then looked up at everyone in the room and said, "OK. As a precaution I'm ordering us up to Defcon 3. Wake up only the people you need to. Thank you everyone, dismissed."

5 THANK YOU FOR YOUR COOPERATION

Time: 1:57 a.m. March 22, 2025
Location: New Mexico State Police Headquarters, Santa Fe

****

ATTENTION!!! URGENT MESSAGE FOLLOWS

FROM: NORAD
TO: NEW MEXICO STATE POLICE

SUBJ: SATELLITE IMPACT

1. BE ADVISED THAT, AT APPROXIMATELY 1:20 A.M. LOCAL TIME, NORAD IDENTIFIED AND TRACKED THE DESCENT AND IMPACT OF AN INTELLIGENCE SATELLITE BELONGING TO THE UNITED STATES GOVERNMENT. WE BELIEVE THE IMPACT SITE IS APPROXIMATELY 40 MILES NORTH/NORTHEAST OF ALAMOGORDO IN THE AREA OF BONITO LAKE.

2. THE SATELLITE, ALONG WITH ITS MATERIALS AND

CONTENTS ARE CONSIDERED TO BE TOP SECRET AND OF VITAL INTEREST TO THE SECURITY OF THE UNITED STATES. WE DO NOT BELIEVE THAT THE SATELLITE REPRESENTS A HAZARD TO CIVILIANS IN ANY WAY, HOWEVER, BECAUSE OF THE SENSITIVE NATURE OF THE SATELLITE AND ITS CONTENTS, IT IS IMPERATIVE THAT NO ONE EXCEPT PROPERLY IDENTIFIED AND APPROVED PERSONNEL OF THE UNITED STATES MILITARY BE ALLOWED TO APPROACH THE CRASH SITE. MILITARY PERSONNEL ARE CURRENTLY EN ROUTE AND SHOULD ARRIVE ON SCENE ON OR ABOUT 4AM LOCAL TIME.

3. UNTIL FURTHER NOTICE, ALL NON-MILITARY TRAFFIC OF ANY KIND WILL BE PROHIBITED ALONG THE FOLLOWING ROADS: HIGHWAY 54 FROM CARRIZOZO SOUTH TO HIGHWAY 70; HIGHWAY 70 FROM HIGHWAY 54 EAST TO HIGHWAY 380; AND HIGHWAY 380 FROM HIGHWAY 54 EAST TO HIGHWAY 70. THIS AREA IS NOW UNDER MILITARY QUARANTINE. NO CIVILIAN TRAFFIC OF ANY KIND IS TO BE PERMITTED IN THE QUARANTINE AREA.

4. THE NEW MEXICO STATE POLICE IS REQUESTED TO PROVIDE ASSISTANCE IN REROUTING TRAFFIC AROUND THE QUARANTINE AREA AND TO PREVENT ANY TRAFFIC WITHIN THE QUARANTINE AREA (EXCEPT TRAFFIC OF AN EMERGENCY MEDICAL OR OTHER PRE-APPROVED NATURE) AND TO COOPERATE WITH ANY AND ALL DOD SUPPORT PERSONNEL WHO MAY ALSO BE CALLED UPON TO ASSIST IN SECURING THE QUARANTINE AREA.

5. WE ANTICIPATE RETURNING FULL CONTROL OF THIS AREA TO NEW MEXICO AUTHORITIES WITHIN 24 HOURS.

6. THANK YOU FOR YOUR COOPERATION.

****

6 THE CHAINS OF COMMAND

Time: 3:33 a.m., MDST, March 22, 2025
Location: Holloman Air Force Base, southeastern New Mexico

Captain Phil Lancaster was preparing to be relieved as the tower Chief at Holloman AFB. He had just poured and started his last cup of coffee and settled in to the last bits of paperwork on his desk when the phone rang. "Holloman Tower Chief, Captain Lancaster, can I help you sir," he said.

"Captain, this is General Mitch Bradley, CINC NORAD," the voice said.

Lancaster nearly fell out of his chair. "Yes sir!" he said.

"Captain," the General began, "you're aware that your tower tracked an inbound from high altitude about two hours ago correct?"

"Yes sir, we did. We reported it to the Palace right away," Lancaster said. The Palace was a nickname the Air Force used for NORAD's control center ... during the Cold War it had been the Crystal Palace but in the ever increasingly abbreviated world, now it was just the Palace ... Lancaster figured within a few years the younger staff would just be calling it "the P" or something equally ridiculous. "We've got a hell of a lot of data on it sir."

"Understood," said the General, "did you alert anyone other than NORAD? Anyone at your command?"

"Uhh, yes sir, I did sir," Lancaster responded, "I alerted the Base Duty Officer, Major Peterson."

"Anyone else?" the General asked.

Lancaster thought the question was odd, but answered right away, "uhh, no sir."

"So your base commander is unaware of it right now?" the General asked.

"Ahhh!" thought Lancaster. It was well known that the base commander, General Colin Bradley and CINC NORAD, General Mitch Bradley were brothers. Most people also knew that the two brothers were *very* different, didn't get along and didn't much like each other. What wasn't clear to Lancaster was why the General Bradley he was talking to cared whether or not his brother knew about the data. "I, uhh, I don't think so sir, not unless Major Peterson told him. Once we alerted the Palace they took over jurisdiction and told us to let it go, so we did."

"Excellent," said the General. "Now, this is very important Captain, I need you to take any and all copies of any data related to that inbound and destroy it."

"Destroy it sir?" Lancaster asked incredulously.

"Yes, destroy it Captain. Erase all evidence of it. Delete any related computer files and then overwrite the free space on the hard drives with zeroes. If there are scraps of paper with notes related to it, burn them. Submit a list of all individuals involved in your watch crew and the previous one to Colonel Gil Jefferson here at NORAD by 0600. Do I make myself clear Captain?" The General seemed as certain in his tone as Lancaster felt confused in his.

"Uhh, yes sir," Lancaster replied.

"Good, do it now Captain," the General ordered.

"Yes sir!" Lancaster said.

"And Captain," the General said, "one more thing."

"Yes sir?" Lancaster said.

"I need you to take all of the base's tracking and recording systems offline, for ... maintenance, right now," he said.

"I beg your pardon sir," Lancaster said.

"All of them, Captain. Shut down every system. Turn off every display in the tower. Do you understand?" asked the General.

"Not really sir, we have ..." he started to say before the General cut him off.

"Stand by Captain," he said. The General sounded exasperated and he heard him cup his hand over the phone and ask if the line had some kind of security that he couldn't make out the name of. The response was apparently affirmative because the General said, "Captain, the data you're about to destroy involves a secret military satellite that came down in your area earlier this evening. It is IMPORTANT that you have NO record of it. Is that clear?"

"Yes sir, very clear sir," said Lancaster, but his mind was thinking, "holy shit."

"Additionally," the General continued, "everyone on duty for the last several hours who was exposed to knowledge of this object will remember this evening as completely uneventful, understood?"

"Yes sir," said Lancaster.

"Excellent," the General went on, "now the reason for taking the base tracking and recording systems offline is that we have some people who are inbound to your area to collect and deal with this top secret device. It is also important that there be no record of their involvement. They were never there. You never saw them, contacted them or tracked them. You never gave them clearance to come or go. There will be no record of it in your log. There will be no recording of any controller even attempting to contact it. Do I make myself clear Captain?"

"Yes sir," he said. "How long should we be performing this ... maintenance, sir?"

The General again cupped his hand over the phone, then he said, "until at least 0500."

"Understood clearly sir. Thank you sir," Lancaster said. The phone line went dead. "Jesus," he said aloud.

Seconds later, Airman Seth Bonner noted that an unknown had just appeared on the approach radar. "It's not scheduled and it's not squawking sir, shall I try to contact it?"

Lancaster stared at him for a second. "No," he said finally. The Airman gave him a puzzled look, and Lancaster quickly added, "but don't let it out of your site, Airman. I want to know where it's going and what it does."

"Yes sir," Bonner replied.

Lancaster's mind was racing. A superior officer has just given him a direct order, and that order had been clear and unambiguous. Part of him wanted to just follow the order, but he was having real trouble wrapping his brain around the story he'd just been told. Why was it so important that his CO not know? He knew that *his* General Bradley was a sonofabitch, capable of literally anything. If he ever found out that Lancaster had kept him in the dark about something ... No, he couldn't do it. He picked up the phone, "get me the Base Commander," he said, and then he looked at one of the Sergeants in the room and said, "and get me all of the tracking data on that bogey that came down earlier, the one we passed on to NORAD, I want to look at it!"

"I see," said General Colin Bradley after listening to Captain Lancaster's report. He was standing in his robe in the office by his bedroom, holding a drink he had just poured for himself. "No no, you did the right thing by contacting me Captain. Have you looked at the data they wanted you to destroy?"

"I have now sir," Lancaster said, "and it's pretty incredible sir."

"In what way?" he asked.

"Well sir," Lancaster began, "their story, I mean NORAD's story sir, the more we analyze this data, the more it just doesn't add up."

"My brother would lie about something?" Colin thought to himself. "Shocking," he said, making no attempt to hide his contempt or his feigned disbelief, "go on Captain."

Lancaster smiled and thought, "Man, they *really* don't like each other." Then he said, "Yes sir, well there's nothing in the telemetry or data that makes it look like it's one of our intel satellites sir ... in fact, well it doesn't appear to be a satellite at all sir."

"What the fuck is he up to?" Colin thought. Now he was sure that his brother was hiding something, something big. "Go on," he said.

"Well, I was thinking sir," Lancaster began, "you know how we're doing all this work on the X-22 project."

"Yes," the General said.

"Well, we know there are other competitors, other parts of the Air Force working with other contractors on competing projects, like the guys over at Edwards," Lancaster said.

"Yes," the General said.

"Well what if this was one of those sir?" Lancaster said. "What if this is a competitor's system that came down."

"If it is, it would mean they're way ahead of us," said General Bradley.

"Yes sir," said Lancaster. "What should we do sir?"

"You said there's another plane inbound?" the General asked.

"Yes sir," replied Lancaster. "We've confirmed it's a C5-D. And we're pretty sure they're going to try to set her down over at Oscura sir. And that can't be that far from where this thing came down."

"So they have a competitor to our candidate for the X-22 which is ahead of ours. And then they crash their experiment in our back yard, then lie to us about it, then further hold out on us by bringing in their own secret guys to try to collect what's left and get out before we can react or do anything?" said the General.

"That does seem pretty likely sir," Lancaster replied.

"How long would it take us to get a couple of our new A-44 surveillance drones in the air Captain?" the General asked.

"20 minutes tops sir," replied Lancaster.

"Do it," said the General. "And I want you personally over at the Drone Control station in 25 minutes to supervise and keep me apprised Captain, understood?"

"Yes sir General," Lancaster replied.

"And Captain," the General said.

"Yes sir?" said Lancaster.

"Keep a lid on this," said the General.

"Yes sir," said Lancaster.

Colin Bradley hung up the phone and stared out his window at the night sky.

7 OFFBASE

Time: 3:01 a.m. MDST, March 22, 2025
Location: Project NEO (Near Earth Orbit) Tracking station, Kirtland AFB, Albuquerque, New Mexico

2nd Lt Nick Lederer was walking up to the Project NEO building in the kind of half-awake state that only happens when you've been woken up in the middle of the night. He had already consumed half of the cup of strong black coffee in his hand, but his eyes were still a little bleary and his head felt fuzzy as he unlocked the front door of the building and proceeded inside. He had been scheduled to take the watch at 4am anyway, of course, so the call from Andy Newton begging him to come over and relieve him early had, in fairness, only robbed him of about an hour of sleep, but that was an hour he had really wanted. Still, Andy really did sound like he wasn't feeling well when he called AND he had promised to pick up Nick's next midwatch in exchange for being relieved an hour early, so he figured he was trading one hour of sleep tonight for four more in a few days. As he walked down the hall to the tracking center's control room, he also told himself that it was his own fault that people were constantly calling him for this kind of thing since he was now the only NEOCON qualified watch officer who still lived on the base (and he again made a mental note to go apartment hunting soon).

As he entered the room, Andy was already standing. "Wow, he really does look like hell," Nick thought, but after exchanging pleasantries and starting to go over the details of turning over the watch, Nick thought he sensed something else, something odd, and that made him suspicious. He took several extra minutes making sure that Andy wasn't dumping some pain in the ass issue on him. When he was finally convinced that, whatever was wrong with Andy, at least he was *not* leaving him with some mess to clean up, Nick assumed the watch.

Andy walked out in as controlled a manner as he could. The control room had a security monitor that showed the front of the building, so Andy continued to do his best acting job all the way to the car until he knew he couldn't be seen anymore.

He had followed the ... whatever it was, far enough to guess roughly where it should have landed, and he had already Google mapped how to get there as quickly as possible. Still, even speeding, it would take up to 2 hours, and by then the ... whatever it was, would have already been on the ground for at least three. It took every ounce of restraint to drive the base speed limit up to the main gate. The guard saluted him, lifted the gate and Andy hit the gas. In moments he was speeding down I-25 southbound towards highway 380. When he turned on to 380 less than an hour later, he took his car up over 100 mph into the darkness.

8 ROADBLOCK

Time: 5:10 a.m. March 22, 2025

Location: New Mexico State Police Roadblock, Carrizozo, New Mexico (Intersection of Highways 54 and 380)

Sergeant Benjamin Martinez shook his head and smiled slightly as he saw the approaching car in the distance. The driver had obviously just realized who and what he was approaching and abruptly slowed down. He figured (correctly) that the car had been doing at least 90. He held up both of his hands to signal the car to stop.

"Shit," Andy Newton said aloud. A roadblock. He should have anticipated this. "Wow," he thought, "this really is a big deal." His mind raced to figure out what to do. At the last moment before he could be seen, he grabbed his phone and held it to his face. As he slowed down and stopped next to the Highway Patrolman he started talking.

"Yes sir, Colonel, I'm almost there sir. I'm at a roadblock. Right, understood clearly sir ... right away, yes sir," Andy said and then tossed the phone onto the car seat next to him. "Officer ... Martinez? I have orders to proceed immediately to the ... site."

"May I see your ID sir?" said Martinez.

"Certainly," Andy said, handing him his military ID while trying to look and sound as normal as possible.

Martinez couldn't put his finger on it, but his instincts told him something was wrong. He stared at the ID, and then looked again at Andy. Normally, he trusted his instincts, but if this kid's presence wasn't legit and he didn't belong out here, why on Earth would he be way out here driving like a bat out of hell in the middle of the night? "You mind telling me what the heck is going on?" he said, testing the young man.

"What do you mean?" said Andy, a little nervously.

"Well, I'm trying to understand why a 2nd Lieutenant from Kirtland is way down here at 5am driving like you were a moment ago," said Martinez, making it clear that he had seen Andy approaching.

Andy's mind raced. He needed a story. Wait! No, he didn't. The State Police were here, that meant someone already had a story. Somehow he had to get the officer to tell him some piece of it so he could figure out what the cover story was and then he could play along with it, "oh that, yeah, well, umm, I'm kind of ... involved ... in what's going on."

Martinez relaxed a bit. He had spent the better part of the last hour, since he'd let that big group of black government trucks go through, trying to figure out what the heck was going on. And now this kid shows up. He figured the satellite story wasn't true at all. The Air Force was always testing crazy ass weapons and things out here, this was probably some drone thing and this kid was maybe the pilot or something. He decided to see if he could confirm his suspicion. "Huh," he said, "was it yours?"

"Was it mine? What the hell does that mean?" Andy wondered. Almost immediately his brain caught up. "He thinks I'm a drone pilot. He thinks it was my drone and that's why I'm here. Perfect!" Andy knew he had to make this convincing. He did his best to sound like he was just a nervous junior officer and didn't know what he could and couldn't say. "Look, Officer Martinez, to be honest I'm not really sure what I'm allowed to say and not say, but yes, you're right. And the ... (he made a gesture with his hands to indicate that he thought he wasn't supposed to say) has some seriously experimental stuff on it and, well, it's really important to my CO that I be onsite ASAP ... and it's totally my ass if I'm not there and, really I need to go."

Sergeant Martinez stared at him for a long moment, then he smiled and handed Andy back his ID, "stay on 380 till you get to 37, turn right and go through a little town called Nogal, then turn right again on 107, that's Bonito Lake Road, and proceed up past the Highway Patrol stop there. Should take you about a half hour. From there, you'll have to ask your people."

"They're onsite already," Andy said nodding, trying to make what was really a question sound like he already knew that.

"Yeah, they blew through here about an hour ago," replied Martinez. "And don't worry, no one else has been up there. They haven't even let us anywhere near it."

"Great!" said Andy, with genuine relief. "Thank you officer," Andy said.

"No problem," replied Martinez, "I'll radio ahead and let them know you're coming."

"Shit!" thought Andy. He knew that any response other than thanks would immediately arouse suspicion. "Great, thanks!" he said as he raised his window and drove off into the night.

About 25 minutes later, Andy was turning on to Bonito Lake Road. It was a crystal clear night and the half moon, just over half way up in the sky was shining brightly on the ground. Andy had been thinking about his next move during the drive to this point. He knew that Officer Martinez had radioed ahead. Whoever was at the roadblock in front of him (which had to be reasonably close to the crash site) knew that Andy was coming. What he didn't know was whether or not they had already figured out that Andy wasn't supposed to be there, and whether or not they were going to arrest him when he drove up. As he proceeded up the road, Andy decided that it was unlikely that they would let him past the second roadblock and, even if they did, Officer Martinez indicated that there were others already on site (and they for *sure* would know that he wasn't supposed to be there). No, if he was going to get a look at this thing, he was going to have to sneak past this last checkpoint. He slowed his car down to under 10 mph and turned off his lights. The moonlight was more than sufficient for him to see and drive by. He drove past a small group of homes. As he passed what Google maps showed was the last house before the lake, he saw the lights from a State Police car in the distance marking the last roadblock. He pulled into an empty lot on his left and turned off his car.

He'd have to hike it from here.

9 BONITO LAKE

Time: 5:17am, March 22, 2025
Location: Bonito Lake, New Mexico

Jim Landrum stood quietly on the north shore of Bonito Lake. He stared across the water at the crash site, trying, and mostly failing, to contain his excitement. Jim was a Special Forces veteran with combat experience dating back to the last days of the Iraq and Afghanistan wars. He had seen and survived some incredible things in his 33 years, but nothing in his life compared to this moment.

Jim had been a top student at West Point in every way, but it was his natural joy and boundless enthusiasm for life that had made him nearly universally liked by his fellow students. He was a man whose inner child simply would not die. It was impossible not to like him, despite his affection for playing elaborate, mischievous practical jokes. His most famous, or infamous trick was once managing to charge the sprinkler system in the Pershing Barracks with shaving cream. How he had accomplished "Operation Hot & Foamy" remained a mystery to this day because, as a somewhat hilarious condition of his comparatively light punishment, he agreed to never disclose to anyone (other than the Commandant, of course) how he did it. Not even war could take away his need to make life fun. In fact, if anything, the incessant near death experiences of combat made him appreciate the wonder and joy of life even more. Jim enjoyed being alive, and his enthusiasm for his mission, whatever the mission, was infectious.

Jim had been recruited into UNCLE, the Unknown Contact Liaison and Examination team, about five years ago. He was a perfect fit: tough, resourceful, smart and naturally curious. Jim had been a good soldier and was proud to serve his country, but he always felt that the real adventure was beyond humanity's sad obsession with what he called "the little stuff." He would never give less than 100% (including his own life if necessary) to accomplish whatever objective his country asked of him, but the truth was that he felt that conflicts between nation states were petty and, in the grand scheme, meaningless. UNCLE gave Jim the opportunity to find the adventure beyond mankind's silly fights with itself, and there was perhaps no one else in the organization who was quite as at home there as he was.

Technically, UNCLE was part of the Defense Department. Its mission was to handle any and all extra terrestrial contact situations. Only a handful of people in the world knew it even existed. The reality of occasional alien contact was, for obvious reasons, a closely guarded secret by the few world governments who knew about it. Fortunately, events weren't that common (although the people who *did* know about them also knew that was about to change). In fact, there hadn't been an "uncontrolled" alien landing on Earth involving a new species (at least not one they were aware of) since 1991, the year before Jim was born. All contact with existing, known species was highly classified and access to even the knowledge of those interactions was restricted to an incredibly small number of people. But everyone involved knew that the day would come when the next new species would arrive, and so the Joint Chiefs, which sometimes had a frankly tenuous relationship with UNCLE regarding the uses of the information and technology that UNCLE possessed, always found a way to make sure that the program was secretly funded, and that the team was trained. And trained. And trained ... for today.

Today, finally, was not a training exercise. This was not a drill. The target was live. Right there, right in front of him, just a few hundred yards away, there was an actual unknown, non-terrestrial craft that had crash landed only a couple of hours ago. The people at UNCLE dedicated their lives to moments like this one. And Jim, promoted to Team Leader only a year ago, was going to be out front when they went in.

About 90 minutes earlier, UNCLE's specially equipped C5-D Galaxy had landed at the Oscura landing strip, dropped them off, and disappeared back into the sky. On their way in they had determined the exact location of the crash site and their 10-truck entourage had crossed the ground from there to here in no time at all. Jim had long since put on his environment suit and was standing on the shore, waiting impatiently for permission to proceed. Behind him, he heard the door of the giant RV that housed UNCLE's command center open and close and he heard footsteps approaching him from behind. He knew who it was.

Jim's best friend and team partner Mike Powell walked up and stood next to him. "Almost," Mike said quietly, understanding that the anticipation was driving Jim crazy, "almost." Jim nodded and continued shifting his weight from side to side.

Dr. Mike Powell was the perfect counterpart for Jim Landrum, and both of them knew it from the moment they first met. Tall and thin, Mike didn't have the rugged good looks or the impressive physical strength of his friend, and he had no military experience at all, but when it came to biology, chemistry or physics, there were very few people on Earth who knew more than Mike. He had literally been born with a voracious appetite for virtually every scientific discipline he was exposed to. A top student at Stanford, Mike went on to get his first two Doctorates at Johns Hopkins University, and it was there that he ended up coming to the attention of UNCLE. Like Jim, Mike had joined UNCLE for the adventure, but it wasn't physical adventure he craved (at all really), it was the mental one. Mike had a scientific curiosity that wouldn't quit, and frankly there was no other job on Earth that could offer him the endless supply of raw, scientific material to study.

It was a little strange, in a way, that Mike and Jim had become such good friends so quickly, but there was no question that their mutual admiration society was instantaneous and strong. When they met, Jim knew immediately that Mike was pretty much always going to be the smartest guy in the room, and he wanted whoever that guy was to be as close to him as possible. And for his part, Mike saw Jim as a pure bred American hero, the guy most likely to ensure that everyone under his command came out of any situation alive and OK. The fact that they ended up having a similar sense of humor and that both had the same approach to life outside of work, well that was just one of those things that happens.

Over the course of the three years since they'd met, they had become largely inseparable, and many of the people at UNCLE jokingly referred to them as "Kirk and Spock" (a comparison made all the more amusingly appropriate because Mike was tall and thin, had short, dark hair and was given to speaking in something of a monotone when lecturing on highly scientific topics).

Finally, their headsets came alive. "Captain Landrum, Dr. Powell," the voice said, "all monitoring sensors are now functioning. We're going to launch the bird here in just a moment. Once we have it in the air and transmitting, we will give you clearance to proceed, is that clear?"

"Roger that Colonel, standing by," Jim replied.

Colonel Jane Wisener was a Marine who had been in charge of the UNCLE strike team since 2009. At age 60, she was one of the very few people left alive with "first contact" alien experience. Among the handful of people who knew of UNCLE's existence, Colonel Wisener was often regarded as the "adult supervision" of this now predominantly much younger group. Wisener had begun her career as one of the first female combat pilots in the Marine Corps. She had a well-earned reputation for being as physically and mentally tough a human being as nature was capable of producing. During operations she was an all business, no bullshit leader with no tolerance for excuses. She demanded the absolute best from everyone who worked for her at all times. But what made her different and special to those who served with her was that she very obviously cared for everyone under her command and treated them like they were her own family. Everyone at UNCLE, in fact everyone who had ever worked for, or even around Colonel Wisener, respected her, liked her, and would frankly follow her off a cliff if she so much as asked.

"Radiation, Dr. Powell?" the Colonel asked.

Mike looked at his gauge. "Almost none ma'am, literally about 10 micro Sieverts," said Powell, "in any case we should be more than safe enough in the suits."

"Alright," said the Colonel, "keep your eye on it as you get close to the ship."

"Yes ma'am," replied Mike.

Finally, it was time. "Alright," the Colonel started, "I want Teams 2 and 3 to set up at 200 yards on either side of our Command Center here, Teams 4 and 5 head south, get up that hill and secure the area. The bird is in the air and we are recording. Team 1, you may proceed ... with CAUTION gentlemen."

The "bird" was an aerial recon drone that looked like a slightly oversized version of a remote control flying toy, but this one was filled with cameras, sensors and monitors and cost the taxpayers about $15 million. "We sure do have cool toys," Jim thought as the bird flew over them and then on to the crash site.

As they walked slowly and carefully around the edge of the small lake and towards the ship, the Colonel spoke up. "Remember gentlemen, this one is new. We've not seen a craft like this before; I want you to proceed with EXTREME caution. We have NO idea what we're going to find here."

"Yes ma'am, " Jim and Mike both said.

The Colonel paused, and then said, "Executing Protocol 1." The Colonel pulled a keychain from her pocket, flipped to a gold key, and inserted it into a panel by her station marked "For Emergency

Use Only." She rotated the key 90 degrees to the right. A red light came on and the panel next to it slid up. Everyone in the vehicle knew why, and a couple of people looked over towards the Colonel. She looked back at them but said nothing.

Protocol 1, of course, meant the priming of a low yield nuclear warhead that was literally sitting under their feet. The protocol existed because of Species 3, which had turned out to be decidedly hostile towards humanity. In the event that Species 3 was encountered again, or anything the Colonel deemed like it, she was under orders to detonate the nuke, thereby killing herself, the entire team, and every living thing within a several mile radius, including, it was hoped, whatever alien threat was discovered. In that case, the only record of events would be from a data stream going from the Command Center truck to a special satellite and then to UNCLE HQ. The data stream used a computer encryption technology that was ... well, "borrowed," from the far more benevolent Species 4.

From what they had been able to see in the moonlight from across the lake while they were waiting, Mike and Jim had both expected the ship to be in pretty rough shape, but as they approached it, both men were surprised by how relatively intact it appeared. In fact, given what Mike assumed were the conditions surrounding the impact, the ship was actually in surprisingly *good* shape. As they finally got close enough to start seeing real detail, Jim noted that the hull appeared to be made of something like a carbon composite.

"Doesn't exactly look like it was made for atmospheric flying does it?" said Mike.

"No," said Jim, "it doesn't. My guess is that it wasn't built to ever land on a planet. Not like this anyway."

"An accident," said Mike.

"Gotta be," Jim agreed.

"Report gentlemen," said the Colonel.

"Yes ma'am," said Jim. "The craft appears to be ... well, surprisingly intact Colonel. We're obviously approaching from what appears to be the rear of the starboard side. There is a significant amount of discoloration and scoring on this side. My guess is that they came in with this side of the ship down."

"Jesus!" said Mike, "Jim, come look at this."

Jim moved and spoke quickly, understanding the importance of narrating their movements for the sake of recording everything. "Colonel, I'm proceeding towards Dr. Powell who is currently standing near the port rear of the craft," Jim said. When he saw what Mike had found, he whistled. "Wow. Ma'am, you're gonna want to get the drone over here to see this."

Moments later, they heard the whispering fan sounds of the drone hovering above them.

"Wow," agreed the Colonel, "I wonder what happened here."

Jim stared at the wreckage for a moment. Then he said, "Well, it's almost certainly not combat related."

"Agreed," said Mike, "the absence of other indicators so far suggests that this was impact related, like something hit it."

"A meteorite?" asked Jim.

"Maybe," said Mike, "but I'm not so sure. Look here," he said, pointing forward. "It looks up here like the hull's structure is turned towards the main body."

"Yeah, but back here," said Jim, pointing to a larger sized hole, "it looks like this area has been blown outward, with the skin peeled out."

Mike looked carefully at what Jim was pointing at. He enjoyed puzzles, and this was a good one. "My guess is that this area back here is the result of something that happened after what we see up here," said Mike, pointing again to the first spot they had looked at.

"What are you saying Doctor?" asked the Colonel.

Jim knew where Mike was going. "Impact followed by explosive decompression," he said.

"Right," said Mike, "but the important point here is that all of this happened *before* they came down, which means these folks almost certainly did *not* intend to be here this morning, or if they did, they probably didn't have any intention of attracting attention. This is an accident ma'am, a crash site."

"I'll tell you something else ma'am," Jim continued, "I'd bet money that someone or something was trying to control the landing."

"Go on," said the Colonel.

"Well ma'am, the nature of the data we already have on the approach suggested an attempt at a landing and not an outright crash. If this had been a single point impact my guess is that we'd be finding tiny pieces of ship and Martian guts all over the place. And frankly, well, the whole ship seems to be in much better shape than I would think it would be if someone wasn't at least trying to control the approach."

"Alright," said the Colonel, "Dr. Powell, what can you tell me about the hull?"

"Well," said Mike, smiling as he thought about the possibilities, "the materials guys and I are going to have a field day figuring out what the hell this surface material is. I don't think it's carbon fiber based, but it's similar." He ran his glove along a piece of the surface, "whatever it is, it's way beyond anything we've ever seen or thought of ... and it's got to be tough as hell to have survived the entry into our atmosphere and still be in this kind of shape. And to hold together ... I mean, look at this," he said, as he gestured to the damage in front of him, "this whole side of the ship should have come tearing off on the way down. I don't know ma'am, but I can't wait to find out."

"Any chance we can move it?" asked the Colonel.

"Well, the skin itself feels amazingly lightweight, but I doubt it Colonel," answered Mike, "certainly not with the equipment we have here right now. We'd need a couple of cranes and a surface big enough to set it on. And there's no telling how heavy the engines are or how stable the overall structural integrity is."

"I agree ma'am," said Jim, "we're going to have to cover it before the commercial satellites pass over. I recommend we go with Operation Hot Rock. Also, it might be a good idea to get a couple of the Bobcats over here and start digging around the front."

"Alright, thank you gentlemen. Stand by." The Colonel looked around the room. All eyes were on her. "OK everyone, we're going to commence Operation Hot Rock. The next civilian satellite pass is at (the Colonel looked at one of her screens) 7:04am, which is right at sunrise ... Move!"

Operation Hot Rock meant that, because their newly discovered spacecraft was going to have to be there for a while, more elaborate measures were going to be needed to maintain the plausibility of the cover story, and the biggest and most immediate threat to that story was from civilian satellites. One of the key drawbacks to the explosion in the number of civilian satellites was that it made hiding things on the Earth's surface much harder. Plus, everyone knew that they were near Alamogordo; the area was literally crawling with "rocket scientists," so every story they told needed to be very plausible and what civilians could see had to support it. In this case that meant using what was basically a giant tarp on a series of poles. This was no normal tarp of course, but rather a gigantic, flexible digital screen that would display an image that could fool even the most sophisticated civilian cameras. By sunrise, from space, the site would appear to have just what they were claiming (impact and debris from a fallen satellite). Everyone at UNCLE understood clearly how important it was to keep the number of people involved as absolutely low as possible (if people even suspected something unusual, more troops would be needed to secure the area, and that would mean a mountain of other security issues).

Mike noticed that Jim was suddenly walking away from the crash site, looking up and around. "You hear that?" Jim asked.

"No, what?" Mike answered. Then he heard it. "Uh oh."

"Yeah, uh oh," Jim said, still scanning the dark sky. "There!" he suddenly said, pointing over to the far side of the lake. "Colonel, we got a pretty big problem here," Jim said very quickly.

"What's wrong Captain?" the Colonel answered back.

"Ma'am we appear to have an Air Force surveillance drone in the area," Jim said. "My guess from the sound is that it's an A-44."

"Shit!" said the Colonel. Then after a pause, she quietly added (with no small amount of contempt in her voice), "Holloman..."

"That's a good bet ma'am," said Jim.

"What the hell is it doing here?" Mike wondered aloud.

"I don't know, but it's a safe bet that it's taking all kinds of pictures right now that we don't want it to," Jim said.

"Alright, that's my problem," the Colonel said into her headset, then she looked at her communications officer and said, "get me CINC NORAD right now Lieutenant."

"Yes ma'am," the Lieutenant replied.

.

10 COMPLICATIONS

Time: 5:35 a.m. March 22, 2025
Location: CINC NORAD's Office, inside Cheyenne Mountain, Colorado

General Mitch Bradley wasn't very good at waiting, but he also knew that no news was generally good news. His people had told him some time ago that "the package" (the strike team from UNCLE) had been successfully delivered and that they were onsite. He still couldn't believe their dumb luck that this, whatever it was, had come down in a remote part of rural New Mexico (the location, because of the obvious historical context, still privately amused him). He was also amazed that they had been able to gain such complete control over the situation so quickly. He was, in fact, so calm about the situation that he was actually reviewing a completely unrelated memo on his desk when his phone beeped.

"General Bradley sir?" said the voice of First Lieutenant Amy Taylor.

"Yes Lieutenant?" the General replied.

"Sir, I have a Colonel Jane Wisener for you on secure channel 1," she said, "she says it's urgent sir."

"Thank you Lieutenant," the General said. He tapped the secure button on his phone's display and then touched line 1. "Bradley."

"Brad, it's Jane," Colonel Wisener said.

"Jane!" the General said in a friendly voice. "Good morning! How are things in New Mexico?" he asked.

"So far so good sir, but we have a potential security issue," the Colonel replied.

"Go ahead," said the General.

"Well sir, a moment ago we spotted an A-44 surveillance drone flying low over the site," the Colonel said, "we're pretty sure it was watching and listening General, and it's a safe bet it wasn't an accident."

"Ya shoot it down?" the General asked, only half joking.

The Colonel let out a slight laugh. "The thought occurred sir," she said, "but no sir, we did not."

"I guess we both know where it came from," the General said.

"Yes sir we do," the Colonel replied.

"OK," said the General, "thank you Colonel, I'll handle it."

"Thank you sir," said Colonel Wisener, and then she hung up.

General Bradley shook his head. "That Goddamn Captain," he thought to himself, "great."

"Amy!" the General barked.

Amy Taylor jumped from her desk and ran to the General's office door, "yes sir?" she said.

"Get my brother, General Colin Bradley, at Holloman on the phone. Tell them it's a priority 1 call from NORAD. Have them wake him up if you have to."

"Yes sir," she said, and rushed back to her desk to make the call.

"Something tells me you won't have to," the General muttered to himself. He looked at his desk. "Shit."

11 FAMILY

Time: 5:40 a.m. March 22, 2025
Location: Home of the base Commander, General Colin Bradley, Holloman AFB, New Mexico

It wasn't as though he hadn't been expecting the call. In fact, he was surprised that it took his brother two entire hours to pick up the phone and try to pull whatever bullshit he was going to try and pull. He picked up his phone and heard the voice of his Deputy say, "I have Priority 1 call from CINC NORAD for you sir."

"I don't doubt it," Colin said dryly, "put him through." There was a two-beep tone that indicated the transfer to a secure line connection. "Morning Mitch," he said, "what can I do for you?"

"I think you know why I'm calling Colin," Mitch replied.

"Do I?" Colin said.

"Colin, you've got at least one A-44 in the air over a crash site that you have no business in or around," Mitch said, already annoyed.

"Why would I do that?" Colin continued.

"Let's cut the crap Colin," Mitch said angrily.

"Oh, you want *me* to cut the crap? That's rich coming from you 'General' " he said derisively, "since you've already been on the phone this morning to my people giving them orders to keep important information about activities within *my* jurisdiction..."

"*Your* jurisdiction?" Mitch shot back.

"Where did that C5 land Mitch? Was it Oscura? I think it was, and yes, the last time I turned around that was in fact part of *my FUCKING* jurisdiction Mitch! So yes, telling people under my command to keep information about activities within my jurisdiction secret from me! And why?!" he said nearly shouting now, "because of a weapons project contract and deal that you shouldn't be involved in and don't really give a shit about. You know what this is about? I'll tell you what this is about; this is about *you*, YOU, going out of your way just to *fuck* me again. Well let me tell you something General, you may have two more stars on your shoulder than I do, a fact which you obviously enjoy shoving down my throat every chance you get, but you are stepping WAY out of line here, and if you think I won't scream absolute bloody murder about this if whatever the fuck you're doing out there interferes with our getting a fair shot at the X-22 contract, then you are out of your God damned, mother fucking mind!"

On his end of the phone Mitch Bradley's eyes widened, his mouth opened slightly, and his face froze. "Oh my God," he thought, "he has no idea what's going on. He thinks this is about the X-22." Maybe the drone was malfunctioning, maybe Colin really didn't know! Mitch knew that the less his brother knew about what was going on at Bonito Lake the better. There was already no love lost between the two of them and hadn't been for years, so if Colin thought it was about the X-22, it was probably best to let him keep thinking that.

"I'm not on anyone's *side* Colin," Mitch said, trying to sound appropriately angry (which wasn't that hard given how much of an asshole his brother was otherwise being anyway). "I'm trying to preserve fairness in this process."

"Holy shit!" thought Colin, "I was right! That means Edwards really is way ahead of us. And here Mitch is claiming to be impartial." He was furious. "Bullshit!" he shouted.

"Colin," Mitch began, trying to sound calmer now, "I'm going to say this once, and I'm giving you a direct fucking order. Get your birds out of the sky and stay OUT of that area. Is that clear?"

"Fuck you Mitch," Colin said and slammed the phone down. He stood there, fuming, continuing the fight with his brother in his head. "There's no way we're not winning that contract," Colin thought to himself. "We will do whatever it takes," he went on, continuing to shout at his brother in his mind, "to win that contract. Those jobs, that program, that power, it's all going to be based HERE and I will *NOT* allow you to *fuck* with me or interfere with our getting it!" His phone beeped again. "What?!" he shouted into it.

"Sorry sir," his Deputy said, "but I've got Captain Lancaster holding for you sir, he said it's urgent."

Colin Bradley's voice and body calmed down rapidly, "put him through," he said. "Bradley."

"Uhh, yes sir General, this is Captain Lancaster sir, I'm over at the Drone Command Center," Lancaster began.

"What is it Captain?" the General said, his voice still irritated from his last conversation.

"Well sir, we've just finished analyzing the camera data from one of the A-44s," Lancaster said.

"And," the General said impatiently.

"Well sir, I think you're going to want to come over here personally and see this sir," Lancaster said.

Colin was starting to get the impression that the Captain was very nervous about something. "Is there a problem Captain?" he asked. "What's the status of their X-22 model?"

"Well, actually that is the problem sir," Lancaster said, clearly now not saying something.

"*What* is the problem Captain?" the General asked impatiently.

"Sir, this is NOT the X-22," Lancaster said flatly. "This is something ... *different*, sir."

"Different?" General Bradley said. He paused, putting it all together, "different like..."

"Yes sir, I think so sir," Lancaster replied.

General Colin Bradley's mouth fell open slightly. His mind quickly churned over the events of the last several minutes. "That sonofabitch," he thought to himself, "I don't believe it, he lied to me again! But why? Whatever this thing is, he must know about it, and he must want it, and I'll bet it's a lot more valuable to whoever has it than the X-22 contract." His eyes narrowed and his jaw tightened, "I'll be right there Captain," he said.

"Yes sir," replied Lancaster, "thank you sir," and he hung up.

12 SPECIES 14

Time: 6:15am, March 22, 2025
Location: Bonito Lake, New Mexico

"Jim!" Mike shouted, "Get over here!"

Jim spun around and ran the 30 feet to Mike as fast as his suit would allow. When he arrived and could see what Mike had been pointing at, he smiled. "Well, that makes it a lot easier," he said

Back in the mobile command center there were several screens that gave the Colonel and her staff a good deal of information about what was happening, but the most important screens, the ones with the helmet cameras, showed frustratingly little due to the lack of light. The Colonel was looking at the screen that displayed the vital readings for the two men on site. The heart rate of both men had just risen noticeably. "What is it gentlemen?" said the Colonel, "talk to me."

"Yes ma'am," said Mike, trying (mostly in vain) to calm himself down, "We've found something that … it's a hatch ma'am."

"A hatch?" the Colonel repeated.

"Yes ma'am," said Jim, "and it's open ma'am. Permission to

proceed?" Jim nearly smacked himself in the forehead, immediately irritated with himself. "Seek forgiveness, not permission bonehead!" he thought, "I should have just said 'proceeding in' or something." Now he had to wait.

"Hang on guys," the Colonel replied, "if the hatch is open, we might have occupants out in the area already." The Colonel turned to everyone around her and said, "Alert the perimeter teams that we may have unknowns in the area, everyone proceed with EXTREME caution. Everyone outside, lock and load your pulse guns NOW." The Colonel looked back at the wall of displays in front of her, the "bird" was arriving at the hatch area giving her a barely better view of it, though she could see Captain Landrum and Doctor Powell turn and look up at it as it arrived. "OK, gentlemen, we can see you but our video feed has got a lot of shadows and our overall vis is poor. Tell us what we can't see."

"Yes ma'am," said Jim, "the hatch is fairly large, I'd say 9 feet across. It's definitely wider than would be necessary for something like a moon buggy or an ROV or a recon vehicle of some kind, but there's no sign of anything."

"Dr. Powell?" asked the Colonel.

Mike wasn't sure why, but he felt sure the hatch wasn't for storing anything like a recon vehicle, "yeah, I don't know ma'am. The ship's obviously sustained some significant damage. It's possible the hatch just opened as a result of the impact, or it could have been part of some automated, emergency procedure. I agree with Captain Landrum; there's no sign of anything and we haven't seen anything that looked like vehicle tracks. The ship appears to be entirely without power. It seems a lot more likely to me that anything that was inside the ship when it arrived is probably still in there, and probably more in need of assistance than anything else."

"Roger that, stand by." The Colonel paused for what seemed to Jim and Mike to be forever (it was, in reality, about 10 seconds). Finally she said, "all right, proceed CAREFULLY gentlemen. All perimeter teams are now in position. Keep your mics hot, your suits locked and your weapons armed, understood?"

"Understood," Landrum said. He smiled, looked at Mike, "Ready?"

Mike was apprehensive to say the least. He looked at Jim. If Jim was nervous too, he didn't show it. He looked up at the dark entrance, then looked back at Jim, smiled and said, "you know what, after you."

Jim smiled and moved towards the hatch. His hand slid as he touched the side of it and he pulled it back immediately. "Colonel, there appears to be some kind of viscous fluid or gel on the edge of the hatch here," he said. "It could be a lubricant for a mechanism, or the ship could be leaking something. There's some of it on the deck inside as well." Jim looked at his glove, then said, "whatever it is, it doesn't appear to be doing any damage to my suit. Proceeding in." Neither of them noticed that there were traces of the substance on the ground outside the hatch.

The UNCLE environment suits that Jim and Mike were wearing were as secure as spacesuits, but a fraction of the weight or bulk. In fact, the sensors, recording devices and other technology attached to the suits weighed as much as the suits themselves. Newcomers to UNCLE often described people wearing them as looking like armored scuba divers. The helmets were entirely transparent except for an area along the height of the eye (and this area was shielded to the inside in order to protect their eyes from the wide angle lights on each side which were designed to illuminate their field of view). To keep the lights in the right position at all times, the helmets were attached by a carbon fiber collar that locked together on a floating ring of bearings, the inner side of which was physically attached to a skull cap each man was wearing. The design was such that there was at least some light being projected everywhere in the wearer's field of vision.

As they stepped into the ship, even in their suits they could sense that the air in the ship was different. Jim spoke up first, "Colonel, the air near the hatch is probably mixed pretty badly with our own at this point, but as we're proceeding in it's clear that the atmospheric pressure is at least a little higher. The air outside my suit feels noticeably heavier."

Mike was looking at his atmospheric sensor. "It's more humid too," he said. "Actually a lot more humid. I can even feel it on my gloves. There's something else Colonel, stand by," Mike said, taking several more steps in.

In the trailer the video from Captain Landrum and Dr. Powell began jumping and freezing. They had anticipated that this might happen. "OK gentlemen," the Colonel said, "your video is breaking up pretty badly already."

Jim frowned. "Damn," he thought. "Do you want us to hold?" he asked.

The Colonel stared hard at the screens in front of her. Everyone knew this was a command decision that *she* had to make. Nothing she was looking at was going to tell her what to do. It wouldn't take long to have them step back outside, run a couple of fiber cables out there and plug them into their suits. Then they'd have a hard wire connection. But they still had audio, and there was still no indication whatsoever that there was any danger. And if there were some catastrophic danger, well then they'd initiate Protocol 1, and whether or not they had a clear picture would pretty much be the least of their problems. The Colonel decided that it wasn't necessary to delay. "No," she said. "But!" she added quickly, "if we start to lose audio you are to retreat out immediately so we can hard wire, is that clear?"

Jim smiled in relief at being allowed to continue. "Very clear ma'am," he said.

"Doctor, talk to me about the air in there," said the Colonel.

"Yes ma'am," said Mike, looking again at the sensor to make sure it was correct. "Uhh, it appears that the amount of oxygen in the air in here is actually significantly higher than is normal for us ma'am. Currently the amount of oxygen outside my suit is at about 35%, and it's still rising." Everyone was thinking the same thing;

they're oxygen breathers.

They walked down the passageway slowly, cautiously, both doing everything they could to keep their heart rates under control. The walls in the passageway were a very dark green color, almost emerald like. Mike stopped and stared at one section, then suddenly deactivated his helmet lights.

Jim noticed immediately and turned his head towards his partner, "What are you doing?"

Mike looked over at Jim, his eyes annoyed by the lights. "Stop that," he said, "turn them off for a second." Jim thought that was a bad idea, but he switched off his lights. The passageway should have been totally black, but it wasn't. It was bathed in a very low dark green glow.

Jim switched his lights back on. "Huh," he said, "I wonder what causes that."

"Report," said the Colonel.

"Yes ma'am," said Mike, "We just switched off our helmet lights for a moment and then turned them back on. The interior walls of the ship appear to be either coated with or maybe made of a compound with a low level, bioluminescent, dark green glow." Mike was about to note that the walls might also be absorbing the light from their helmets, but before he could speak, the Colonel interrupted.

"You've turned your lights back on now?" the Colonel asked.

"Yes ma'am," Mike responded. "We're at roughly the middle of the ship now Colonel. In front of us the ship evidently splits into two decks, and there's a short stairway leading to the upper deck. Behind us is what I'm guessing is the engineering area."

"Let's have a look in there first please," the Colonel directed.

"Yes ma'am," Mike said, and both men walked into the main

engine room. There was silence for several moments.

"Doctor Powell?" the Colonel said a little impatiently.

"Yes ma'am," Mike replied, "sorry, I was just trying to get a grip on what I'm looking at."

"What do we have?" the Colonel asked.

"Well, this is pretty interesting," Mike said, still looking intently at the equipment in front of him. "If you just look at the engines outside, it would seem pretty obvious that this craft was not meant for long, interstellar journeys, which is why we were all kind of wondering whether or not this was just a scout ship or something like that."

"And?" the Colonel asked.

"Well," Mike continued, "in looking in here, we *could* be wrong, this ship could be out here on its own."

"Explain," the Colonel said.

"Yes ma'am," Mike continued. "It looks to me like what I'm looking at does something a LOT more massive than simply power the two engines on the sides of this ship."

Jim looked at all of the equipment in front of him. He was a smart guy, but he had no idea what he was looking at. This sort of thing was *exactly* why he was so glad to have someone like Mike with him. "Like what?" he asked.

"Well, how would you move a ship like this across vast distances without giant engines?" Mike asked.

Jim shrugged, "are we talking warp drive or something here?"

"Not exactly," Mike said as he stared at the massive equipment in front of them. "Actually, if I had to guess, I'd guess that they use this thing to generate a wormhole and then just pop through it."

"Wouldn't you need an unbelievable amount of energy to do that?" Jim asked. Mike raised an eyebrow at him. "What?"

Mike laughed a little, and then nodded, "yes, you would actually."

"Which means this thing might be able to generate enough power to..." Jim started.

"Supply the entire power needs of the United States for ... I don't know, a few centuries?" Mike said, finishing the sentence.

"Oh boy," the Colonel said.

"Yeah," said Mike.

Everyone knew what that meant. It meant that the technology present on this ship was *way* beyond where the human race was at that moment, and thus it needed to be hidden and protected. A new level of urgency came over Jim, and he was suddenly on the move. He looked at Mike. "Come on," he said. Then he spoke to the Colonel directly, "proceeding up and forward ma'am. If they think at all like us we should find the bridge there." They went up the stairs and then down a passageway, passing several closed compartments until they came to what a hatch toward the very front of the ship. As Jim stepped through and turned to his left, his heart rate shot up. "Mike!"

Just about every sensor Jim was wearing went crazy back in the Colonel's command center. "Captain!" barked the Colonel, obviously concerned.

Jim wanted to respond immediately, but his mind was simply too busy processing what he was seeing. The mix of emotions was entirely new. He was finally face to face with an alien species, but just as clearly, this wasn't going to be an opportunity to actually have the "first contact" he wanted.

"Bodies Colonel. Two of them." Jim immediately felt a sense of loss. He was sad for himself, but also sad for whomever these creatures were. They'd almost certainly traveled from farther than he could imagine, only to die in an accident on some other planet, impossibly far from home.

"Status!?" barked the Colonel, who had moved over towards the emergency panel and placed her left hand on the gold key.

Jim quickly pulled himself back into the moment. "Sorry ma'am." His voice was sad, solemn. "They do not appear to be alive ma'am."

In the Command trailer, alarms were appearing on the screens tracking the vital signs, brain waves, stress levels, just about everything in both men. One of the med techs monitoring them turned and looked back at the Colonel and said "ma'am?" The Colonel shook her head very slightly, and raised her hand just a bit, as if to say, "let's give them a moment here." Until this moment, the Colonel was one of the very few humans left alive who had been through a first contact experience. Suddenly encountering alien corpses wasn't anything a human could prepare for or predict their reaction to.

Mike wasn't quite as hardened as Jim was to the appearance of blood and guts and death. He had certainly seen his fair share of dead things, but nothing like the scene in front of them. His stomach churned uncomfortably for a moment, but he quickly recovered and his second reaction was similar to Jim's. As he looked at the bodies he felt a sudden need to treat the place with more respect and reverence. He too had hoped there might be a chance to communicate. He felt certain that anyone in the ship would probably need medical attention and had been mentally gearing up for a chance to help a living being. But it was clearly too late for that. He tried to sound dispassionate, but the disappointment was obvious in his voice when he said, "Colonel, I concur with Captain Landrum's assessment," he said, "the subjects are deceased."

"Are they 3s?" asked the Colonel anxiously.

"Definitely not ma'am," said Mike, who shivered a little as he realized that the Colonel had probably just been ready to nuke them all. "I repeat, they are definitely NOT Species 3. In fact, I am quite certain that we've just discovered Species 13."

The Colonel exhaled in relief; something she was decidedly not alone in doing. "Your video is still too choppy to be of any real use to us Doctor, describe them," she said.

"Actually, they're pretty amazingly like us ma'am," Mike began. "They're about our size, bipedal, two arms, similar cranium, a little wider, with a small ridge in the skull that goes from above one eye around the back of the head to the other. Their eyes are different than ours, wider and thinner. Their digits are also longer and thinner than ours. They appear to have seven on each hand, with one opposable. Umm, one of them even appears to have two breasts, perhaps indicating a two gender species like us. Their skin has a kind of aquamarine tint to it, and their hair isn't really hair ... it's very thin and more, well, almost scale like." Mike crossed the room to examine the other one. "The one I presume is male looks like he died from a pre-crash trauma."

"What makes you say that?" asked the Colonel, who was no longer standing by the emergency panel, but hadn't disengaged the weapon either.

"There wouldn't have been time to get him over there," said Jim.

"Right," Mike agreed. "Colonel, he's not near what I'm guessing was his station. He's lying on what appears to be some kind of emergency medical table. He definitely appears to have been receiving medical attention. And his blood is all over the place here. Whatever happened to him, if it happened during the crash, he wouldn't be over here or you'd think the other one wouldn't be at her station."

"What about the one you think is female?" was the next question.

"She died on impact sir. It appears that a structural rod below the deck broke off and impaled her. There's also quite a mark here on the top of her cranium. The good news is that both bodies appear to be relatively whole and ..."

"Mike!" said Jim, "I got something else here. You should see this."

Mike hadn't even noticed that Jim had left the room and was startled when he turned and saw Jim halfway back down the passageway staring into another room. He walked quickly down and stared in. "Wow."

"Talk to me gentlemen," said the Colonel impatiently.

Mike spoke first, "Colonel, we've found a room near the bridge that's open and appears very different from the others."

"Explain," said the Colonel.

"Well," Mike began, "the other occupants we saw are obviously very like us, but whatever stayed in here, well, wasn't. Whatever was here had to be much larger. Also, there are no chairs in here, but clearly there's a large, well, it looks like a living area, maybe a bed of some kind, but it has to be 30 feet long and 10 feet wide."

"Hey Mike," said Jim, over along the bulkhead, "get a load of this. Whaddaya think, some kind of feeding tube or something?"

Mike was now going over towards what he thought was the bed area to see what Jim was referring to, but as he stepped he slipped slightly on a patch of goo on the floor. He stopped, looked down, then bent over to touch it. "Colonel, we've found more of that viscous stuff in here. In fact it appears to ..." he and Jim were both shining their flashlights down on the floor and following the path of the stuff as it went out of the room and back down the passageway towards....

"Code 10! Code 10! Colonel, tell the backup teams they may not be alone!" shouted Landrum as the two of them now ran for the escape hatch.

"What's wrong?" said the Colonel.

Jim spoke as he ran, "Whatever this thing is sir, it's probably big, it's different, and it's very likely OUT ma'am."

"Out?! Shit! Tell the border teams to look alive, they may have company," the Colonel moved back towards the emergency panel.

Mike added, "Colonel, I recommend everyone proceed with extreme caution. Whatever it is, it's likely injured and it may react defensively."

"Agreed," said the Colonel, who was made both more and less worried by the thought. "Captain Landrum, do you think you can track it?" asked the Colonel.

"Maybe," Jim replied, "it does seem to be occasionally trailing this material. Son of a bitch!" Emerging back outside and looking down where his feet had been, Jim realized that they had both missed the clue when they had entered. "C'mon!" He and Mike followed the patchy path of goo about 30 feet to the edge of the water and then they looked northeast down the shoreline. Suddenly Jim grabbed Mike's arm and gestured in front of them. At first Mike didn't see it. The shore became narrower and rockier in front of them as it approached the dam, and there were a couple of big rocks.... and then he saw it. They and the other teams had all literally been looking at it for an hour now in the darkness. Of the two big "rocks" in front of them, one was very normal looking, but the other was nothing like the other rocks in the area, it was rounded and smooth, like you'd see after eons of water flowing. It wasn't a rock at all.

"Found it," Landrum said softly into his mic. He raised his weapon and began quietly, slowly, carefully walking towards it. "Wow, this is gonna be Species 14 ma'am ... and it is *definitely* not from around here."

"Is it alive?" asked the Colonel.

"Unknown Colonel," said Jim. They were now just a few feet away from it. It wasn't moving.

Mike reached out and touched it with his glove. He thought it reacted almost imperceptibly to his touch. "I believe it may be Colonel," said Mike, "but if it is, my guess, based on the conditions in the ship compared to the conditions out here, is that it won't be for long unless we do something."

"Can we move it?" asked the Colonel, looking at the clock on the wall. Sunrise was literally minutes away. "Time is NOT our friend here."

Jim looked at the size of the creature. "If it cooperates, I think so, but we're going to need the small auto lifter, and the supplies truck is gonna need to be completely emptied, fast!"

The Colonel looked at one of her aides, snapped her fingers and pointed at him. The aide moved quickly.

Mike spoke up, "Colonel, I recommend we get this creature into a secure and environmentally contained facility as soon as possible. My guess is that it is almost certainly suffering from severe moisture and oxygen deprivation."

"Do you have a place in mind Dr. Powell?" asked the Colonel.

"As a matter of fact I do ma'am," said Mike.

Suddenly, around the corner by the dam, Jim thought he heard a sound, like a rock falling. He spun, his hand instinctively going to his weapon. He saw part of a dark figure in the distance looking their way and he thought he heard a faint, "shit!" but before whoever it was could turn, Jim had locked in on him and fired the EM pulse gun. The figure fell.

"What was that?" the Colonel demanded.

Jim trotted over and found himself looking at the unconscious body of Air Force 2nd Lieutenant Andy Newton. "Uh oh," was all he could say.

13 BIOSEC INC.

Time: 11:00 p.m., March 22, 2025
Location: BioSec Inc. Campus (just north of Alamogordo, New Mexico)

Heather Carson was driving out to work at the BioSec campus just outside Alamogordo, and she wasn't very excited about it. She had worked for BioSec for almost three years now. Technically, she was a "lab technician," but on the night shift that usually meant little more than "experiment maid." She knew that most people in her position only stayed a year or two before returning to school (there was no upward mobility in the job, you did it for the experience and then moved on). She also knew that, even though she was only 26, her chances of having the kind of career she wanted were going to fade fast if she didn't pick a direction for her life soon ... and the search for that direction wasn't going well. Despite her intelligence and her talent for the work, Heather's career had stalled, and she knew why. The truth was that she just wasn't very good at playing "the game" with the senior research staff, and she had become increasingly disillusioned about how much of advancement in the biotech field was linked to who you knew (and sometimes who you screwed). She had begun to wonder if she wanted to change careers altogether, but she had convinced herself that the story wouldn't be any different anywhere else.

And then there was her Grandmother. Grandma Carson was one of the last remnants of the now very old "you get a job so you can meet a nice man, get married and settle down" school of thought. She drove Heather crazy, but she was the only living relative that Heather had, so when she had called a few hours ago, Heather felt compelled to again go through the whole "what are you doing with your life" conversation *again*. At least she didn't ask Heather if she was gay this time (you know your love life isn't going well when the conversation ends up including the phrase, "no Grandma, I'm not a lesbian"). Heather liked men, and she liked having sex with men, there just hadn't been one in her life for a long time, and the last one had been a REALLY bad idea. The fact was that Heather was beginning to wonder if the right man for her was even out there and, if he was, if she would ever meet him. Heather's Grandmother clearly worried about this possibility a lot more than Heather did, but the truth was that, when it came up, it did rather force the point in Heather's mind that she was, metaphorically, standing at this big fork in the road of her life, unable to decide which way to go.

As she drove towards BioSec she was replaying the evening's conversation in her head, *again*, and questioning just what the hell she was doing with her life, *again*, and the only answer she could give herself was that it was a "good job", it paid pretty well, it was in an exciting field and BioSec was definitely a prestigious company to work for in the biotech industry. If nothing else, it would look good on a résumé or graduate school application ... as long as she didn't linger in the job too long ... and even though that day was approaching, it was not today, so she told herself to shut up about it.

She pulled into the long drive up to the BioSec campus, and to change the subject in her mind, she looked up at the sky. It was another beautiful, star filled night. She had very few memories of her father, but looking up at the stars always provoked the strongest one. Her Dad had been an avid, amateur astronomer. On special nights, her Dad would go into the backyard and set up this big telescope they had. She and her Mom would bring a blanket and snacks out, and her Dad would find all of these interesting things in the sky and tell them all kinds of stories about whatever he was showing them. She remembered that her Dad had wanted her to be an astronaut, traveling out into the stars. Heather would ask how long it would take to get to this place or that, and her Dad would figure it out and tell her (and it was always some impossible number of years). It was a very happy memory, and she smiled a little as she looked up at the stars and remembered.

As the main gate came into view, what Heather saw quickly shook all other thoughts from her mind. Normally there was one security guard at the gate to the complex, tonight there were three, and they weren't from the security company. They were armed, military looking guards. Looking past the gate, she could also see several unfamiliar trucks, including a large, funky looking RV kind of vehicle in the parking lot. She immediately assumed that they were government trucks of some kind (though these were unusual in that they were all black with no markings or logos). She had seen this kind of security at BioSec before of course, but these weren't uniforms she recognized (they weren't Air Force, that's for sure). Heather wasn't especially concerned about what part of the military they were from though. BioSec did secret work for the government all the time and, when they did they almost always had extra guards all over the place. All the locals thought BioSec was involved with some secret, biological weapons work or something. It was a rumor Heather did not discourage (mostly because the rumors made her job sound more interesting than it was). Most often, however, the truth was far more mundane. The last time Heather remembered the company being called on to do something top secret, it was really just to help clean up a chemical mess that had been created by using the wrong paint in an industrial area. Anyway, she knew that the presence of all of these extra, armed guards would send everyone into high stress and paranoia mode, so she prepared herself for the silliness of 'heightened security.'

The guards checked her name and ID against a list they had and waved her through with only slightly more than the normal level of elevated effort. As she walked up to the main entrance, Heather looked again at all the trucks and equipment and wondered if something genuinely interesting might be going on after all. She had heard on the news that the Air Force had, suddenly and rather mysteriously, sealed off a large area north of town. But this was New Mexico, home of Roswell, and that meant that every time some stray experimental jet went down, nearly every crazy UFO person for hundreds of miles in every direction dusted off their best conspiracy theories and aired them out. She figured some military experiment had come crashing to Earth and the military, once again, needed BioSec's help to clean up whatever radioactive, biological or chemical mess they had created.

It didn't really matter of course. It was very unlikely that she would ever get to know what it was. She worked in the horticulture experimentation lab. As a result, she felt certain that, unless something had gone horribly wrong with a secret Air Force experiment to launch a pot of geraniums into orbit, it wasn't terribly likely that she'd ever get to know what all the excitement was about. As she walked in the main entrance, however, it was clear that a *much* higher than normal level of security was in place there too. In fact, the more she looked around, the more it appeared that all the extra attention was centered on her part of the building. To get in, she had to go through *another* identity check, and there were armed guards *inside* the building as well. "Now that is strange," she thought as she walked in. They cleared her to go to work, but told her to report to some Doctor whose name she'd never heard of at the security desk after changing into her lab clothes.

She went to the locker room to change into her sterile "lab blues." Heather was about 5' 7" with very straight, slightly more than shoulder length, "dirty" blonde hair (tied back, of course, into a single, very neat pony tail). She felt like she was just a bit on the small and thin side, but she was in good shape, and most men found her attractive, not that she cared that much about that. Suddenly she was explaining her sexuality to her Grandma again in her head and she almost said aloud, "Look, I like a good fuck as much as the next girl, I just don't have time right now."

One of the reasons she enjoyed the night shift was the solitude away from all the Doctors and other Researchers. The ones who weren't married generally weren't interested in a serious relationship with the lab techs, and the ones who were interested were invariably married, and she'd been there and done that (that would be the aforementioned relationship a year ago that was REALLY wrong ... "*never* again," she had promised herself about a thousand times since). As usual, Heather was alone in the dressing room as she changed clothes. She liked her lab clothes; they were large and comfortable like sweats, but thinner and lighter. And she always wore her white lab coat. She told herself that she did that because the lab coat kept her warmer in the air conditioned labs, but the real reason was because it made her feel more important.

She approached the security area and there met Doctor Stern. She quickly decided that he was well named. Dr. Stern clearly worked for some secret government agency or another and, from his attitude when he said her name, she decided that he hadn't agreed with whoever had made the decision to allow her to work tonight. She had already noticed that, inside the building, the night staff was much smaller than normal. While he was giving her the standard military secrets nonsense (you saw nothing, you heard nothing, which never did anything but increase anyone's curiosity about what the heck was going on), she glanced past him into the security area. The guard who was normally watching all the video monitors of the labs wasn't there. That all by itself was odd enough, but what was really odd was that at least half of the screens were dark. They'd turned *off* the video monitors? She completely tuned out Dr. Stern and began concentrating on trying to figure out which cameras weren't on. It was B-Wing! In fact, all the cameras leading to and in B-Wing were off. That was *definitely* strange. Her office (OK, a glorified storage closet) was in B-Wing. Suddenly, her ears tuned back in to Dr. Stern as he said, "and under no circumstances whatsoever are you to enter B-Wing this evening, is that clear?" Heather wanted to laugh at the guy because she knew that there was pretty much nothing in the world that could make a person more interested in what the heck was going on in B-Wing than to forbid them to go there. She also really disliked the idea of being locked out of her office space (where she liked to hang out when she was done with her work), but she knew the game and very solemnly said, "understood clearly sir."

With fewer people and less to do, she finished her rounds in A-Wing much faster than normal. This was normally the time that she would sneak down to her "office" in B-Wing for a while and wondered what she would do instead. She found herself genuinely curious about what could have happened that would have led to this level of security in what was essentially a plant lab. Whatever was going on in B-Wing, it must be serious. So she walked over to the hallway intersection that she usually took to B-Wing. As she approached, two men who were obviously from the government were walking away from B-Wing. One was an attractive, muscular, "American hero" looking type, and the other was tall and thin with short black hair. They were talking animatedly to one another and didn't seem to even notice her as they walked by. They were wearing light green lab coats with some special writing on it that she didn't quite catch. She had to look down and smile right after they passed. "My God, it's Kirk and Spock," she said to herself. She quickly glanced down the hall as she walked past the entrance area to B-Wing. There was a desk with a video monitor and an armed Guard. "Another guard?" she thought. She decided that they must be guarding some *thing* in B-Wing. "Maybe they created or found some kind of bio hazard," she thought. She was starting to get concerned for the company work that was going on in the labs. She knew these military types, they wouldn't give a crap about whether or not BioSec's equipment or experiments in progress got damaged or destroyed in the process of whatever the hell they were doing. Now she really wanted to find out what was going on (and make sure that the company's experiments were all OK), but she wasn't going to get in the normal way.

Suddenly she realized that she might know something the military guys didn't. When BioSec built the smaller C-Wing (which was between A and B-Wings), among other cost cutting measures, they had decided that the two wings would share the same custodial closet ... a closet whose door in B-Wing was past the guard and giant the bio hazard door behind him (she had always thought that this was an incredibly *stupid* design decision because, if anything ever "got loose" in either wing, it could easily infect the other ... but that flaw might do her growing curiosity a real favor tonight). And her access card would get her into C-Wing, so she decided to go there.

When she entered C-Wing, the hall was empty and the door to the custodial closet was open. She couldn't believe her luck. Heather was used to government people making stupid mistakes, but she was still amazed that they could make a mistake this big. Then she heard voices coming from the closet. "Damn," she thought. She quickly realized that they had probably discovered this security issue just as she had thought of it and they were fixing it. As the men were leaving the closet, she decided to walk down the hall and do her best to make it look like she belonged there and that she was going somewhere specific on purpose. Fortunately, the lab door across the hall from the closet was open and she immediately walked in that direction. As she passed by and into the lab, the two men (also dressed in the strange, light green lab coats) stepped out of the closet. One of them ran a security card through the closet door's handle mechanism and said, "That should do it."

She was sure that they had seen her walk by, but they completely ignored her. She heard one of them kick the up the pedestal to the closet door and heard their footsteps as they walked away. Her eyes raced around the room, frantically looking for something, anything to block the door before it closed. She turned to look at the door. She had only seconds left. Her lab coat! She stripped it off and wadded it up with lightning speed. She aimed as best she could and then tossed it towards the floor by the edge of the closet door and held her breath. Perfect! The closing door reached the wadded up coat and stopped. She looked down the hall just in time to see the door to C-Wing close. The two men, whoever they were, hadn't heard or turned around. Still, Heather sprinted across the hall, grabbed the door and pulled it open just enough to get through it while reaching down and grabbing her lab coat all in one motion. The door closed and latched behind her.

Her heart was pumping much faster now, not just because of what she had just done, but because she suddenly realized that, if she were discovered here, she would almost certainly lose her job.

She walked across the closet to the door that opened into B-Wing, and very slowly, very carefully, turned the handle.

14 B-WING

Time: 12:02 a.m., March 23, 2025
Location: B-Wing, BioSec Inc. Campus

B-Wing was strangely dark. Not black, but the lights were dimmed down to about 15% of normal, giving the hallway a kind of strange, moonlit feeling. She stuck her head out. No one. She looked to her right (towards the bio-hazard proof door). She knew the guard she had seen earlier was standing watch on the other side. The door was several inches thick and she knew there was no chance that she could be seen or heard, but she wanted to make sure there was no one coming. She turned and looked down the hallway. The far end of the hall was a *mess* of big, fat cables. Several of these cables ran into the labs where they were attached to equipment she had never seen and didn't recognize. Heather knew immediately that she had been right about these people, whoever they were. Whole areas had obviously just been commandeered, and clearly these people had absolutely no respect for what had been in the labs (experiments and equipment had been just pushed aside). A number of the cables went to generators that were running in labs (with their exhaust coupled to lab vents).

The generators were making the wing much warmer than normal. And clearly some of these cables were high voltage or something, almost certainly very dangerous. Heather began to wonder about what could be worth this level of effort. Whatever it was, she was starting to be concerned that she was already in way over her head. For the first time, part of her thought about turning around and just going back. If she were caught by anyone other than the guys who had locked the closet moments ago, she figured that she could still play the lost, "dumb blonde" card and maybe talk her way out of trouble (tell them she'd wandered over via C-Wing by accident, etc. ... it would be worth a try anyway). But when she was about 10 feet from her office door, she heard voices from the lab at the end of the hall, and they seemed to be on the move. "Shit!" she thought. She ran to her door. There was yellow tape crossing her door (as well as the other doors in the hall that hadn't been commandeered). She slid her key card through the lock. The light turned green and the latch clicked. "Thank God they didn't change the lock codes," she thought as she carefully and quickly stepped over and under the two stripes of yellow tape crossing her doorway. Once in, she silently spun and held the door open by just a crack. She strained to hear as much of the conversation as she could as they walked by.

"That's it for tonight then?" the one voice said.

"Probably," the other replied. "Powell and Landrum said they were going to get a bite. Said they might come back to check on it, but basically we're supposed to just let it acclimate some more and ... I don't know, hope I guess."

As they passed her, she opened the door a little wider to hear better (figuring they wouldn't turn or look back).

"I think it's a mistake to leave it alone," said the first one.

"Oh, I doubt it's going anywhere," said the other, "it would have done it by now. I don't think it's gonna make it anyway." Everything after that she couldn't make out, but she was still processing what she heard; let *IT* acclimate? What the heck was "it"? What did they find out there?

Heather was completely overcome by curiosity. She forgot

about her job, forgot about feeling that she shouldn't be there ... she was there and WAY past the point of no return, she *had* to find out now.

She waited until she heard the big door at the end of the hall close before sticking her head back out. She was alone in B-Wing ... with "it." She stepped back out into the hall and walked very slowly towards lab #8, the last lab on the right at the end of the hall. It made total sense to her that they would use lab #8, it was the only lab with the ability to access it from outside the building (via a very large, very heavy door that was basically more airtight and stronger than the building it was attached to). Many of the big cables and things seemed to converge in that doorway. As she passed the door to lab #6 she noticed that it was closed and locked, but had to tape over the door and obviously no cables running in or out of it ... and for a moment she thought she heard something or someone in it. She froze, but after several moments of hearing nothing more, she very quietly moved on. As she got closer to the door to lab #8, she could feel the air getting very humid and heavy. The room had kind of a black light glow to it ... except black light always looked kind of purple to her, where the ambient light here was clearly a subdued electric green color. The air smelled like both something and nothing at the same time. Almost as if the air itself was different, not just warmer and wetter, but like a different mix of gases. It took more effort to breathe, but clearly there was more than enough oxygen. As she walked in, the first thing she saw was several massive dark green lights pointed at the ceiling. And there was some strange looking equipment that she had never seen before. They looked a little like humidifiers, but they were doing something to the air. Then she saw it.

It was hard to make out what it was at first. "Whatever it is," she thought, "it's big." Suddenly, she was overwhelmed by the feeling that she was in WAY over her head. Her heart rate was now racing, but as afraid as she was, she was now insatiably curious about what she was looking at, and needed to see it better. The light was too low though, and even with her eyes fully adjusted, she was going to have to step into the room to get a good enough look at whatever the heck this thing was.

As quietly, softly and slowly as she could, she walked into the room. Her eyes strained to see, and with her next step she suddenly got an outline. She figured it had to be at least 20-30 feet long, at least six feet tall in the middle, and sort of cylindrical, but flattened on the ends. Its outer surface wasn't like anything she'd ever seen. It seemed sort of plant like (like wet leaves in places). Her mind struggled to compare it to something. It was the size of a small whale, but it was like some sort of giant worm/plant/whale hybrid thing. Its skin was a brownish green in the green light of the room. At the end of it closest to her was what she guessed was a massive mouth, easily large enough to open and consume a person. Then, ever so slightly, it moved. It was alive! And NOT from around here! "Holy shit!" she thought, "They really did it! This is some kind of alien thing!" The mix of feelings was incredible! There was fear, excitement, and a massive rush of adrenaline running through her body. Some part of her knew that she could be in incredible danger, but another part couldn't turn away. Was it breathing? Sort of. It was definitely moving, VERY slowly, like it was asleep or something.

"Wow," she whispered aloud. She was startled by her own voice, and quickly looked behind her (sensing there might be someone there). Nothing, she was alone with whatever this thing was. But when she turned back, something was different. Not a lot different, in fact only very slightly different, and she struggled to figure out what it was. It was the "mouth" … it was *open!* Only very slightly, but unmistakably, it was open. And while she couldn't quite make it out, there appeared to be several soft antennae like things at the edge of the inside of the mouth. Heather froze, she had no idea whether she was imagining that it was aware of her, but her survival instinct took over and said, "Time to go!" She took one step backward with her right foot, which made a crinkling noise on the plastic sheeting covering the floor, and that, was all the creature needed to figure out where she was.

15 CUSTODY

Time: 11:55 p.m., March 22, 2025
Location: B-Wing Lab #6, BioSec Inc. Campus

Andy Newton was in *big* trouble, and he knew it. At this point he was sure that, if his military career weren't already over, it certainly would be shortly. He felt *incredibly* stupid as he replayed the events of the weekend in his head for the one-thousandth time. Of course, there weren't that many events to replay since he had literally slept through most of it after getting zapped by whatever super secret, stun gun thing it was that they had shot him with. He couldn't believe how much he wanted to go back to the moment when Major Anderson had ordered him to forget about the target and just do what he was told. And then what had he done? He had gone charging off after this thing in the middle of the night, he lied to a *State Trooper* ("God only knows what the penalty is for that," he thought, but he was sure it was *not* good), and then he had gone sneaking around in the wilderness up to this lake with a dam where ... well, zap.

When he had finally woken up, almost 8 hours ago now, he was on a cot in a strange room. His head hurt, in fact his whole body was kind of achy. He felt groggy, fuzzy and disoriented, and the fact that he had no damn idea where in the world he was didn't help either. He appeared to be in some kind of laboratory. He was only awake for a few minutes when they came in. Three of them. When Andy saw one was wearing a Marine Officer's uniform, he got up and did his best to stand at attention.

"Good afternoon Lieutenant," she said, "At ease, I'm Colonel Jane Wisener."

"Lieutenant Andrew Newton ma'am," Andy responded. The other two men appeared to be in uniform too, but it wasn't a uniform Andy recognized.

"Oh, we know who you are Lieutenant," the Colonel said, "what we don't know is what the hell you were doing up at Bonito Lake this morning."

Andy suddenly realized that he had no idea what time it was or how long he had been unconscious. There was a clock on the wall behind the Colonel. It said it was 4:10pm. He'd been unconscious for about ten hours. "No wonder I'm so hungry," he thought, momentarily avoiding the reality of the situation. He had no idea how to answer the Colonel's question. "I, umm..."

"Yes, well, suffice it to say that you're in what we would normally call a shitstorm of trouble Lieutenant," the Colonel continued, "but I'd like to hear your side of the story."

Andy explained what had happened. He told them that he worked at the Project NEO station up at Kirtland (they knew that) and that he had been the one on watch when the unknown had been detected (they knew that too). Then he told them how he had disobeyed orders and placed the station's equipment in diagnostic mode so that he could track the unknown AND how he had hidden that fact from NORAD. Andy wasn't sure, but he thought he saw the Colonel suppress a smile when he told them about that. Then he told them about how he had called Nick and made up a story about being sick so that Nick would come in early and relieve him so he could go drive out and see this thing. He told them that he hadn't really intended to lie to the trooper at the first roadblock, but he figured he had come this far, and he was really curious, and he wanted to see whatever it was. Then he told them about how he hid his car when he got to the lake area and then quietly hiked up the side of the hill to the site ... where he obviously he got hit by whatever had knocked him out for the last half of the day. Finally, he told them that he realized that it was really wrong for him to have done ALL of that, that he was really sorry and that he really just wanted to go back to his base and face whatever punishment he had coming to him there.

Colonel Wisener stared at him for what seemed like an eternity, and then she said, "Well you're not going anywhere Lieutenant, at least not for the moment."

"Yes ma'am," Andy said, resigned to his fate. "What's going to happen to me ma'am?"

The Colonel looked at him sharply. "To be honest Lieutenant, we haven't decided yet," the Colonel replied, clearly implying to Andy that his behavior and cooperation were still *very* important.

"I'll be expected back at Kirtland..." Andy began.

"Well, don't worry about that," the Colonel replied, "we've already spoken to them *and* to your superiors at NORAD."

Andy looked surprised. "Well," he thought, "that's it for my career then."

The Colonel decided it was time to let the kid off the hook a bit. "What we've told them is that, for the moment, despite your inability to do what you're told, or rather because of it, you are temporarily assigned to this unit for at least a few days while we sort this shit out."

Andy's face changed and he suddenly felt more confused than scared.

"Oh yes," the Colonel said, "I can do that. You see, what you've stumbled into and on to here is something that is WAY over your head and pay grade."

"Well *that's* certainly true," Andy thought. "Yes ma'am," he said as respectfully as possible.

"But," the Colonel continued, "at the same time you also demonstrated some characteristics that most people in the military don't like, but *we* actually look for. AND, since your boss's boss's boss is a personal friend of mine, we've decided to hold off on the decision of what to do with you and/or whether to send you to some God forsaken duty station in the middle of nowhere forever, until we are in a better position to make that decision. So until we have that time, you will sit here."

"Yes ma'am," said Andy, "for how long ma'am?"

"For as long as I Goddamn well say Lieutenant," the Colonel answered in a calm yet annoyed and stern voice. It was clear that the Colonel was very well practiced at being able to put someone in their place while at the same time not completely shutting them down.

One of the two men was looking at Andy with a face that made it clear that he had just asked the *wrong* question. "Yes ma'am," said Andy apologetically.

Colonel Wisener found herself having to actively suppress the fact that at least part of her liked this kid. She couldn't say it or let him know it of course, but she was impressed. He had demonstrated brains, ingenuity and guts in what he had done. "*And* he evaded our strike teams before getting caught only a few feet from the alien," she thought. And she felt like he had been completely honest with her. Clearly this young man had potential. The Colonel was already wondering if she might not even try to recruit him into UNCLE before this was over. "You look hungry," she said.

"Yes ma'am," Andy said, smiling a little.

"Alright," the Colonel said understandingly. "The Captain here will see to it that you get some food, washcloth, towel, and ... I don't know maybe a book to read or something?"

"Yes ma'am," Captain Landrum said.

"There's a bathroom right over there when you need it," the Colonel continued. "Until further notice, you are confined to this room, is that clear?"

"Yes ma'am!" Andy said.

"Alright, carry on then. Gentlemen..." she said to Captain Landrum and Dr. Powell, and the three of them turned and left. The door closed and locked behind them.

The rest of the day had been pretty boring. From several of the materials in the lab that were in unlocked drawers and laying around, Andy determined that he was being held inside the labs of a company called BioSec. In the back of his mind he thought he knew the name but couldn't place why. He guessed that they were a defense contractor that had something to do with whatever they had found at the crash site. About 20 minutes after the Colonel had left, two other individuals (also wearing the same uniform that Andy had never seen before) entered with a tray of food, a towel, and a few magazines. Andy spent the rest of the day sitting on the cot, reading, wandering around the lab, and generally trying to avoid thinking about how much trouble he was in (which was not easy) ... but no matter what he did, his mind kept coming back to the moment just before he'd gotten zapped. "There was a ship," he thought, "it was a *definitely* a *ship* of some kind." And that meant one incredible and undeniable truth; he *had* in fact tracked some kind of alien craft crashing down to Earth. Andy realized that he was now part of one of the biggest events in human history. No wonder they were keeping him here! "Heck they might be deciding whether or not to let me *live!*" Andy thought nervously. He wondered if anyone had survived the crash. And then, at the very edge of his mind, he remembered something he couldn't quite get his brain to latch on to, something *immediately* before he had lost consciousness. He kept trying, but it wouldn't come.

Which brought him back to now. Having spent the better part of 10 hours that day unconscious, he was having difficulty getting to sleep. He assumed that there was stuff going on related to the alien ship in this part of the BioSec building. Outside his lab door he would occasionally hear footsteps and voices, but at about 11pm, everything seemed to settle down. Andy had been trying to get to sleep for a while, but then he heard what sounded like someone in the hall. He got up slowly, but as he did his cot made a noise. He froze, and then after a few moments he thought he heard the very faint sound of someone continuing, almost as if they were sneaking by his room.

A few minutes later he heard a woman scream, and it wasn't just any scream. It was the kind of scream that meant real danger. Then, unmistakably, there was a brief cry for help that stopped as suddenly as it started. Andy jumped to his feet, ran to the door and tried to force it open. Nothing. He shouted for help and pounded on the door. Nothing. His eyes raced around the room. He felt the urgent need to try to help whoever it was, but he couldn't see any way out. Then he looked up. Ceiling tiles! He jumped up on the lab counter that ran along the wall and punched the tile out of the way. He looked up. The wall did NOT go all the way up to the upper ceiling! Andy kept moving quickly but couldn't help thinking about how dumb that was for a lab (clearly some sort of cost cutting design flaw). He pulled himself up above the suspended ceiling and forced the front of his body over the cinderblock wall between his room and the one next to it (where he was certain the screams had come from). Since he had first heard the screams there had been total silence. The quiet only made him more afraid for whoever it was and more determined to help quickly. Amazingly, the suspended ceiling in the next room held his weight as he moved onto it. And then it didn't.

Crash! It was *not* Andy's most graceful entrance into a room, but he did manage to grab one of the drop ceiling suspension rods on his way down, which allowed him some control as he fell. He landed mostly on his feet before crumpling in a heap. He got up as quickly as he could and tried to focus in the very low light of the room. Almost immediately his eyes focused on a very large *thing* to his right. *"HOLY SHIT!"* he yelled. Adrenaline flooded into Andy's body and he involuntarily recoiled and jumped backwards. After a moment, he made the first effort to calm himself. It wasn't very successful. "Holy shit holy shit holy shit!" he thought, "That's an *alien*!" He was instantly overwhelmed by both fear and curiosity. The more he stared at it, the more he decided it probably wasn't much of a threat and started to calm down a little. It also looked asleep or dormant or something. It was barely moving, but towards the front (or what he assumed was the front anyway) appeared to be...

Andy's heart rate doubled again as his mind jumped to the only conclusion it could. The room was empty now, but moments ago it couldn't have been. He *had* heard a scream, and there was no one there but the alien now. He looked at the creature. "Oh my God," he thought, "this thing just ate whoever that person was!" He was immediately gripped with fear but also overwhelmed by the need to try to help, even if that meant endangering himself. The problem was that he had no idea what he could do to help. The creature seemed to move again, like it was moving whomever it had just eaten down along its, whatever. In a panic he went over to the creature and started hitting and pushing it on the side where it was moving and bulging. He shouted, "no!" and pushed as hard as he could in the spot that appeared to be where the bulge was moving.

And that's when he felt a sharp shock, followed by the sense of flying for just an instant and then a BANG as, once again, the world went totally black.

16 CONTACT

Time: unknown
Location: The Plain

Heather was only vaguely aware of her own existence. Her mind was a jumbled and confused mess. With what little awareness she had, she felt bodiless, like she was gently floating and spinning through an endless void. She reached out to her senses for input, but got back only a very general feeling that didn't answer the only question she was capable of thinking: "where am I?" Slowly, she felt the outline of her consciousness returning to her, but she couldn't concentrate on anything long enough to get a grip on ... anything. She couldn't see or really feel her body, but she felt like it *was* there. Then suddenly, at the base of her spine she felt a very specific sensation. It was both very painful and yet not painful at all. It was a sharp, tingling sensation, like acupuncture needles. It was there, and yet, not there. The "feeling" proceeded up her spine, and then her neck ... and then, very suddenly, it felt like someone shot a thousand tiny needles into the back of her head right at the base of her skull. The pain was instantaneous and incredibly intense yet, again, it was also like she wasn't feeling it at all, but rather watching it or hearing someone tell her about it.

Suddenly the world went from all black to all blinding white.

Then black again. Then white again. Then much faster: black white black white black white black white ... and then black. There was a pause, and Heather was able to use the moment to identify herself. "I'm Heather Carson," she thought. "I..." and then RED. It was such an overpowering sensation that the only word to describe it was loud ... in fact, it almost seemed like there was a sound to the color. There was nothing but red. A deep red. Then all of a sudden it was blue. Then yellow. Then green. Then violet. Then orange. These colors repeated several times. Then mixtures of the colors in various combinations. It was like a kaleidoscope of colors; some were unspeakable beautiful, others were grotesque and disturbing. Heather was powerless to do or think anything other than to react to what she was sensing. And then it stopped.

NOISE! An instantaneous, incredibly loud, jarring, "jump straight up out of your seat" cacophony of noise unlike anything she had ever heard. She wanted to raise her hands to her ears, but while she knew she had hands and ears, she couldn't see them or control them. And then it stopped, and in its place was the most beautiful soft musical sound she had ever heard. It was music so pure and perfect that it would have brought tears to her eyes. And then a horn, and then something that sounded like a construction site, and then a loud crash, and then a bell, and then a whole string of various, unrelated sounds that were just long enough to identify.

After another pause she smelled flowers, and then the most awfully putrid sulfur dioxide (rotten egg) smell, and then a pizza, and then chocolate, and then a host of other foods and chemicals and smells of all kinds, again all coming and going so quickly that there was barely enough time to identify them before they were gone. All of them were incredibly intense but so fast that there was no time to react.

Then she tasted her Grandmother's fudge, and after that a barrage of foods and things, some beyond delicious, some absolutely vomit inducing.

Finally she felt something touch her hand. Startled, she tried to recoil, but she had no idea where her hand was, and even if she could see it and/or identify it, she couldn't control it. Soft things, hard things, sharp things, smooth things. She felt like something cut her hand open but then it was instantly fine again. She felt the most mind-bending headache, and then nothing. Several of her body parts ached and then felt great. She had an incredible menstrual cramp and then an explosive orgasm, but it was all happening with such speed that there was no time to feel lasting pleasure or pain in any of it.

And then, again, there was total blackness, and she again felt weightless and bodiless, floating gently and silently and peacefully through an endless void. But it wasn't endless this time. And it wasn't black. There was color here this time. Slowly at first, and then much more rapidly she saw a gentle swirl of pleasant, light colors. And there was sound! It was like music but at the same time not music. But it was beautiful and peaceful. Heather was instantly calmed by it. Then, within the endless, pleasantly colored world, a shape began appearing. It was darker, which made it easier to distinguish it from its background. It was a circle, but the moment she recognized it as a circle it became a square, and then a triangle and then a sphere and then a cone and then a pyramid and then a dozen other shapes. Finally there was a shape that she didn't recognize (she thought it was like a cube but with the tops of a bunch of pyramids sticking out of it) and it didn't change. After a moment, the shape gently divided itself into two identical shapes, and then a third, and a fourth, and so on. She counted them until there were ten shapes. Then the entire row split into a second, identical row and she thought, "20." And then there were thirty and forty and so on. The shapes got smaller until there were one hundred.

Every now and then, Heather's conscious mind would try to think, but every time it did she'd get as far as remembering who she was, "I'm Heather Carson," and then it would be gone.

All of the shapes disappeared except one. Then two more appeared at a distance. They came together into a single grouping of all three shapes, and then they disappeared. Then there were two groups of two, and they came together to form a single group of four. Then three and two, then three and three, and so on, but this time when they got to ten shapes, below the shapes appeared the number "10". And then all of the shapes disappeared, and in their place she saw "10 +10 = " and immediately again thought "20."

Examples of the four basic mathematics functions began appearing and disappearing in front of her at staggering speed. As quickly as they would appear she would think of the answer and the question would disappear and be replaced with another. And then everything stopped once again.

From off in the distance another shape appeared. It was a sphere with a smaller sphere in an irregular and constantly wobbly orbit around it. Heather thought of a planet orbiting a star, but the image did not go away. Instead, the "star" in the middle suddenly broke into four smaller spheres all mashed together and now two smaller spheres raced around it. "Hydrogen and Helium!" Heather thought. It was apparently the right "answer" because suddenly the images began changing quickly again, but this time when she didn't know what something was, the image continued to change anyway.

And then, again, everything faded slowly and calmly back into blackness. Suddenly, in front of her was a cat. But it wasn't just any cat; it was Porter, a cat that had belonged to her friend Kathy in grade school. Then she was looking at Kathy, but not Kathy as she had to be now, it was Kathy the way she was the last time she saw her (about 6th grade).

And that's when the "show" *really* started. Images and moments from Heather's memory appeared in front of her, all of them appearing and changing at absolutely staggering speed. She relived an incredibly fast, rapid-fire series of snapshot memories of her life from her earliest memory to the present day. Most of the images were so fast that she couldn't keep up, but every now and then it would seem to slow down enough for her to see one and concentrate on it (she saw the alphabet along the top of the write and wipe board in her 1st grade classroom, she heard a piece of music from a school musical in 9th grade).

The images stopped as abruptly as they had started, and their absence was as jarring to Heather as their presence had been moments before. Then she sensed the darkness giving way to light again. The light was warm and gentle, but there were different colors this time. There were light colors, but also darker ones. There were primary colors, but also richer, more complex colors. And there was a soothing sound, it wasn't music, but it felt restful. Far more importantly, Heather finally felt control of her conscious mind returning to her. She could *think* again, and *control* what she was thinking. She got past her name, her address, and her phone number. She quizzed herself for several moments and felt a sense of relief when she finally had the mental strength to ask, "Where the hell am I?"

"Hello," a voice said, "I am Gopto."

The voice startled Heather. It was different, deeper than most male voices she could think of, but not booming or ethereal and, after the initial shock of hearing it, not really frightening either. "My, my name is Heather Carson," she said. She could hear her own voice and yet she was sure that she wasn't really speaking.

"You are ... concerned ... for your safety," Gopto said, "you are ... fine."

"Where am I?" Heather asked.

"We are one," Gopto replied.

Heather thought about that, and as she did, her last moments in the lab before she lost consciousness slowly came back to her. "Am I dead?" she asked.

"You are ... fine," Gopto replied.

Heather didn't think that was an answer to her question, but she definitely didn't *feel* dead, and the voice made her feel oddly calm and safe.

"I ... apologize," Gopto continued, "I am learning you. It will get better."

"Why can't I see or feel my body?" Heather asked.

There was a pause, and then slowly, like a camera coming in to focus, Heather could see herself. She was naked but otherwise seemed in tact. She looked at her hands, moved them around, open and closed her fists, moved her head around. She noted that she had been right. She was floating. "I should be standing," she thought, and immediately, wherever she was suddenly seemed to have an up and down for the first time. There was a sensation of gravity. She felt her feet contacting a surface, and then she was standing on it.

"Where am I?" Heather asked again, and then it occurred to her to ask the question in a different way. "What is this place?"

"It is the beginning," Gopto replied.

"The beginning of what?" Heather asked.

"The beginning of anything," Gopto replied.

"I don't understand," Heather said.

"I am sorry," Gopto replied. "I am still learning you, it will get better."

Despite the fact that her conscious mind was returning to her very quickly now, she was still confused and getting more frustrated by the moment. She had no idea where she was, who this Gopto was or what the hell was going on. The whole thing felt like a very surreal dream, except that, as each moment wore on she felt more and more sure that, despite how bizarre and inexplicable it all was, it was not a dream. She struggled to put the last things she remembered into some kind of context.

"It is ... OK," Gopto said. "You ... can ... remember now."

Heather focused on the last thing she remembered. "I was ... I was in a lab," she said.

"Yes," Gopto said.

Heather was still not sure who or what Gopto was, but elaborate dream or not, it did seem as though he was helping her, or at least trying to. She concentrated again. "I was in B-Wing at BioSec," she continued. "I wasn't supposed to be there. I went into the lab at the end of the hall and..." suddenly Heather felt a physical chill run through her entire body and a sense of absolute terror.

"You are fine," Gopto said.

Immediately, Heather's sense of fear was wiped from her mind, but so was her entire train of thought. She went through the events again, this time trying harder to control herself.

"I will ... help," Gopto said.

Heather had no idea what that meant, but as she went through the events again, this time she did feel oddly calmer and more dispassionate about her own memories. "I went into the lab and I saw a ... creature of some kind. It was ... alien!" She paused. "What I saw was you wasn't it?"

"Yes," replied Gopto.

"Where are we?" Heather asked.

"We are one," replied Gopto.

Heather was frustrated. She understood that Gopto was, to some degree, reading her mind, and she felt certain that he didn't mean her any harm; he was simply trying to communicate. Then it hit her; he doesn't understand the question! "That's not what I mean," Heather said, this time trying to rephrase her question, "Where are we *physically*?"

There was a long pause. Heather felt a minor tingling sensation in the back of her head. "I understand," Gopto said. "We are, in the same place."

"We're still in the lab?" Heather said.

"Yes," Gopto replied.

"Well, if I'm still in the lab, and I'm not dead and you didn't eat me or something, where is my real body?" Heather asked.

"We..." Gopto started.

"... are one," Heather finished, frustrated again, "yeah, I got that. What does that *mean*?" There was a long pause, and Heather now felt an almost uncomfortable amount of tingling in the back of her head, and at this point she basically understood why. "He's somehow searching my mind," she thought. Normally this would be incredibly invasive and offensive to her, but she knew that he was simply trying to communicate with her and something about that made it OK.

"You are correct," Gopto said. "My vocabulary will ... improve, in time. Some words are harder, but I am ... learning." There was a long pause, and then a black rectangle appeared in space in front of her. It grew rapidly until it resembled a big screen display. On it, an image appeared. It was what she remembered seeing in the lab.

"That's you," she said.

"Yes," Gopto said.

Suddenly, the image changed. It rotated away from what was in Heather's memory and moved along the far wall of the lab (to an angle that Heather had never observed Gopto from). She guessed that the creature had to be at least 25 feet long. She thought it resembled a giant worm with relatively small ends and a really big fat middle. "This is some kind of computer generated animation," Heather thought. Then, in the image, a woman appeared by the lab door. "That's me?" she asked.

"Yes," said Gopto.

Then, very rapidly, two long, thin, tendril like appendages shot out of the image of Gopto's front, wrapped around the image of Heather's ankles, and pulled. The image of Heather fell and Heather watched as her head hit the floor with a powerful "whack!" Heather gasped and instinctively pulled her right hand up to touch the spot behind and above her right ear where her head had hit the floor. She could remember the moment now, but she couldn't feel the bump on her head. Heather focused on the image in front of her because she knew what she would see next was what she *couldn't* remember. Gopto's tendrils pulled her, literally *inside* the creature.

"You ate me," she said in a kind of quiet shock, "I *am* dead."

"No," said Gopto. "Look."

As Heather watched the screen, it again rotated so that it showed her the side view of the creature. Then Gopto's skin faded and disappeared. The image looked far more like an animation now, and Heather felt a bit like she was watching a movie from a school science class. It was hard to tell what everything was, but there was a very large mass in the upper middle of the creature that looked like it was connected to *everything* else. The screen pulled in on this area and "highlighted" it with a kind of glow around it.

"Gopto," Gopto said.

"That's its brain," Heather thought. The animation pulled back and showed the whole creature again. But this time it wasn't in the lab; it was in the middle of some kind of tropical rain forest. There was lots of lush vegetation. With quick, decisive moves, tendrils from the creature's mouth whipped out, grabbed the vegetation, and sucked it in. The image then centered on Gopto again. The skin disappeared and she was looking at its insides. A pathway highlighted from the mouth along the bottom of the creature, under the brain and beyond. There were many chambers and tubes.

"Food," Gopto said, "need food."

Heather understood and was relieved to be increasingly certain that she was not on the menu. The animation pulled back a third time. This time it was back in the lab again. Heather could again see herself standing in front of it. The creature grabbed her and pulled her inside, but instead of going where the food went she saw her body being moved into a bubble like chamber that was above the digestive tract and next to the brain. The chamber ballooned to accommodate her size, and she was tucked into it in a fetal like position.

"Heather," Gopto said.

Heather understood, "And how are we able to...?" she asked tentatively, but as she asked, the animation continued. Her body rotated onto its right side, so Heather was looking at her own back from her butt to her skull. She watched with apprehension as a very long tendril attached itself to the base of her spine and then worked its way up to the skull, where the end became flat and square and then slapped into the base of her skull. She remembered the sensations as she watched them. "That's how we're talking," Heather said.

"Yes," Gopto replied.

"And you can do all this," Heather said, looking around, "create this ... place, in your mind?"

"This?" Gopto said, "This is nothing. This is what we call The Plain. It is ... (there was a pause as Gopto clearly searched Heather's mind for the words) like a blank slate. It is the beginning point from which we ... create."

"Create what?" Heather asked.

"Anything," Gopto said.

"Anything?" Heather said. There was a pause, and then the

screen in front of Heather faded away. And then the color of the space faded to black. Heather still felt like she was standing, but where she had felt like she had been in a normal sized "room" (even though the "edges" weren't really well defined) she now felt like she was standing on a black pedestal in a vast empty space.

BOOM!!! Heather was instantly standing in what appeared to be the vastness of outer space. There were stars and galaxies everywhere. "Holy fuck!" she said. Her eyes soaked in the incredible beauty of the infinite landscape in front of her. Tears came to her eyes.

"Anything," Gopto said, "everything."

Tears streamed down Heather's face as she fought to soak in what she was seeing. She wanted to speak, but she couldn't. She just stood there. There was no frame of reference for the experience. It was beauty on a scale that her brain simply didn't know how to react to. Finally, she whispered, "my God."

Very gently, she had the sensation of moving. The stars around her began changing position relative to her. There was no question, she was moving ... faster, and faster. Like a roller coaster ride but without any sensation of danger. Heather was now flying through space at incredible speeds, zipping through nebulae, flying by planets, seeing things no human had ever seen or even dreamed of before. "Is this real?" she asked, still barely able to get the words out of her mouth.

"Yes," Gopto replied. "Here..." he said, and as he spoke she "approached" a particular star with several planets. Most of them appeared cold, dark, rocky and lifeless, but two of the inner ones (the second and third in distance from the star) clearly had life. The farther one from the star had more blue, the closer one had more green, but both had clouds and, apparently, life. She continued towards the inner, green planet. It got bigger and bigger, and then suddenly, with a "whoosh" she felt like she was inside the atmosphere and had a sense of falling to the ground. But instead of crashing, the sensation slowed, and she felt herself "land" like a feather. She felt the tips of the grass like surface on the ground poke up at her bare feet. "Gopto's home," he said, "Morta."

"Wow...." Heather whispered, then she was hit with a wave of excitement like she'd never felt before in her life. "Oh my God, this is so REAL!" she exclaimed. This wasn't like any virtual reality she had ever seen; this was indistinguishable from *actual* reality! She could see, feel, hear and smell the world around her. The area around her was lush. She was standing in a small meadow on the edge of a forest that was thicker and richer than anything she'd ever even seen pictures of on Earth. She reached out to touch the leaf on a giant plant. It looked and felt a bit like a rubber plant, but a bit thicker. "This is amazing," she said. "And I'm not even really here am I?"

"You are asking if you are still one with me in the lab?" Gopto asked.

"Yes," Heather said.

"Good," Gopto said, "we are learning each other faster already. Yes, we are still one in the lab."

"How is this possible?" Heather asked.

"If you will permit me," Gopto said, "I will ... explain."

"OK," Heather said, but she was completely unprepared for what happened next. First, she felt a massive shockwave shoot through her entire mind and body, instantly overwhelming all of her senses. She was mentally and physically paralyzed, unable to move, feel or even think. And then it came; a sensation unlike anything she had ever experienced in her life. It was as if someone had literally opened up a door in the back of her head and began pumping massive amounts of data into her brain.

The raw amount of information was incredible, but even more incredible was the fact that it seemed to organize itself as quickly as it "downloaded" into her mind. Heather immediately just ... *knew* everything that had been transmitted. She knew that Gopto was a Mortub, the dominant species on the planet Morta (where she appeared to "be" at the moment). And she knew all about them. She knew that all Mortubs looked very similar to one another. She knew that they grew to about 5 to 6 feet tall and wide, up to about 25 feet long and that they looked kind of wormlike to her. Like most of the planet's animal inhabitants, they were vegetarians, and voracious ones at that. In fact, the Mortubs served a vital role in keeping the planet's ecosystem in balance as, without them, the otherwise incredibly prolific plant life on the planet would have long since completely taken over. From their outside appearance, it would be easy to dismiss the Mortubs as nothing more than large, slow, harmless, vegetarian ... well, vacuum cleaners for the planet. But they were more than that. Much more.

The Mortubs had an incredibly detailed, complex and extensive mental existence. Their entire culture; music, art, literature, science, architecture, history, everything, all existed in a nearly inconceivably vast, interconnected telepathic communications network. Within their world there were literally structures in thought. There were concert halls, libraries, entire cities, all in thought and all maintained in a giant, shared consciousness.

Heather now knew that the Mortubs communicated telepathically with each other over a range of many miles. Each Mortub mind could also serve as a conduit to any other Mortub mind in range of any other Mortub. Together, they formed the galaxy's largest known interconnected, collective consciousness. Each individual Mortub possessed its own consciousness and was capable of computational multi-tasking on a truly incredible scale, but they also functioned as a sort of wireless router, capable of a nearly infinite number of simultaneous connections to each other.

Heather continued to inventory the vast amount of new information in her head. She saw the history and culture of the Mortubs. She saw the virtual cities they built with their minds, the art and music and history and science they had accumulated. She learned how they evolved the extraordinary capabilities they had. She saw them millennia ago, using the chamber that her body was now in as a means of communicating with and pacifying some of the few, aggressive animal species of their world. Heather started to think, "but how..." but before she could even get the question out, the information was there.

Suddenly Heather was floating out in space again, high above Gopto's planet. Then her view turned and she was looking at the next planet back from their sun. It was the mostly blue (oceanic) one and was also quite beautiful to look at.

"Japella," Gopto said.

A spaceship appeared from Japella and traveled to Gopto's world. She "followed" it in and saw them arrive on the planet. They looked much more like what Heather thought an alien would look like, which is to say that they looked much more like humans. They had thicker skin that was aquamarine in color and their eyes were larger and black. There was also a strange ridge that started at their temples and went around the backs of their heads, and their hair was, well, not really hair but more like layers of small, thin scales. But in just about every other way they appeared quite similar to humans. They were called the Japel.

Not surprisingly, the first Japel to visit Morta discovered, but then essentially ignored the Mortubs. As Heather watched the "first contact" between their species, she couldn't help but smile as she related to the confusion, fear and intensity of the experience. It was the first time that either species had encountered another intelligent one. Fortunately, in an impressive example of cosmic dumb luck, it turned out that the Japel and the Mortubs were not only telepathically compatible, but both had built societies with compatible *values*. Most importantly, both valued cooperation over competition and exploration over conquest. Together, the knowledge, experience and capabilities of both species expanded exponentially.

The Mortubs had never been unhappy with their existence. Their collective consciousness was a completely harmonious flow of thought. But their experiences and interactions with the physical world were not only very limited, but something they almost completely ignored. The introduction of the Japel into their culture was the most significant, transformational event in millennia. The Japel represented something that, for all of the vast knowledge and beauty that comprised the Mortubs' existence, they had never known or considered; the Japel were something *new* and *different* in the *physical* world. Within their collective consciousness, the Mortubs had created a vast world filled with everything they could conceive. The Japel introduced them to the possibilities of experiences beyond their world, filled with things they *couldn't* conceive. To the Mortubs, the physical world had always been uninteresting, certainly unworthy of their intellectual attention. But now the Japel had shown them that the physical universe was in fact far more vast than any of them had ever considered.

For their part, the Japel had managed to advance and build spaceships capable of reaching Morta. But like so many other species, they lacked the ability to cross the vast distances of interstellar space in a practical timeframe. In the Mortubs, the Japel found a species that had already accumulated a vast amount of knowledge of mathematical structure. The Mortubs quickly applied the knowledge that they already had from the construction and maintenance of their virtual world to the things they learned from the Japel about the external universe. This combination, along with the ability to use and augment existing Japel technology, led to the discovery of the ability to fold space, and suddenly long distance space travel became possible. Thus began one of the most remarkable symbiotic relationships in the galaxy. With the Mortubs' assistance, the Japel could explore the galaxy on a scale that would have taken them millennia to accomplish on their own (if ever). And with the Japel's help, individual Mortubs could actually leave the collective, learn new things, have external experiences, and then return and share them.

There was more, of course, a LOT more, but Heather's mind was exhausted. She had just been forced to instantaneously process an unbelievable amount of data. When it stopped, Heather found herself crying out, and immediately began panting. "Oh my God," she said, still very much out of breath, "what the hell was that?!"

"You are upset?" Gopto said, "I am sorry, you said you wanted to know."

Heather was more mentally out of breath than anything else, but she was also calming down quickly. "It's OK," she said, "I just ... I just wasn't expecting ... *that.*" She took a deep breath and exhaled loudly. "Wow! That was quite a rush. That's amazing! So, so you can just ... transmit stuff like that into my head?"

"Yes," replied Gopto, "we are fortunate that we are compatible."

"Yeah," said Heather, "wow." She thought for a moment. The feeling was still very strange. She had all this new information in her head that she could access at will, and yet, when she did, there was a part of her consciousness that seemed to be hearing it for the first time, like she was reading a book. She wanted time to just sit and think about all the new information she had, but her mind was also reeling at the possibilities in front of her. It was pretty obvious that there was so much to see and learn and do with Gopto that it would take a lifetime (and an apparently amazing one at that) to explore a fraction of it. She could now learn and do more than she had ever hoped to in her entire life! Even if her body had to be stuck in that little spot for the rest of her life, it would almost certainly be worth it.

But then she wondered if she was giving up reality in the process. Gopto's abilities to read her thoughts and literally just blast information into her head were truly incredible things, but they also made her a little uneasy. "If I stay here forever, how much of me will really be me?" she wondered.

"I mean you no harm, Heather Carson," Gopto said.

"I believe you," Heather replied, "I'm ... I'm just a little uncomfortable with your *always* being in my head like this."

There was a pause. "You want ... privacy," Gopto said.

"Yes," Heather said, grateful that he understood.

"I understand," Gopto said.

Heather momentarily felt the irony of the situation. She *knew* that Gopto was telling the truth, that he *did* understand, but the reason she knew it was because of the information he had already shared and the link they currently had. She knew that, while it was in their nature for the Mortubs to share everything, it was also important to them that communication be entirely consensual. Prior to encountering the Japel, the concept of wanting mental privacy was basically unknown to them. The nearest equivalent had been that sometimes Mortubs would not share a thought because the idea was still "under construction" and its creator, out of respect, simply wanted to complete it before sharing. Still, while they had no interest in it for themselves, the Mortubs rejoiced in the introduction of the concept of privacy for others. They respected it without question and went out of their way to accommodate it, confident that doing so would improve their relationship with the Japel and, by extension, their own society and culture.

"Do not worry," Gopto continued, "you have the ability to ... turn me off, and I will not be one with you when you do."

In her mind, Heather suddenly felt the presence of what can only be described as a switch, and she understood immediately that it was *the* switch, the one that would disconnect or reconnect her link with Gopto. She went in her mind to flip the switch and test it.

"I need to warn you," Gopto began, "if you disconnect now, your senses and your mind will work as they have before."

"OK," Heather said, thinking that was obvious and not understanding the implication (given where her actual body happened to be at that moment). But before she flipped the switch she asked, "what would happen if I didn't come back?"

"Then I cannot communicate with the humans and I will die," Gopto replied. "I do not have the energy to link with another."

Heather felt badly for even asking it, "OK, well, don't worry, I'll be right back," she said, and then she flipped the switch.

The return to her actual body was instant and jarring. She tried to open her eyes, but they (and the rest of her) were covered in a thick, gel like fluid. What she could see was very dark and blurry. She was immediately aware of two small tendrils, one in each of her nostrils, pumping oxygen into her. Her first reaction was basically shock. She felt frightened and confused, but just as quickly she also felt a sense of calm and warmth and safety. She put together in her mind where she obviously was and that, bizarre as it was, if she trusted Gopto (and at this point she had very little choice), she was safe. She closed her eyes, breathed in deeply, and calmly flipped the switch again. When she opened her eyes she was back on The Plain, and everything felt normal again. "Wow!" She paused as she re-acclimated to her virtual world. "So," she began, "that's where I *really* am?"

"Yes," Gopto replied.

"And here, this place, The Plain, when we're here you can show me..." she began.

"Everything," Gopto said, "but first, I need your help."

"Wow," Heather thought, "*everything*! OK, well, let's not do everything right now. I'm going to need some time to soak all of this in." Then she came back to what Gopto had just said.

"You need *my* help?" she asked.

"I am dying here," Gopto said. "I believe that the humans that found me and brought me to this place mean well. They have ... saved my life and made it so I could reach out to you, but if I do not leave soon, I will die."

Heather was immediately committed to helping. She knew that her mind and body had just been through an incredible experience that certainly could be clouding her judgment, and she knew that Gopto was almost certainly capable of manipulating her mind in any way he wanted to if he wanted ... but it seemed just as clear that he in fact *didn't* want to manipulate her. He had done what he had done because he needed a way to communicate. She felt like she had a special responsibility now to be the first intermediary between Mortubs and humans (as in fact she was). She thought about the incredible opportunities for mankind, how Earth shatteringly significant this could be. Yes, she *had* to help Gopto. "What can I do?"

"You must, be my voice," Gopto said. "When we are connected, I can see what you see, hear what you hear, feel what you feel."

"Don't I have to stay here, inside you ... to have access to all of this?" she asked.

"No," replied Gopto. "It helps though, for now. The longer we are one like this, the stronger the link becomes. Unfortunately you must go now."

"Why?" Heather asked.

"The time has come," Gopto replied, "other humans have just arrived. There was another before. He tried to hurt Gopto when I found you. I think he meant only to help you. I disabled him, but he will be conscious again soon. Others are coming now, they will find him. You will need to speak for me. We must leave The Plain now, but please do not turn off our link."

"Umm," Heather wasn't sure how to ask her next question, "how do I get, you know ... out?"

"I will ... spit you up," Gopto said.

Heather nodded her head and suppressed a laugh. Clearly Gopto also understood humor.

"I am very grateful to you Heather Carson," Gopto said, "thank you."

Heather smiled, then closed her eyes. "I'm ready," she said.

17 EMERGENCE

Time: 7:03 a.m., March 23, 2025
Location: Lab #8, B-Wing, BioSec

Colonel Wisener had finished her workout, cleaned up and was just sitting down to breakfast in the BioSec cafeteria when she heard, "Colonel Wisener, please report to lab 8 immediately." The message repeated, but she was already running down the hallway to B-Wing. As she entered the lab, she quickly scanned the room. The look on her face clearly said, "what the hell?" To her right, a section of the ceiling had fallen in and there was a mess of ceiling tiles and metal on the floor. In the middle she saw the alien, which appeared largely the same, although it did seem noticeably bigger towards the front. And on her left she saw Captain Landrum and Dr. Powell. They were assisting and talking to someone who was sitting on the floor, leaned up against the far wall. He had a cut on his head. It was Lieutenant Newton. "What the hell is he doing in here?" she asked immediately.

Jim Landrum stood and faced her. "We were just kind of putting that story together ourselves Colonel," he replied.

"Well?" she said impatiently.

"Well ma'am," Jim began, "as near as we can tell, somewhere

around midnight, the Lieutenant here claims he heard a woman's voice screaming for help in here."

"How is that possible?" the Colonel interrupted.

"We're not sure ma'am," Dr. Powell answered, "But we have confirmed that there is an employee missing from the overnight shift. A lab technician named Heather Carson. How she could have gotten past our security, into B-Wing and down here is unknown, but if she did, it is ... possible."

"Who was on watch?" the Colonel asked pointedly.

"Staff Sergeant Thompson ma'am," Captain Landrum answered.

"And before I go find him and tear him a new one...?" the Colonel asked.

"That's what Mike and I were just discussing ma'am," the Captain continued. "If the Lieutenant here is right about the time, the Staff Sergeant went for midrats (midnight rations) right about the same time as Newton here heard the screams. Thompson had a relief to watch the security door while he was gone, so we don't know how she would have gotten in, but if she had, obviously you can't hear anything through that door, and it's not likely his temporary relief was ever sitting at or watching the video monitor."

"And the Staff Sergeant didn't see anything unusual on his return?" the Colonel asked incredulously.

"Also possible," Dr. Powell replied, "and frankly our fault ma'am."

"Explain," said the Colonel.

"The building's video security system," Mike went on, "obviously, this wing is used primarily for horticultural and other biological experiments, which is, of course, why we chose it."

"Go on," the Colonel said.

"Well, the video monitors are set during normal working hours to record and display about 3 frames per second," Dr. Powell said.

"OK," the Colonel said, getting a bit impatient for Dr. Powell to get to the point.

"But at night, and on weekends, the system switches to just one frame every 10 minutes. It saves on storage space," Mike said.

"So you think..." the Colonel started.

"Yes ma'am," Jim stepped in, relieving his friend, "we think all of this happened inside 10 minutes and that by the time the next frame posted to the monitor, or whenever the next time was that Staff Sergeant Thompson looked at it, there was nothing significantly different to see."

The Colonel looked around the room and then stared at Captain Landrum in disbelief at that last statement. "Nothing that different to see?!"

Jim pointed to a space over the door, behind where the Colonel was standing, "nothing he could see ma'am. As you can see, we left the camera statically pointed at the alien." Jim motioned to the part of the floor with broken ceiling tiles and metal, "This area here would have been out of the frame to the right," then Jim motioned to where Andy was, "and when we found the Lieutenant here, he was unconscious on the floor on the far side of the room and would have been out of frame to the left."

"Which brings me back to the question of what the hell you're doing in here young man?" the Colonel asked, looking directly at Andy with eyes that said "you are in *trouble*."

Andy was nervous. "Yes ma'am, I know, and I'm *really* sorry. But I heard this scream, and it was *bad*. Whoever I heard was in real trouble ma'am. I shouted and tried to get someone's attention, but no one could hear me, and then she screamed for help, and ... I didn't know what else to do. So I looked around to try to figure out a way I could get over here to help and, well, then I saw the ceiling tiles. So I jumped on the table by the wall, pushed the tiles out of the way, pulled myself up and over the wall and then, well, sort of fell in here ma'am."

As the Colonel listened to the earnestness and sincerity of Lieutenant Newton's defense (and the rather incredible story), she suddenly found it difficult to keep a straight face. At this point, she had to admit it; she just plain liked this kid. Not only was he smart and talented, he was *brave* in exactly the right way, and he had a moral compass she admired. With effort, she held her face solid and said nothing, waiting for him to continue.

Andy was made even more nervous by the Colonel's silence, but he was sure that she was waiting for him to continue, so he did. "And well, once I got in here, I sort of, well, figured, that this creature thing here had basically *eaten* whoever was in here. And so I went over to it and I tried to get it to stop and ... well that's when everything went black again."

At this point the Colonel couldn't contain herself anymore. She looked down and placed her thumb and index finger along her eyebrows, using her hand to shield her face and hide the smile she could no longer suppress. Andy thought she looked thoroughly disgusted with him. "I'm going to get Court Martialed for this," he thought. In desperation he started to say, "ma'am I..." but the Colonel quickly held up her other hand indicating that she didn't want him to say another word. "I'm finished," he thought.

"Let me ... let me get this straight," the Colonel said, still looking down and hiding her face. "You heard a scream in here. You thought someone was in real danger." In more control now she moved her hand away and looked at Andy. "So, unable to get help, on your own, and in direct violation of *my* orders, you took it upon yourself to break through a *ceiling*? You then hoisted yourself over a *wall*, crashed through *another* ceiling where you encountered something that clearly didn't originate on this *planet* and then attempted to what? Heimlich? ... this several ton alien so that you could try to save whoever it was who you thought was in danger? Is that about it?"

Andy thought the whole story sounded a lot better the way the Colonel explained it. In fact it sounded kind of awesome and brave and, even though he was still scared out of his mind, he took a moment to realize that, no matter what happened, he would surely remember this experience for the rest of his life as something really amazing he once did. "Yes ma'am, I..."

Again, the Colonel put her other hand up to silence Andy ... but this time, after a pause, she couldn't hold it in any longer. She shook her head slowly and began to laugh. Andy was confused. Then he noticed that no one was looking at him. The Colonel was looking down, pinching the top of her nose and had started laughing. Captain Landrum was looking up and off to his left and appeared to be suppressing a smile, and Dr. Powell was looking at the floor and pursing his lips. A sense of relief flooded over him as it suddenly dawned on him that they weren't really upset with him, they were *impressed* ... and for the very first time in his life, Andy felt something he'd never felt before; he felt like he was with people that he *belonged* with.

Colonel Wisener finally looked up, and when Andy could see her face he could see that she wasn't really upset with him at all. She looked at Andy, shook her head again, and then said to Captain Landrum, "well, what do you think Captain?"

Jim Landrum shook his head, shrugged, then smiled and said, "Sounds like UNCLE material to me ma'am."

"Dr. Powell?" the Colonel asked.

"Yes ma'am," Mike said, raising his hand a little to indicate that he too agreed.

"OK," the Colonel said, "Lieutenant Andrew Newton, assuming you're interested, and you'd better be, by a soon to be given order of the President of the United States, you are hereby transferred from duty in the United States Air Force to the Department of

Defense's very top secret Unknown Contact Liaison and Examination team, otherwise known as UNCLE ... and *this*," she said, indicating over to the alien, "this, is what we do."

Andy felt 12 feet tall. He swallowed and blinked, fighting back a tear that was coming to one of his eyes. "Yes ma'am," he said, "thank you ma'am."

Jim looked at him, "Jim Landrum," he said as he smiled and shook his hand, "I'm the one who shot you yesterday."

"Oh," Andy said, "nice shot!"

"Mike Powell," Mike said, extending his hand, "resident egghead."

"Andy Newton," Andy said smiling back.

"Alright," the Colonel said, "well, let's get this young man a uniform and..."

She was just about to say something when the alien clearly moved and made a gurgling sound, and then the slightly enlarged "hump" area towards the front of the creature began to shrink and move towards them. Powell and Landrum immediately spun around. Jim unholstered and charged his weapon. Its mouth opened, and a human body emerged. The Colonel's first thought was that it was not unlike witnessing a birth, except this was no baby. The body was an adult female and it was covered in a translucent gel like substance. It came out feet first, in a fetal like position, with its back facing the creature and not them. Dr. Powell stepped forward and dropped to his knees next to her. He grabbed her wrist, feeling for a pulse. He looked at the Colonel.

"She's alive ma'am," Mike said.

They were all wondering the same things. Who was this? Was this the missing lab technician? Was it some kind of copy of her? Had the creature manufactured her somehow? What had happened? As they sat there staring at her for a moment, the woman suddenly sputtered and coughed, spitting out and away some of the substance that covered her. Her eyes opened, but they too were covered, so she raised her hand to wipe them. Then she looked around the room, her eyes adjusting.

"Are you alright ma'am?" Dr. Powell asked her.

Heather paused, still looking around the room and trying to process everything. It was like waking up from an incredible dream, and yet she knew it wasn't a dream. "Yes," she said, "I think so." She started to try to get up.

"Here, let us help you," Dr. Powell said as he and Captain Landrum helped her to her feet. As she stood, both men noticed that there was something from the creature that was still attached to her. They looked behind her and saw a tube-like tendril. It was slightly thicker than a man's thumb and it extended from the creature's mouth to the base of the woman's spine. At the base of her spine the tendril was connected to a thin, flat membrane that was about two inches wide and four inches long. The membrane was clearly, physically attached to the woman. From there the membrane got thinner and ran up the woman's spine and neck where it disappeared under her hair.

As Heather stood and got her bearings, she was immediately conscious of the fact that the men were checking out her backside, which made her instantly aware of the fact that she was totally naked! This made her extremely self-conscious. Immediately a voice came to her.

"I am here," said Gopto.

"Gopto," she thought without speaking, "can you hear me without my having to speak?"

"Yes," Gopto replied.

"Gopto, I am *naked*," Heather thought.

There was a pause. "Yes," Gopto said, clearly not

understanding why this was a concern.

"Where are my *clothes*?" she thought earnestly.

There was another pause. "I am sorry," he said. " I was ... hungry."

"You ATE my clothes?!" she thought.

"Yes," said Gopto, almost apologetically. "They did not ... taste, very good, but I need food."

"I understand," she thought, suddenly feeling badly about having made a big deal of it and realizing the gravity of the situation. There were bigger things in life now. Everything was different now. "Gopto is clearly fighting for his life and I'm worried about clothing" she thought.

Andrew was captivated. He looked at her and thought that she was, without question, the most beautiful woman he had ever seen. But when he looked at her face, he could immediately see that she was very uncomfortable with the fact that she was naked. He quickly looked around the room. In the corner there was a coat rack with several lab coats on the hooks. He quickly ran over, retrieved one and brought it to Heather. "Here," he said as he placed it over her shoulders. He tried not to look at her naked body, but it was impossible not to get at least a little look. "I'm Andy."

"Thank you," Heather said, putting on the lab coat and buttoning it. She looked at all of them. She immediately recognized the two who had helped her up as the "Kirk and Spock" looking duo that she had passed in the hall the night before. Behind them was a very serious looking older woman who appeared to be in charge. And the one who had just given her the lab coat, Andy, she hadn't seen him before. She could tell that he thought she was attractive by the way he was acting. She thought he was sort of cute, in a sweet and sheepish kind of way, and certainly he had been both kind and thoughtful to get her the lab coat.

"Heather Carson, I presume?" Colonel Wisener asked.

"Yes," Heather replied.

"Miss Carson, I'm Colonel Jane Wisener," the Colonel started.

"Are you in charge here?" Heather interrupted.

"Uhh, yes," the Colonel said a little surprised by the question.

"Good," Heather said.

"Miss Carson, would you mind explaining to us exactly what happened and how you came to be here this morning?" the Colonel asked.

"This morning?" Heather thought. "What time is it?" She looked up at the clock on the wall. It was nearly 7:30 in the morning. She had been inside Gopto for over 7 hours. In a way it seemed like it must have been much longer, and in another like it couldn't have been nearly that long.

Heather explained who she was, what she did for BioSec, how she got into B-Wing, and what had happened. She knew that she would be fired and that her entire career was basically ruined, but she didn't care about her job or anything else in the entire world anymore. She knew that *everything* was different now. *Nothing* that had mattered in her life 8 hours ago mattered now. And then she told them about Gopto. She decided that she needed to frame the events a little bit. She said that she was initially frightened but that she was convinced that Gopto's intentions were peaceful and that right now, he just needed to get home.

"And it can hear us?" the Colonel asked, "Right now, through you?"

"Yes," Heather replied.

"And it understands English already?" the Colonel asked.

"Yes," said Heather, "he said he's still having some trouble with certain words for some reason ... but he's getting better very fast, and he can definitely understand you."

"Can it speak through you?" Wisener asked.

Heather wasn't sure, but said, "Not ... directly. He's not controlling my mind if that's what you mean. But I can repeat what he says. In fact, I'm sure that's why all of this happened." As she thought about what the Colonel had just asked, she said to Gopto in her mind, "You can't control my mind completely can you?"

There was a pause, "not in the way you are thinking," Gopto replied.

"May I speak to it?" the Colonel asked Heather.

"Of course," said Heather, and she looked at and focused directly on the Colonel.

"Gopto?" the Colonel began, looking at Heather to make sure she was addressing him correctly. Heather nodded. "Gopto, my name is Jane Wisener. It is my great pleasure to meet you. I am a special representative of the human race. I am specifically in charge of meeting and coordinating the relationship between the people of Earth and species from other worlds such as yours."

"Thank you, Jane Wisener," Gopto replied. "I am happy to be welcomed to your planet and for your efforts to ... assist me."

Heather repeated what Gopto said throughout the conversation, word for word.

"May I ask you a few questions?" Colonel Wisener asked.

"Of course," Gopto replied.

"Was it your intention in coming to Earth to make direct contact with us and establish a relationship?" the Colonel asked.

"No," Gopto replied. "Our mission was one of observation. We have visited your planet several times before and were ... checking in, to monitor your progress. Our peoples do not believe that your planet is ready for a relationship yet."

"I am very happy to hear you say that," Colonel Wisener said, with genuine relief, "because we agree. In fact, part of my mission is to help protect the natural progress of our planet."

"That is wise," said Gopto.

"Thank you," replied the Colonel. "Do you know what happened to your ship?"

"Our ship was badly ... damaged, shortly after arriving." Gopto answered. "We attempted to self-destruct the ship to avoid detection or polluting your culture, but my fellow crew members, Neja and Taynar, were killed during the crash and the self-destruct obviously failed."

"Neja and Taynar?" the Colonel said, "those are the names of the two you were traveling with?"

"Yes," Gopto replied.

"We have brought their bodies here," the Colonel continued. "We were about to examine them, but obviously now that we can communicate with you, we will respect your wishes of course."

"It would be better for all of us if they were to return with me," Gopto said.

"As you wish," the Colonel replied, "but we're not sure how you can return. Your ship is currently under our protection, but it was badly damaged in the landing and we do not think it can be made spaceworthy again."

"I appreciate your opinion Jane Wisener," Gopto said, "but I believe the ship can be made to return."

"OK," the Colonel said, "but I'd like to know more about what your role was on the ship, what you know about its condition and why you think that's possible."

"Of course," said Gopto. "My species has a number of unique abilities," Gopto said. "As you can see from the way I appear to you, our interaction with the universe as you see it is quite basic. Neja and Taynar are members of a species called the Japel. As you have probably guessed, we and the Japel have a complimentary relationship. They have abilities we lack, and we have abilities they lack. Together we can travel where neither of us could ever go alone."

"And how do you do that?" the Colonel asked.

"We have the ability to use our minds to create a perfect mathematical representation of any object or group of objects that we are exposed to in all of space-time. We use our individual and, when together, collective consciousness to ... build, representations. We can also synthesize and imagine, using existing ideas to invent and create structures that we, and species that we are compatible with, can interact with in a way that is indistinguishable from reality as you perceive it."

"If I may ask Miss Carson for a moment," the Colonel said, clearly intending to address Heather, "is this true, have you seen this?"

Speaking for herself Heather nodded and said, "oh, yes ma'am! Earlier this morning I was walking on the surface of another *planet*, and I totally couldn't tell the difference between that and this."

"OK, thank you," the Colonel said, "and now, to Gopto again, go on please."

Heather reverted back to speaking for Gopto.

"We also have the ability to use our mathematical skill, in

combination with the energy generated by our ship's engines, to fold the space between any two known points. We build a momentary bridge between them and the ship travels instantly from point to point," Gopto said.

Jim Landrum shot a look at Mike, shook his head slightly and smiled, amazed that his friend had correctly guessed how the ship traveled.

Mike was also pleased that he'd figured it out, but he was already doing the math in his head. He whistled slightly and said, "The amount of energy required to do that would be fantastic."

"Creating the energy needed is far less difficult than you think," Gopto replied, "but building the bridge requires mathematical skills which you do not possess. In any case, to answer your original question Jane Wisener, only one of the ship's engines is needed to ... execute a jump between two points. We have redundant emergency power units on the ship that have the ability to recharge. If I am correct about how long I have been here, just more than one of the planet's full rotations, those systems should now have enough power to start the generators which can restart that engine. With just that one engine, my capabilities and a little assistance, the ship should be able to jump to an emergency rescue point that is always closely monitored. It only needs to survive there for moments before a rescue team can get to the ship."

"Assistance?" Heather thought. She was stunned by the words as they came out of her mouth and her mind as immediately reeling over the possibility that she might actually be able to travel in space with Gopto.

"Assuming you can provide safe return passage," the Colonel said, "we would be happy to provide assistance."

"Thank you, that is a kind offer," Gopto said, "however, I require only Heather Carson's assistance."

The Colonel frowned but accepted Gopto's word on the subject immediately. "Miss Carson," she said, "are you willing to do this?"

Heather looked at the Colonel and realized that she had the power to say no. That fact frightened her, but she looked directly at the Colonel and said, "yes ma'am I am. In fact I want to, more than anything."

The Colonel stared at Heather, "and how can I know that you're making this decision of your own free will?" she asked.

Heather was a little panicked by the question because she had no idea how to prove that she was in control of her mind. "Uhh, I, I don't know Colonel," she said honestly and with more than a little emotion in her voice, "but I *am* the only one that can help. Gopto doesn't have the strength to bond with anyone else."

"All the more reason to be concerned," the Colonel said.

"I, I don't know what to tell you Colonel," Heather said quietly, "I want to go."

The Colonel paused, then looked over at Mike. "Dr. Powell?" she said.

Mike looked at the Colonel directly and not at Heather, "well ma'am, Captain Landrum and I have observed that the alien *is* physically connected to Miss Carson."

The Colonel had seen the tube like structure that appeared to be dangling along the back of Heather's right leg. "May I...?" she said.

"Of course," Heather said. She turned around and faced Gopto. She felt Dr. Powell lift up the back of the lab coat she was wearing. He pulled it all the way up to the connection point at the base of her spine.

The four of them got a good look at Heather's backside. Once again Andy tried to ignore how unbelievably attractive she was to him, a task made easier when he took his eyes off her ass and focused instead on the connection point. It was a thin, flat, plate like membrane that was clearly embedded in the base of her spine, but something odd had happened in the minutes since Jim and Mike had first observed it. Dr. Powell looked more closely. Heather's skin appeared to be starting to grow around the edges of the plate as well as around the cord as it ran up her spine. Mike released the lab coat and lifted up Heather's hair at the base of her skull. Here again he saw a plate like object, but this one was more square in shape. It too appeared to be being absorbed in some way by Heather's body.

The Colonel looked concerned. "OK, thank you," she said. Heather turned back around to face them. "Doctor?"

"Well ma'am," Mike started, "as you can see it appears to be some kind of biological connection, and Miss Carson appears to be literally assimilating it in some way."

Heather was visibly startled by Dr. Powell's statement. Immediately she thought, "Gopto?"

"Part of me will remain part of you for as long as you wish it," Gopto said. "If you no longer wish it or we are separated for too long, it will die. And no, it will not harm you."

"Can we determine if she is acting of her own free will?" the Colonel asked, getting to the point.

"No ma'am," Mike replied, looking slightly apologetically at Heather, "we cannot." Then he looked back at the Colonel and added, "further, we have no way of knowing what, if any, short or long term medical or other consequences there may be from this connection."

"Colonel Wisener," Heather began, "I assure you ma'am, I am in complete control of my own mind. Yes, what Gopto did to me, he did without my permission at first, but it was the only way to communicate with us. I don't object now, and he has given me the power to basically turn on and off the connection to him."

The Colonel raised an eyebrow at that. "And how do you do that?" the Colonel asked.

"It's a ... a switch," Heather replied. "It's hard to explain ma'am, but I *can* do it."

"And this physical connection?" the Colonel asked.

Heather thought to Gopto, "can you disconnect this ... cable, thing, to me?" she asked. "It might help them believe that I really am telling the truth."

"We are not quite ready," Gopto said, "it will be more challenging for us to ... talk ... but yes, it is possible."

"Would you believe us if Gopto were no longer physically connected to me?" Heather asked.

"It would help," the Colonel answered.

Heather felt an instant sensation in her lower back. It was as if all of her muscles were suddenly failing her. She felt like a machine that was leaking a critical fluid or power. She staggered a little bit. Captain Landrum and Doctor Powell both moved in immediately to grab her arms and stabilize her. And then she felt a tearing sensation, like a cut. "Unh!" she said as her face cringed at the pain.

Plop. The connection between Gopto and Heather fell to the floor. It immediately recoiled inside Gopto and disappeared. Mike reached around her and lifted up her lab coat again. When he reached the base of her spine he stopped, there was a roughly one inch long scab along the base of the plate. He lowered the lab coat, turned to the Colonel and nodded.

"Gopto," Heather said in her mind. No response. "Gopto are you there?!" Her face looked panicked. She spun around, dropped to her knees and moved towards Gopto's mouth. "No!" she shouted. Captain Landrum and Doctor Powell grabbed her arms to restrain her.

"No!" she shouted again, "you don't understand! I have to go back!" Tears filled her eyes and panic gripped her entire body.

They pulled her back and away from Gopto.

"I am here," she heard in her mind. She immediately stopped struggling and Captain Landrum and Doctor Powell just as quickly released her. "Gopto?" she said hopefully and out loud.

The voice was more distant to be sure, almost like it was traveling over a static filled radio, but it was definitely Gopto. "Do not be afraid," Gopto said, "I am here."

Heather smiled in relief and exhaled loudly.

"You can still hear him?" Colonel Wisener asked.

"Yes," Heather said with relief. She was pretty certain that the Colonel and her people meant well, but she was just as sure that the demonstration had been a frightening and unnecessary one. "Barely," she added.

"And you believe you have the ability to turn the connection to him on and off at will?" the Colonel asked.

"Yes, of course," Heather replied. "Colonel, he means us no harm," she said earnestly. "Gopto is sick and getting sicker by the minute here. He just wants to go home."

"And I am prepared to help him do that," the Colonel said firmly. "I am even prepared to let you go too, but *only* when I am as convinced as I can be that you are acting of your own free will," the Colonel said. "Miss Carson the experience you've just been through is ... unprecedented in human history."

"I know Colonel," Heather interrupted, "and the truth is that there's nothing I can do to totally convince you that I'm making this decision entirely on my own except to say that, yesterday I was a nobody lab tech at a dead end in my career and, based on what

I've already done, pretty much no matter what, my career here is totally over ... but then *this* happened, and now I have the chance to literally see and learn things that no one has had the chance to do before. I mean, wouldn't you ... ma'am? Wouldn't *anyone* choose to go with Gopto?"

The Colonel paused again. "Not bad," she thought, and then very matter of factly said, "Yes, I suppose I would." Heather sighed in relief. "OK," the Colonel said.

"Thank you," Heather said, then after a pause and afraid that she might be pushing her luck a bit, she added, "Ma'am, I can hear him, but it's much harder for us to communicate like this right now. Gopto has told me several times that this will get better over time, but in his weakened state it's ... it's hard to hear. We've already demonstrated that we can be separate, can we please reconnect?"

The Colonel stared directly into Heather's eyes for a long moment. Then nodded. Immediately a cord like tendril emerged from Gopto's mouth. It wrapped around Heather's right leg as it went up this time, disappearing under the lab coat until it reached the connecting point. Heather again felt a kind of tearing sensation, but then a sudden cool and powerful rush through her whole body.

"So I can go?" Heather said.

"Yes," the Colonel replied, "but not alone."

Heather's eyebrows lowered a bit and she looked confused.

"Miss Carson," the Colonel began, "I'm perfectly content to let you go based on the extraordinary circumstances of this experience and because, for whatever reason, you've basically been chosen to be the first translator between our species *and* because I'm reasonably convinced by the arguments you've just made, but the fact is that this is not the first time that humanity has encountered extra-terrestrial life, and the further fact is that there are protocols and processes which we, the representatives of the people of Earth, want followed in these situations, protocols and processes that you know nothing about. So, if you want to go, you're not going alone, is that clear?"

Heather could immediately see that the Colonel was not going to argue this point. This was a "my way or the highway" moment for her.

"Yes ma'am," Heather said.

"It's alright," said Gopto, "they are welcome to come."

Heather smiled, "Gopto says you are welcome to come too."

"Oh, sadly no," Colonel Wisener said, "it won't be me. Captain Landrum and Doctor Powell will accompany you on your journey and will represent Earth under any and all circumstances is that clear?"

"Yes ma'am," Heather replied. Jim Landrum was well practiced at hiding his emotions, but when Colonel Wisener said his name, even he couldn't keep his eyes from getting noticeably wider with excitement. Mike Powell's left eyebrow raised. Heather looked at the two men's reactions and couldn't refrain from stating the obvious any longer, "has anyone ever told the two of you that you're a lot like..."

"Yes," Mike Powell said, cutting her off, "they have."

Heather looked down and smiled, realizing that, yes, they must get that a *lot*. She then looked at the Colonel and asked, "then you'll let us go?"

"Yes," Colonel Wisener said.

"Ohhh, let's not let them go ... not just yet," said a voice behind them. They all turned to see General Colin Bradley standing in the doorway.

18 POWER PLAY

Time: 8:15 a.m., March 23, 2025
Location: Lab #8, B-Wing, BioSec

"Good morning everyone," General Bradley said as he walked into the room. He looked to his right, glancing at the ceiling tiles and metal on the floor. He shook his head in a dismissive manner, then he looked at the group, smiled and said, "I'm General Colin Bradley. And who might you be?"

"Colonel Jane Wisener," the Colonel said, introducing herself and stepping forward to intentionally cut the General off from getting farther into the room, "and I'm in charge here General," she said authoritatively.

The General smiled and said, "oh, I think that, if you have a look around this facility right now Colonel, you'll find that, actually, *I* am in charge here."

"I'm sorry sir," the Colonel said, already losing the battle to control her temper, "but frankly you have no idea what's going on here. Further, you have neither the clearance nor the authority to be in here. And if you don't leave immediately, I'm going to call our guards at the end of the hall, who shouldn't have let you down here in the first place, and have you escorted out."

"Oh, but I want to know what's going on here, Colonel," the General said confidently, "very much in fact. And as for your men who would escort me out, I think that, if you run down the hall right now, you'll find that your guards there, and pretty much all of your personnel in this facility, are now under the armed control of my personnel." In the hallway behind the General they could see two armed Air Force security guards.

As the Colonel and the General were arguing, Andy noticed that Captain Landrum had moved directly between them, making it harder for them to see him. Andy was confused. The Captain was very slightly sticking his butt out at Andy, back and forth. Clearly he was trying to get Andy to see or do something, but Andy didn't have a clue what it was. Then he looked at his belt. There was something that looked like a very odd pair of handcuffs. Andy very slowly and carefully reached for them. He had *no* idea what the Captain had in mind. "Surely he doesn't intend for me to try to handcuff the General," Andy thought.

"What on Earth makes you think that you have the authority or the right...?" the Colonel began.

The General cut her off and quickly, angrily snarled, "*I* give *myself* the authority and the right here Colonel." He quickly calmed back down and stepped around the Colonel to the right, towards the others and Gopto. "Now, what do we have here?" The General looked at Gopto and shook his head. "My my my..." he said, "and to think that just over 24 hours ago, I was stupid enough to think that all the hubbub was about a competing version of the X-22."

As the General moved, Captain Landrum quickly shifted to continue blocking most of the General's view of Andy. Andy was able to use the movement to brush up against the Captain's backside and release the snap holding the cuffs. "Got 'em!" he thought triumphantly, "now what?"

"And what's this?" the General said, noticing Gopto's connection to Heather. "What kind of weird ass experiment do we have going on here? You," he said pointedly to Heather, "who the hell are you and what are you doing here?"

"She's a technician here," the Colonel answered for Heather, "she made contact with the alien and is now our only means of communicating with it."

"Is that so?" said the General, and then in an uncaring voice he added, "Huh ... can't wait to hear how you lost your clothes and got covered with all that crap in the process."

Heather was too terrified to speak. She'd never met the General in person before, but being a resident of the area, she knew who he was. He was known in the community for being a very powerful man with a nasty temper. In any case, she knew he was a bad man whose arrival obviously threatened everything, most importantly Gopto's very survival. She knew that Gopto was still seeing and hearing everything through her, but he wasn't speaking to her anymore. She (correctly) assumed that he was exhausted and trying to conserve his strength. For the moment she was on her own. She also wondered why the Colonel had just said what she had said. Then it hit her, "she's trying to make sure that the General keeps me and Gopto together."

The Colonel was rapidly running out of patience. "General," she began, "I don't know how long you think you can maintain control here,"

"Long enough Colonel," he replied, "but go on."

"At some point sir," the Colonel continued, "your actions right now are going to come to the attention of, at the very least, the Joint Chiefs, and at that point, sir, your ass is going to be in a really major sling ... sir."

The General looked unfazed. "Wellllll, we'll see about that Colonel," he replied. "You see, I know something about the Joint Chiefs that you don't. There's a little saying about possession being nine tenths of the law, and as long as I have this big fella right here," he said, then looking at Heather, "along with what is now apparently his pet human, who we'll be taking with us as well." Heather looked terrified. "Sorry young lady..." he said, and then returned to his train of thought, "and his ship, of course, which, incidentally, my men are also securing as we speak ... a ship which probably also has lots of technological capabilities that might be considered, shall we say, exceptionally valuable? Well, once we have all of them back at Holloman and under our complete control, we'll be in a far better position to discuss access to these ... assets, as well as my future, don't you think Colonel?"

Sadly, they all knew that it was all too possible that he was right.

"And how do you plan to do that?" the Colonel asked.

"Why, with the very same equipment you used to get him here, Colonel," the General said logically. "As soon as I've dealt with you, we'll open that lab door over there to the loading dock and load our new space friend here into the very same truck you brought him in. Then it's just a quick trip down the road to Holloman."

Andy looked down at the handcuffs in his hands, still not knowing what to do with them. Then he noticed that Captain Landrum's left hand was now at his side, and he was very carefully pointing his index finger (in a way that only Andy could see) at Andy. "He wants me to put the handcuffs on myself?!" Andy thought. "What on Earth for?" Andy couldn't imagine what the Captain had in mind but, very slowly and carefully, he slid his hands into the cuffs. As each went in there was a tiny "tick" sound as they secured around his wrists. No one appeared to see or take notice. His timing was perfect, because at that exact moment, the General finally seemed to notice he was there.

"And what about you," the General said to Andrew, "the quiet one in the back, what are you doing here?"

"This man is in our custody General," Captain Landrum said, stepping aside to reveal Andy standing there in handcuffs.

"Is he?" the General said in a "well, we'll see about that" kind of way.

"He came down from Kirtland General," the Colonel volunteered, "he interfered, we arrested him."

The General looked suspiciously at Andy for a moment. He wondered what a kid from Kirtland was doing all the way down here, but the kid looked whipped and scared so he decided that he'd get those questions answered later. The important thing was that he probably had no love for the people who had him in handcuffs, and that made him a potential asset right when the General needed one. The General relaxed a bit. "You're in some pretty deep shit aren't you young man?" he said.

Andy looked down. "Yes sir," he said solemnly.

The General smiled a somewhat sinister smile and said, "Well, I can always use one more junior officer who owes me his life. Tell you what, you do what I say and help me gain control of everything you've seen here, and I'll see to it that you don't get in any trouble over it. And if you don't do what I say, then I'll shoot you myself, deal?"

Andy looked up and did his best to look and sound genuinely excited. "Yes sir!" he said.

"Uncuff him," the General said.

Captain Landrum looked at the Colonel. She nodded. Landrum pulled the key from his pocket and unlocked the cuffs. They popped open. Andy pulled his wrists clear and sneered slightly at Jim as he took them away.

"You won't get away with this, General," the Colonel said flatly.

Without warning the General exploded with anger, "do you think for a moment that I give a *shit* about what you think I will or won't get away with, Colonel!? Do you have any idea who I am here? You are in MY backyard. My base is the largest employer in this part of the *state*. The Mayor, every City Council Member, every member of the fucking Chamber of Commerce Board, they're all right here in my phone, and if you give them a choice of listening to me or you, who do you think they're going to listen to? Especially when I have *them*," he said indicating over to Heather and Gopto. "Can you imagine what this thing and its technology represents to the future of this area? Can you fathom how important this entire region could become? How many jobs? How much money? Can you even guess? And even more importantly, can you guess whose side all the people who might be positively affected by that will be on? So if you want to get into a pissing contest with me here on my turf Colonel, if you want to try to wrestle control of my men and this company and this community from me, well then you go right ahead and roll those dice, but be prepared to find yourself with *very* few people willing to help you." He paused, "so, what's it going to be Colonel?"

Colonel Wisener stared coldly and directly at the General.

"Fine," said the General. "Colonel, you and your men are now under arrest and in custody until such time as *I* say otherwise."

The Captain began to step forward at which point both MPs in the hallway reached for their guns. The Colonel held up her hand. Landrum stopped.

"Lieutenant," the General barked at Andy.

"Yes sir," Andy said obediently.

"Disarm this man," the General said.

"Yes sir," said Andy. "I'll have that weapon please, Captain." Landrum handed him the pulse gun.

"You have any idea how to use that thing Lieutenant?" the General asked.

"Yes sir," Andy replied. "They used it on me yesterday sir, I saw how it works."

"Alright, excellent, make sure it comes with us. I have no idea how they got ray gun technology, but I'm sure we can figure it out and use that too," the General said and turned to leave.

"Yes sir," Andy said. His mind was racing, he had to help his friends but he didn't know how. And then he had a thought. "General sir," he said. The General turned and looked back. "Sir, may I recommend that we temporarily lock the prisoners up in the lab next door?" The General looked at him. Andy tilted his head and said a little sheepishly, "They had me locked up in there all day yesterday sir."

The General smiled slightly. "Payback huh?" he said. Andy shrugged slightly. "Why not," the General said, "do it, but get right back in here and get that back door open to the loading dock."

"Yes sir," Andy said.

"I'll have two of my men come over to the outside of the dock," the General said, "you'll use whatever equipment these people used to load this thing onto it and get it in the truck, then the three of you will take it straight to Holloman, understood?"

"Understood sir," Andy said.

"All right then," the General said, then he looked at the Colonel with an "I win" smile. "Lock 'em up Lieutenant. MPs you're with me," he said and walked out of the lab and down the hall.

"Yes sir," Andy said, smiling broadly. "Colonel, if you and your men will lead the way please."

Colonel Wisener looked pissed, but she did as she was told.

19 THE ASSIGNMENT

Time: 8:45 a.m., March 23, 2025
Location: Lab #6, B-Wing, BioSec

Colonel Wisener waited until the security door to Lab #6 was securely closed and locked behind her before she spoke.

"OK, *that* was impressive," she said with a smile.

"Yeah, who knew he had that kind of talent?" Jim Landrum said. "I have to say, I had no idea whether or not that was going to work."

"How'd you get him the cuffs?" Mike asked.

"When the General moved, we both turned and he got them," Jim replied.

"Nice," said Mike.

Jim shrugged and then looked at Colonel Wisener, "what do we do now Colonel?"

"Well let's give him a few minutes," the Colonel started. "Obviously I need to get out of here and get to some place where I can communicate with NORAD."

"You want us to cover you?" Jim asked.

"No," the Colonel replied, "I need you to stay with Gopto and the girl."

"Were you serious about our going with them Colonel?" asked Mike.

"Yes I was," Colonel Wisener replied.

"But Colonel," Mike said, "all that stuff about processes and procedures for relations with aliens, that was all bullshit right? We don't have any of that."

The Colonel paused, and both men looked at her. She smiled, "actually, yes, we do," she said.

"But we've never heard ... " Mike said.

"You've never heard about them because we've not had a live contact situation with a new species since before either of you joined UNCLE," the Colonel said.

"But no one has ever gone *with* any of the species we've encountered before," Mike said.

"Sure they have," the Colonel replied. "You know the memorial wall we have back at HQ?"

"No!" said Mike.

"Yes," said the Colonel tilting her head, "a number of those folks aren't really dead, they're ... on assignment."

"No shit!" said Mike.

"No shit," said the Colonel.

"Need to know," Jim said, looking down.

"Correct Captain," said the Colonel, "but now you need to know. So yes, I want you to go with the alien. And there *are* actual instructions to follow gentlemen, and I expect you to follow them."

"Yes ma'am," said Jim. The very idea that he was about to go out into deep space with an alien life form had him as excited as he had ever been in his life. This was IT! This was what he had trained and waited his entire *life* for. "Where are the instructions ma'am?" he asked.

"They're on your identity file chips," the Colonel said smiling.

"No way," said Mike, shaking his head again.

Each UNCLE member had a small identity chip sewed into their right shoulder. It contained a nanodisc with a number of files on it. The files could be accessed wirelessly from any UNCLE device in range (watch, phone, computer), as long as you had the code.

"The file name is Offworld1 and the access code is A1742," the Colonel said. "Make sure you read it and do what it says."

"Yes ma'am," said Jim.

"We will," added Mike.

"Good," said the Colonel, "now, I think we've given our young friend about all the time he should need. So Captain, if you would be so kind as to follow the Lieutenant's escape route, we can get the hell out of here."

"Yes ma'am," Jim said.

20 LOADING UP

Time: 8:45 a.m., March 23, 2025
Location: Lab #8, B-Wing, BioSec

As Andy closed and locked the door to Lab #6, he looked down the hall towards the security door. He was right; one of the MPs had the door open and was looking back at him. Andy waved and shouted, "They're secure!" The MP waved back. Andy turned away and walked back towards Lab #8. He heard the security door close behind the MP. He turned his head and looked down the hall to make sure he was gone. As he entered Lab #8, he set the pulse gun down on the counter to his right (right next to where he had come through the ceiling). Then he went back to the doorway, jumped up and yanked the cable out of the video camera that was pointed at Heather and Gopto. He looked at Heather. She was sitting on the floor, leaning on Gopto and touching him with her hand. She stood up and looked at him uncertainly. Andy smiled.

"Sorry about that," he said.

Heather felt an unbelievable wave of relief sweep over her, and her face showed it. She *thought* Andy was still on their side, but he had been so convincing just now that she just wasn't absolutely sure.

"I wanted to tell you or signal you somehow," Andy said, continuing to apologize, "I just didn't think we could risk..."

"It's OK," Heather said quickly, relief still washing over her. She stopped him, held his hand and looked Andy straight in the eyes, "thank you," she said sincerely.

Andy stared straight back into Heather's eyes and swallowed hard. "You're welcome," he said softly. And for just that instant, time seemed to stop. He already felt a deep attachment and affection for Heather. It was unlike anything he had ever known. Suddenly, his feelings for her combined with his knowledge of the situation and flipped some kind of switch inside him. Two days ago he had been nothing more than a frustrated and disillusioned kid with a bad attitude and no control or direction in his life. Now he was literally *filled* with purpose, direction and conviction. The last few hours of his life had included a whole string of defining moments, but rather than exhausting him, they were energizing him. Andy felt more *alive* right now than at any other moment in his life. And even more importantly, *he* was starting to really believe in himself. *He* was removing the limits on his potential. His desire to live up to his new self-image and to help his friends was overpowering. He had no idea where he was getting the strength, concentration and focus he needed for the task at hand, but wherever it was coming from, it was flowing through him like a river.

"HEY!" came a shout from down the hall.

Andy's heart rate shot up. He looked at Heather. She looked afraid, but her concern simply fueled his determination. He raised his hand slightly to her as if to say, "don't panic" and walked to the door. He stuck his head out. One of General Bradley's men stood at the far end of B-Wing holding the security door open. "Yeah?" Andy shouted back.

"Your video just went out, is everything OK?" the Guard asked.

Andy tucked his head back in the room for several seconds. He looked up at the dangling wire he'd just yanked from the wall. He raised an eyebrow and shot a look at Heather as if to say, "watch this." Heather smiled. Andy leaned his head into the hall again, "looks fine from here!" Andy shouted. "Could be a short or something."

"Yeah," said the Guard, obviously trying to decide what to do.

"I wouldn't worry about it," Andy offered, "the General is sending two guys around to help me in just a minute anyway, and we'll be out of here just after that. I can run down or shout at you or something if I need anything."

The Guard paused. The Lieutenant was right; he *had* just heard the General give the order for two men to come around outside and assist the Lieutenant in getting that ... whatever it was ... out of the lab. "Yeah, OK sir, just holler if you need me."

"Will do!" Andy said.

The Guard closed the security door and disappeared. Andy stepped back into Lab #8, looked up with both eyes, shook his head and blew all of the air out of his mouth. Then, just as quickly, he looked at Heather and returned to the task at hand. "OK," he said walking towards and then past her towards the rear of the lab, "we don't have much time. In a couple of minutes, those two guys that the General is sending are gonna be here to help me get Gopto back in whatever truck he came in." Andy pointed to the huge security door at the rear of the lab and said, "I assume there's some kind of loading dock on the other side of this big ass door here?"

Heather was really starting to like Andrew, but she also knew the seriousness of the situation. "I can like him later," she thought, "now we have to save Gopto." She cleared her mind and became equally serious. "Yes," she replied to Andy, "we use this lab for big stuff, you know, stuff we can't or don't want to truck through the building. There's a narrow loading dock on the other side of the door. When I pulled in for work last night I saw a big black truck pulled up to it."

Andy looked at Gopto and frowned. "He's got to weigh at least a couple of tons," Andy said. "How the heck did they get him in here, and how do we get him out?"

"The General said something about using the same equipment?" Heather volunteered.

"Right," Andy said. "UNCLE must have some kind of lift or something on the truck. So we don't have to figure that out. All we have to do is figure out how to keep the truck from going to Holloman and instead get it back to Bonito Lake."

"How are we going to do that?" Heather asked.

Andy was asking himself that very question, and the truth was that he didn't have a clue. He looked at her and said honestly, "I don't know..." but then he added, "yet, but don't worry, we'll figure it out."

Tick tick tick! Someone was knocking on the rear door. Andy looked at Heather. She pointed him to the door's release mechanism. A loud alarm sounded, followed by several beeps, then a whooshing sound as the door at the rear of the lab began to open. The warm, moist air of the room seemed to suck out, and the cool, dry, desert air of the outside world rushed in. Andy and Heather squinted as their eyes fought to adjust. It was a bright, sunny morning outside, and the light was jarring. As the door moved away, Andy could see the legs of three men standing on the other side of the door. As it went up, it revealed the rest of them. Two of the men were enlisted soldiers in work fatigues, but the third was General Bradley. The door stopped, and the men moved forward.

"You ready to go Lieutenant?" the General said.

Andy hadn't really been prepared to see the General again so quickly, but he regained his composure instantly, "yes sir General," he replied.

"Alright, well, this is Staff Sergeant Thorn and Sergeant Black. They're men that I know and trust a lot more than you, OK?" the General said.

"Yes sir," Andy replied.

"Good," the General said, "and hopefully that will change fast, but for now I want you to work with them, understood?"

"Yes sir," Andy said. Thorn and Black were both rugged and tough looking men, and Andy was suddenly very nervous about how he was going to get control of the truck once they had Gopto on board.

The General pointed to the inside of the truck. "We found some equipment in the truck that we assume was used to get our alien friend here off the truck and into the building. You three need to figure out how to use it and get that thing from there," the General said, pointing at Gopto, "back to there," he said pointing to the truck.

"Yes sir," Andy said along with Black and Thorn.

The device was extremely odd looking. It was essentially, a very long, giant claw with a plate on the bottom. It was about 15 feet long with an operator area in the middle. There was a pole that was about 8 feet in the air that ran along the length of the plate and was attached to the control area in the middle. The thin, metal, claw-like arms were attached to the pole. The device looked a bit "erector set" like and probably could be built and configured to do all manner of things (it was also clearly collapsible in some way and was probably far more compact when being stored). The large plate on the bottom also appeared to have sections that could be compacted in some way, and under each section there were lots of ball like wheels.

Turning it on was easy enough (Andy hit the button marked "Power"). The directional controls to make the whole thing move were pretty self-explanatory too. Andy was relieved that the device was so easy to figure out; in only a couple of minutes he was able to get it to move and make the "claw" portion open and close.

"I think we've got this General," Andy shouted from the truck to the General, who was standing just inside the door to the lab staring at Gopto and Heather.

The General looked at Thorn, who had been standing next to and observing Andy. Thorn nodded in agreement.

"Alright then," the General said. "I'm heading back to Holloman to make sure we're ready there. You men are now in charge of getting our big friend here loaded up and on his way to his new home, got it?"

"Yes sir General," Andy said.

"Load the truck, check out with the main gate, and the three of you drive directly to Hangar 3 at Holloman, understood?" asked the General.

"Yes sir," all three men replied.

Andy turned back towards the controls of the device again and started moving it from the truck into the lab. While he was doing that, the General motioned to Thorn. Thorn nodded and walked towards the General.

"Keep your eye on him, Thorn," the General said quietly, "I think he's with us, but, just keep your eye on him."

"Yes sir General," Thorn replied.

"Alright," the General said loudly, "good luck, we'll see you back at the base ... for the dawn of a whole new world!"

"Yes sir," Andy, Thorn and Black all replied.

The device made beeping noises as it moved from the truck. The General watched for a moment, then walked to the side of the loading dock (which was barely wider than the truck and had protective walls on both sides), went down the steps, and out of sight.

Andy steered the claw sideways into the lab and lined it up with Gopto at a distance so that he could raise the "claw" side all the way up.

"Ugly sonofabitch isn't it?" Thorn said.

"Yep," agreed Andy, "but it's got all of our futures sitting inside it doesn't it?"

Thorn relaxed a little bit and started trusting Andy just a little bit, "I guess so," he replied.

"The General's gonna make this work for all of us," Andy said, "which is a good thing cuz I'm gonna need it."

"Just stick with the General L-T," Thorn said, "he's a genuine sonofabitch sometimes, but he takes care of his people." Then he paused and added, "and if you're not one of his people, he can make you wish you were never born, know what I mean?"

"I do," said Andy seriously, doing his best to convey a "you don't need to worry about me" message to Thorn.

Thorn looked hard at Andy again. He couldn't decide if he wasn't to be trusted or if he was just another scared, stupid junior officer ... but based on experience, he figured that the odds favored the latter. "Well, as the General says, alright then, let's load this fat ass up on the truck," said Thorn.

Andy moved the device towards Gopto until the lower plates were pushing up against Gopto's outer skin and making it bulge. Then he lowered the claw arms until they reached Gopto. "Sorry big fella," he thought, "hope this doesn't hurt too much." The claw arms made contact with Gopto's side. At first, Gopto's skin bent with the claws, but then, slowly but surely, the claws began to move Gopto until he was rolled on his side onto the plates.

Tears were in Heather's eyes as she watched all of this play out. She still believed Andy was trying to help, but she didn't know how they were going to get out of the predicament they were in. Gopto was clearly getting worse by the minute. She knew that the outside air wasn't good for him and she was sure that moving him on his side with this giant claw thing wasn't helping either and she just ... felt ... despair.

Still, she walked along with the device carrying Gopto into the truck. Once Andy had Gopto safely in the truck he released the claw (allowing Gopto to roll off the plates) and powered down the device.

"Whoa!" Thorn said, noticing for the first time that Heather and Gopto were physically attached to each other. "Are you fuckin' for real?! Black, check this out ... the chick is *attached* to this thing."

Black, who had been helping guide Andy into the truck and was in the very back (checking out the end of Gopto that was resting against the far inside wall of the truck) moved forward and looked at Heather. "Wow," he said, "now that's fucked up."

Thorn moved towards Heather. Heather backed up. He leered at her and said, "so, how are you ... hooked up there sweetheart? Mind if I have a look?"

Andrew's blood began to boil, but he knew he had to control himself. Instead he said, as matter of factly as he could, "I think we should leave her alone Thorn."

"Relax L-T," Thorn said in a "mind your own fucking business" tone, "we're just talking." He moved towards Heather again. It was clear what he intended to do next.

"Shit!" thought Andrew, "well, so much for my plan." He ran at Thorn, lowered his shoulder and tackled him at full speed. Both men went flying out of the truck, across the short loading dock and onto the floor in the lab.

Sergeant Black immediately started running towards them.

Heather panicked, and in her mind shouted, "GOPTO!"

Like lightning, a tendril shot out of Gopto's mouth. It barely touched Black's leg. Heather heard a "pop" sound, like an electrical fuse box blowing. Sergeant Black's body was picked up off the ground and thrown hard into the side of the truck. He dropped to the floor in a heap, already unconscious.

Andy pushed off Thorn and jumped to his feet. He'd never been in a real fist fight before and figured Thorn could almost certainly kick his ass, but he didn't think he had any other real options, so he summoned all the rage and strength he could find and prepared to fight.

Thorn looked at Andy with absolute fire in his eyes. The General was right about this guy. "I am going to kick your fuckin' ass," he said as he scrambled to his feet. Then he glanced to his right and saw Black's body collapsed on the floor of the truck. Thorn clearly wasn't worried about Andy, but Gopto was another matter. "ALERT THE GENERAL!" he shouted at the top of his lungs.

They stood about 6 feet apart. Andy prepared himself for a fight he was pretty sure he couldn't win. And then his eyes picked up movement. "Jesus!" he exclaimed, looking beyond and behind Thorn, "you scared me!"

Thorn looked at him incredulously, "you really think I'm that stupid?" he said.

"Well," said the voice behind him. Thorn spun around just in time to watch Captain Landrum pull the trigger on his pulse gun. The blast sent him flying several feet before he crumpled to the ground, unconscious. Jim Landrum shrugged, "yes," he said.

"Hey!" a voice said from beyond the loading dock.

Andy ran over to the dock and peered around he edge of the truck. It was an MP. He had a rifle and he was walking towards the truck.

"Everything OK in there?" he shouted.

"Yeah!" Andy replied.

"You said alert the General?" the MP asked.

Andy thought fast. "Yeah," he said as if he was giving an order to the MP, "alert the General that we're finished loading and should be ready to go in a few minutes."

The MP looked annoyed. "Oh! Yeah, OK." He turned and walked away. "Alert the General?!" he said to himself while shaking his head and looking down. "Where do they find these idiot JOs?" he thought. "You *finish* the job first, *then* YOU tell him yourself ... dickhead." He walked back towards the parking lot to continue his rounds.

Andrew was overwhelmed with relief. He stepped away from the side of the dock and back into the lab. As he walked back into the room he looked at Jim, he raised his palm to his forehead and again blew all the air out of his lungs. "Well it's about fucking time!" he said in mock frustration with the man who had just saved his ass.

Jim smiled broadly, "What?" he replied, "you were doing alright. I was impressed."

"Are you kidding me?" Andy said, "that guy was totally gonna kick my ass."

"Nah," said Jim, "I can teach you how deal with guys like that."

"Yeah?! ... good," said Andy, admitting to himself that being able to defend himself like that would be totally cool. He was calming down but still felt quite a bit of adrenaline and the need to share some exasperation. He looked around and then at Jim again. "And I totally want one of those things," he said, referring to the pulse gun.

Thump! Mike Powell's boots hit the counter top behind Jim, "yeah, me too" he said hopping down from the counter.

"Gentlemen," Colonel Wisener said. The men looked up and saw her face peering through the hole between the labs above the ceiling line. "If you're done in there..." she said.

"Yes ma'am," Captain Landrum said over his shoulder, then he looked at Andy and smiled again, "the Lieutenant will be right there."

21 HIJACK!

Time: 9:15 a.m., March 23, 2025
Location: B-Wing, BioSec

Andy opened the door to Lab #6.

"Thank you Lieutenant," Colonel Wisener said as she walked out.

"Yes ma'am," Andy said.

They walked into Lab #8. Jim and Mike had already dragged Black and Thorn's bodies into the middle of the lab and were stripping them out of their uniforms. It appeared that the men were close enough in size that the obvious plan in progress might work. The Colonel walked right by them, out to the loading dock and into the truck to check on Heather and Gopto. Heather looked very relieved to see the Colonel.

"How's everybody doing in here?" the Colonel asked.

"Better now," Heather said, and then she thought about that and added, "for the moment."

"I understand," said the Colonel. "How is Gopto?"

Heather was clearly very worried as she said, "he's not talking ma'am. He's trying to conserve his strength."

"We did all we could to try to create an environment like his on the ship here in the lab," the Colonel said a little apologetically.

"He knows that ma'am," Heather said, "thank you."

"Well, make sure he knows that we're going to do everything we can to get him out of here and back home alive," the Colonel said.

Heather nodded. Behind the Colonel she saw Captain Landrum and Dr. Powell approaching. They were already wearing the uniforms of the two Air Force men who were now unconscious. The Colonel saw Heather's eyes move and turned to see the men approaching her.

"What do you think?" Captain Landrum said.

Thorn and Landrum were close enough to the same size that Landrum's new uniform fit pretty well, but Mike Powell was several inches taller Black, and the uniform showed it. The Colonel looked up and down at both of them, frowned a little and said, "well, it's the best shot we've got."

"I agree ma'am," Landrum said. "I also think that, the longer we're here, the higher the risk."

"Agreed, we need to get you on the road," the Colonel replied. "Lieutenant," the Colonel said, to Andy.

"Yes ma'am," Andy replied, walking towards them.

"I'm afraid you're going to need to do at least one more acting job today," the Colonel said.

Andy smiled, "I'll do my best ma'am," he replied.

"Good, because that's what we'll need," the Colonel continued. "With Bradley's people in charge, I'm sure gate security will be expecting three men, but you're the only one whose ID matches your picture, so you'll be the driver and it will be your job to get the three of you and your cargo out of here safely."

"Yes ma'am," Andy said.

"As you get to the gate," the Colonel went on, "Captain Landrum and Doctor Powell here will do their best to keep their faces out of view, but you're going to have to do whatever is necessary to get through security and *not* arouse suspicion."

"Understood, Colonel," Andy replied.

"Alright, anything else we need?" the Colonel asked.

Heather spoke up from behind them, "the bodies," she said quickly and solemnly.

"Right," said Mike Powell. "They're across the hall in Lab #7. I was actually just about to start the formal autopsy on them this morning. Can you give me a hand Jim?"

"Sure," Jim replied, and they walked off to collect the two bodies.

"What about those two?" Andy asked, pointing to Thorn and Black.

"They'll be out for hours," the Colonel said, "but you'd better drag them over into Lab #6 and lock them in there."

"Yes ma'am," Andy said and went to do so.

Jim and Mike walked in to Lab #7. It had been barely 24 hours since they had discovered the two corpses in front of them on the alien ship. Neja and Taynar's bodies were still both in body bags (though the bags were unzipped). As they zipped up the bags, both men again felt regret that their first encounter with these creatures had come too late to even try to save either of them.

They carried Taynar's body to the truck first. Jim had to smile as he looked down the hall to see Andy struggling to keep hold of Thorn's body (which he had obviously just dragged to the door of Lab #6) while trying to unlock the door.

They laid Taynar's body carefully and respectfully as far into the truck as possible. In her mind, Heather told Gopto what was happening, but when she said that they were in Lab #7, her mind quickly drifted to the fact that there were a number of experiments there that she had been helping to monitor for the last week, which made her picture the inside of the lab in her mind. Gopto reacted instantly.

"There!" Gopto said.

Heather nearly jumped, delighted to hear from him again, but she didn't understand. Suddenly Gopto forced a picture into her mind. On the far side of the lab were several rubber tree plants. Heather thought it was weird that Gopto would choose that image. The plants weren't part of any experiment that was currently in progress but ... before she could finish her thought, Gopto showed her an image she had seen earlier when she was inside him. When he had recreated his world for her, she was standing in a meadow near the edge of a forest ... and she reached out and touched a huge leaf on a tree ... and it had felt like a rubber tree leaf.

"Maybe food," was all Gopto could say weakly.

"Guys!" Heather nearly shouted at Mike and Jim as they were walking out of the truck and back for Neja's body. They turned. "In the back of the lab there are several rubber tree plants," she said quickly, "they may work as food for Gopto. Can you bring them please?"

"Right away," Jim said.

As they loaded Neja's body onto the truck, Heather felt

something from Gopto. It was an emptiness ... confusion ... as if he didn't know what to feel.

"Twellock," Gopto said faintly to Heather.

"Oh my God," Heather thought, "of course."

Included in the knowledge that Gopto had already given Heather was information about the bonding experience between the Mortubs and the Japel. Mortubs refer to the Japel which they successfully join with as Twellocks, a term which best translates as "outsiders now inside." As she already knew, the connection is a great deal deeper than just telepathic communication. Over time, the two individuals usually develop a deep and multi-faceted bond with biological, emotional, mental and physical components. The relationship goes far beyond any kind of intimacy known to most species. The two end up knowing each other in a completely unique way.

Heather also knew that, for reasons that neither species could explain yet, Mortubs could only bond with females. For whatever reason, males were simply incapable of maintaining a strong enough connection for a long enough time to be of any value. That was why Gopto had chosen her. The Twellock (and Heather assumed that this would be true of her as well) could only communicate with the Mortub Collective via the specific Mortub they were bonded with. Similarly, the Mortub Collective could only communicate with that Twellock when she was connected through her Mortub.

For those who successfully join, the universe is never the same again. For the Mortub involved, the Japel they are bonded with become their eyes and ears to the outside, physical universe (senses that can be startling to many Mortubs as they gain the chance to see and hear their world (and others) in a completely new way for the first time). The Mortub also gains access to the thoughts and life experiences shared by that Japel. And for the Japel involved in the bonding, the access they gain to the Mortub Collective expands their consciousness in ways that no one else can understand. Heather already knew that voluntarily leaving something like that behind would be nearly impossible for any intelligent being.

From the moment she found out that the bodies of Gopto's crewmates were at BioSec, Heather had known that one of them had to be Gopto's Twellock, but what that meant hadn't really hit her until that moment. She cleared her mind and focused for a moment on feeling compassion.

Jim and Mike loaded three large rubber tree plants into the truck, and then the entire group gathered near Heather by the rear door.

"It's time to go," the Colonel said to Heather.

"How are you going to get out of here Colonel?" Jim asked.

"Not sure," the Colonel replied. "I could risk trying to just walk out of the loading dock after all of you leave, make it to our comms truck and try to contact NORAD from there."

"There's MPs patrolling the parking lot ma'am," Andy said.

"Well, the only way out through the building is down the way we came, and if the General has a guard on the other side of that door it's not likely I'm going to get past him without a pretty major problem," the Colonel said, "you got any better ideas?"

"I do!" Heather suddenly interjected.

They all looked at her. Heather reminded them how she got into B-Wing, through the custodial closet that was linked to C-Wing, where there was no guard.

"You could take one of those lab coats on the wall and walk out of C-Wing," Heather said. "It's not likely anyone would stop you between there and the staff locker room. My locker number is 35, and my phone, ID and car keys are all on the top shelf. The phone code is 0401. My car is a light blue 2019 Corolla. It's in the second row of B-lot."

They all looked at each other. The Colonel looked at Heather, tilted her head and said, "not bad Miss Carson."

Heather smiled. She was delighted to be able to help.

"Alright, let's do it," the Colonel said decisively. "Good luck gentlemen," she said, and then she turned, walked into the lab, grabbed a lab coat, and disappeared down the hall in B-Wing.

Andy reached for the door and started pulling it down, closing Heather and Gopto into the back of the truck. Before it reached the bottom, Mike stopped him, handed Andy his walkie-talkie, and gestured for him to give it to Heather. Andy took it and crouched down to hand it to Heather. "Here," he said, "in case we need to talk."

"Thanks," she said, taking it and putting it in one of the pockets of her lab coat.

"You ready? You OK?" Andy asked.

Heather wasn't really sure about the answer to either question, but she smiled and nodded.

Andy smiled. "It's gonna be OK," he said, and then he closed and locked the door.

The men got in to the front of the truck. Mike sat on the right side, Jim in the middle, and Andy took the driver's seat. They pulled out of the loading dock and made their way to the BioSec main gate. It seemed like there were guards everywhere. Andy fought to control his fear. On the one hand, he'd already lived through a bunch of things this morning that were probably more dangerous than what he was about to do, but on the other this was really the biggest and most important piece, and there was zero room for error and very few options if it didn't work. Having his new friends, Jim and Mike, with him helped a lot (particularly Jim, who he figured could probably get them out of just about anything), but it was weird to have so many people depending on him, and totally surreal to have gone from a job where he felt so ignored and unimportant just two days ago to having one that he felt was so incredibly important now.

Jim glanced over at Andy and immediately sensed his apprehension. Andy felt him looking and glanced back. "Relax kid," Jim said, "you've got this."

Andy wasn't sure if Jim was just blowing sunshine up his backside or not, but there was so much confidence in Jim's voice that Andy instantly felt better.

As they pulled up to the gate, the MP in front of them held up his hand and signaled for them to stop. Andy stopped, lowered the window and looked down at the MP as he approached the truck.

"Where you headed?" the MP asked.

"Lieutenant Andrew Newton under orders from General Bradley to take this cargo directly to Holloman," Andy said.

"ID sir?" the MP said in a professional and yet bored voice.

Andy handed him his ID. The MP looked at it. He looked up. He could see there were others in the truck but couldn't see their faces. "Who's with you Lieutenant?" he asked.

"Staff Sergeant Thorn and Sergeant Black," Andy answered.

"OK, standby sir," the MP said and went back into the guard shack.

The MP was gone for at least a minute, and Andy was starting to get really nervous that something had gone wrong.

Jim looked down and away and said quietly, "patience."

The MP returned and handed Andy his ID, "OK Lieutenant, you're cleared. Your orders are to proceed directly to Holloman, no stops, understood?"

"Yep, got it," said Andy, "thank you."

"Have a good day sir," the MP said, and the gate went up.

Andy raised the window and drove forward. As they reached the main road away from BioSec, Mike Powell exhaled, looked out the window, shook his head slightly and smiled. "OK," he said, "you can stay."

Andy smiled.

22 ON THE ROAD

Time: 9:50 a.m., March 23, 2025
Location: UNCLE Truck #6, En Route to Bonito Lake (northeast of Tularosa, New Mexico on highway 70)

The ride had been unusually quiet since they left BioSec. Each of the men was thinking about the rather incredible events of the day. Andy was thinking about his new life with UNCLE, while Jim and Mike were contemplating their last moments on Earth. Jim in particular was trying to soak in everything he was seeing, trying to remember every detail, not sure when, or if, he would ever return. Andy spoke first.

"So, is this like a ... typical weekend for you guys?" Andy asked, clearly trying to make light of the situation and start a conversation.

Jim laughed a little, grateful to be snapped out of his melancholy fog. "Oh, yeah," he replied.

"Well, do you guys mind if I ask you a few questions about UNCLE?" Andy asked.

"No, of course not," answered Jim, "shoot."

"Well, everything happened so fast this morning, I just suddenly realized that I don't have a clue in the world what I've just signed myself up for," Andy said.

"So?" said Jim.

"So ... what in the world have I just signed myself up for?" Andy said.

"Well, UNCLE's been around for a long time," Jim began, "since the 1960s actually, but it's only been in its current form since the late 90s. It has three key missions. First, of course, is to do what the name says, to serve as the first and primary point of contact, liaison and examination for human encounters with extra-terrestrial life."

"And how often does that happen?" Andy asked.

"Not often enough for me," replied Mike.

"Me either," said Jim, "but more often than you might think. And in the not too distant future, it's going to start happening a LOT more often."

"Why is that?" asked Andy.

"Because we talk too much," said Mike dryly.

"What do you mean?" asked Andy.

"We've been broadcasting signals powerful enough to reach out into deep space for almost 100 years now," Mike explained. "So imagine an ever expanding spherical bubble around the Earth."

"OK," said Andy.

"Well that bubble is now about 100 light years out in every direction," said Mike.

"That's a big bubble," said Andy.

"Well, that depends on your perspective," continued Mike, "but yeah, it's big and it gets bigger every day. The good news is that, relatively speaking, our planet is located in the pretty distant suburbs of our galaxy, so there's not a lot of traffic out this way."

"Makes sense," said Andy, "so what's the bad news?"

"The bad news is that, thanks to the contacts we've already had, we know that a good deal of traffic passes through a part of the galaxy where our bubble is about to reach," said Mike.

"Ahh," said Andy, "so..."

"So yes, it's just a matter of time," Jim said, completing Andy's sentence for him, "before we start attracting a LOT more attention."

"How much time?" asked Andy.

"Well, I could tell you in Galactic Time if I had a calculator," said Mike, who did, of course, have a calculator on him but had no interest in doing the math at the moment, "but it's about 25 more years."

"Galactic Time?" said Andrew

"It's a standard measure that most every species converts to when talking to each other about time," said Mike. "There's an agreed upon border of the center of our galaxy. Each time any specific point on that border's equator fully rotates on its axis back to the same position is one unit. From there down everyone uses base 10 mathematics for increments of that unit in groups of 100. Obviously most measures of time are many groups of increments down from that one, so there's a kind of shorthand where the first number is almost always zero with a subscript number to indicate the number of sets of zeroes before the first non-zero number."

"Huh," said Andy, "and there's some galactic federation or

something that determines this?"

Mike paused, "not that we know of," he answered. "Actually, we don't know who started it, or how or why, but every species we've encountered so far uses it when talking to each other."

"Right," said Andy. His brain was taking in everything Mike had said, but he wanted to get back to what he felt was clearly the bigger issue. "So, at some point in the next 25 years or so, our ancient radio signals are going to start crossing some intra-galactic highway and...?"

"And some of those folks are gonna come check us out," finished Jim. "And when that starts to happen, and those species start checking us out in large enough numbers ... well, we're not gonna be able to keep it hidden."

"And, as a species," Mike continued, "we are obviously NOT ready for that, which brings us to the second mission that UNCLE has. We have to protect humanity from being exposed to even the awareness of extra-terrestrial life, including how much of it there is, until its ready to accept and deal with that fact without causing massive societal problems."

"Yeah, good luck with that," Andy said.

"It's a challenge," Jim said with a smile, "but not an impossible one."

Andy was really starting to like Jim. He wasn't just a really competent, hero type of guy; he was also an optimistic, "glass is half full" kind of guy. That was pretty cool, and Andy made a mental note to try to be more like that himself.

"And finally," Mike concluded, "UNCLE's third mission is to help push humanity along so that it progresses at a speed that's faster than it otherwise would, and as fast as possible, but not so fast that it causes bigger problems than it solves."

"And how the hell do you do that?" Andy asked.

"Welllllll," Mike said, "*that's* kinda tricky."

"I'll bet," said Andy, "can you give me an example?"

"Sure," Mike said, and then after a pause, "velcro."

"What?!" said Andy, scrunching up his entire face, "no way."

"Yep," said Mike, and then after a longer pause, "most Wi-Fi network technologies."

"Oh get the fuck out of here!" Andy said. "Really?!"

"That was us," Mike said.

"Wow ..." said Andy, soaking this new information in. "That's just so ... I don't know, conspiracy theory like."

"And it's *important* that it stays like that," interjected Jim. "Whacky. Out there. Ridiculous. Understand?"

"Yeah ... yeah I do," Andy said, and he did understand.

"UNCLE's success is totally dependent on integrating technological advances into society in a totally seamless, natural and *undetected* way," Jim said.

"With a zero error rate," Andy added.

Mike scoffed and blew air quickly out of his mouth. "Yeah," he said almost sarcastically, "well...."

"Not exactly," Jim conceded. "We make mistakes. But when we do, we have to make any evidence of our screw ups or leaks look rationally explainable by some explanation other than the truth."

"Right. So, how do you do that?" Andy asked. "I mean the technologies thing. How do you integrate technologies into society like that?"

"Oh, there's a number of ways to do it," Mike said. "As I'm sure you can understand, the majority of UNCLE is not made up of people like Captain America here." Jim gave Mike a look. Mike smiled. "It's got a lot more people like me."

"Do they ever get to invent or discover anything?" Andy asked.

"Oh no!" Mike said, "of course not. But we do go out into the field. We attend seminars here, conferences there. We meet up with someone in a relevant industry and ... have a conversation. We share some research, plant an idea, we ... suggest."

"Wow," said Andy, "so all those people, they just *think* that they invented something that they really didn't."

"Oh, I don't think I'd go *that* far," Mike said. "In a number of cases, they still do a lot of the work, they 'discovered' it ... they just did it because we were there..."

"Pushing the human race forward," Andy said, finishing Mike's sentence with a smile.

"Exactly," said Mike. "So, what do you think?"

"I think you have the coolest fucking job in the world!" Andy said.

"Well good," said Mike, and then his face fell a little bit, "because you'll be there to see some truly cool shit come out in the next few years."

"Really?!" said Andy, "what's coming?"

Mike smiled and looked at Andy with a face told him a *major* secret was coming, "AI" he said. And then he added, "real AI."

"No way!" Andy said, "cool! How are you going to do that?"

"Well, actually we've been doing it over the last several years," said Mike. "Introducing it has been, by far, the most complex project UNCLE has ever undertaken."

"Why is that?" Andy asked.

"Multiple companies in multiple disciplines in multiple countries acting and converging simultaneously?" said Mike, "it's been hell to coordinate."

"Are you part of it?" asked Andy, already impressed.

"I'm part of one part," Mike answered, "a *small* part."

Andy saw Jim look up and roll his eyes a bit. Clearly Mike was being modest. "So who's going to get the credit?" Andy asked.

"Eden," said Jim.

"Wow," said Andy. Eden Corporation was already one of the largest companies in the world and been a key player in technology for decades. "Wish I could buy some of their stock," he added.

"Well you *can*," said Jim, "once."

"Oh, yeah, right," said Andy. It made perfect sense to him that anyone who ever abused the knowledge that they had because they were part of UNCLE could and would be quickly killed for doing so. They rode on in silence for a moment, then Andy spoke again, "so what's your story then?" he asked Jim.

"Me?" said Jim, "no ... story really."

"Oh no, of course not," Andy said sarcastically, "ray gun wielding American hero types with nerves of steel just ... grow on trees."

Jim laughed a little, "well, thanks, but I'm just here to keep the smart guys safe."

"Were you in the Green Berets or something?" Andy asked.

Jim was clearly a guy who didn't enjoy blowing his own horn. "I ... spent some time in Special Forces, yes," he said, answering as modestly as he could.

"Were you ever in combat?" Andy asked.

"Yes," Jim said, his face suddenly very serious, "right out of West Point, when I was about your age."

"Is that why you're so cool under pressure here?" Andy asked.

Jim laughed a little at that, then said, "not really."

"How do you do it?" Andy asked.

"Seriously?" Jim asked.

"Yeah," said Andy, now thinking there might actually be a real secret to it.

"Well, I became a Buddhist while I was overseas," Jim said.

"Really?" Andy said, "so, meditation and shit?"

"Yes," Jim said, smiling at the way Andy had put it, "meditation and shit."

"And you?" Andy said to Mike.

"Me *what*?" said Mike, "am I a Buddhist? No ... but buy him three beers and he'll talk your ear off about it."

Andy laughed. "I'll do that."

"Follow your own path," said Jim, "which you're doing pretty well at by the way. I have to say, you did *really* well this morning. We were all *really* impressed."

"I was scared out of my damn mind," Andy said.

"Fear is just a fantasy," Jim said.

Andy looked at him quizzically.

"You were afraid of the fight with Thorn," Jim started, "Why?"

"Because he was going to kick my ass!" Andy replied.

"Maybe," said Jim, "but the point is that you were afraid of being hurt. You feared the pain and consequences of that possibility."

"OK?" said Andy.

"Your fear," said Jim, "in fact, ALL fear, is based on something that hasn't happened yet. So it's really just a fantasy of your mind rather than fact."

"Hmm," said Andy, realizing he was going to need a LOT longer to think about that one. "OK, and that's Buddhism?"

Jim laughed out loud, "yes, that's it, right there, congratulations, you're done. No, obviously that's just one very small piece, but that's how everything starts."

The more they spoke, the more Andy was regretting the fact that he wouldn't get to know these people a lot better.

"What brought you to UNCLE?" Andy asked.

"Colonel Wisener recruited me when I came back from Afghanistan," Jim said.

"Why did you say yes?" Andy asked.

Jim paused and looked out at the mountains in front of them for a long moment. Finally he said, "I guess ... I guess I just figured that I'd seen the worst and dumbest of what we do as humans, and I wanted to be part of the best and the smartest of what we do as humans."

"And now you're going to get to go and represent humanity," Andy said. "Well that's cool, I don't really know you that well but I can tell you that I feel pretty good about that."

"Thanks Andy," Jim said, and then he added, "You know, in a way, it's kind of all I ever really wanted."

"What about you Doctor Powell?" Andy asked.

"Mike," Mike said, making it clear to Andy that he wanted Andy to use his first name. "Yeah, I'm maybe a little more nervous than Jim here, but the things we'll have the chance to learn are just so far beyond anything else on Earth that I'd be batshit crazy not to jump at it."

"Hmm," said Andy as he thought about that. "How long have the two of you been working together?"

"I met Mike on my first day at UNCLE," Jim said, "about five years ago. He's been stuck with me ever since."

"And when did the Kirk and Spock jokes start?" Andy asked, knowing he was treading on a delicate subject.

Mike shook his head and said dryly, "about five minutes after that."

Andy smiled and then let the truck go silent again for a moment. He had about a million more questions but didn't want to be annoying. He waited before asking the next one. "So, where do you, live?"

"Umm, Mike and I both live near Vegas actually," said Jim, "but most of the UNCLE folks, and almost all the science and research staff, live in or around either Palm Desert, Phoenix or Tucson."

"How'd you guys get out here so fast?" Andy asked.

"The strike teams alternate in two week duty sections," Jim answered. "You live on base 24/7 when you're on duty, the barracks and the hangar are connected, you have to be ready to be wheels up in less than 30 minutes at all times."

"And what do you do for the *years* between contact situations?" Andy asked, knowing but sort of dreading the answer.

"You train," said Jim, "and work ... constantly."

"Ech," said Andy, "another job with endless training," he thought, "Well, at least this one is a LOT cooler."

"Oh no," said Jim, "you're forgetting the best part."

"What's that?" Andy asked.

Mike looked up and shook his head slightly, "he's talking about the toys kid."

"Ohhhh!" said Andy as his eyes got bigger.

"Yeah!" said Jim, "and things like this pulse gun here ... that's just the *beginning* of the stockpile of cool crap you'll get to play with at UNCLE. We have the coolest toys in the world!"

"Yes," agreed Mike, "and, more importantly, you'll get to enjoy them without worrying that someone will take a mobile anti-grav unit and dump twenty pounds of shaving cream on you in the shower."

Andy burst out laughing. Jim smiled, pointed at Andy while looking at Mike and said, "See?"

Mike smirked, shook his head and said, "*Never* get on his bad side kid."

"Important tip!" Andy replied ... and then there was more silence as Andy realized it was a tip he was likely never going to need. "So where's the base?" he asked.

"Real 51" said Jim.

"Figures," said Andy.

Jim shook his head, "no, not that Area 51, the real one."

"Where is that?" Andy asked.

"You'll see," Jim answered with a smile, "but it's not where everyone thinks it is."

"Oh man!" Andy said.

"C'mon, we can't tell you everything," Jim said.

"Yeah OK," said Andy.

Just that moment the truck hit a pothole that bounced the truck a little.

"We're gonna be missed at Holloman pretty much any minute now aren't we?" said Andy.

"Yep," said Jim.

Andy thought he heard something in the back of the truck. "Did you hear that?" he asked.

Mike shook his head but Jim nodded, "she might have shouted something."

"I hope they're doing OK back there," said Andy, reaching for the walkie-talkie. "Heather this is Andy, is everything OK back there?"

"Verrata!" a voice shouted back. It was definitely Heather's voice. "Non koppa be flanchilay."

The guys all looked at each other with concern.

"Heather! Are you alright?!" Andy asked again.

23 KLANNA, HIFE DU NEJA

Time: 9:50 a.m., March 23, 2025
Location: UNCLE Truck #6, En Route to Bonito Lake (northeast of Tularosa, New Mexico on highway 70)

Once she was certain that they were clear of BioSec, Heather spent the first several minutes of the ride tearing the rubber tree plants to shreds. She then began slowly and carefully feeding the pieces to Gopto. It was quickly obvious that there was something in the plant that was similar enough to something from his world to be both edible and useful. Gopto was still having trouble breathing, "and it's going to get worse as we go uphill," Heather thought, but the fact was that Gopto seemed to be getting a little bit stronger from the feeding. Finally he spoke.

"I am feeling a little bit better now," Gopto said.

"I can tell," Heather said. "That's really weird how I can *feel* you somehow."

"We will not need the physical connection at all soon," Gopto said.

"I know," Heather said. "Gopto, are we really going to be able to get you home?"

"I believe so," said Gopto.

"How badly damaged is the ship?" Heather asked. She knew from her own experience that Gopto had the ability to see and hear through the eyes of the Twellock, Neja, so he probably knew what she knew when she died.

"Most of the ship is not repairable," Gopto said. "One of the two main engines has been completely destroyed, and I don't know how much of the hull's integrity has been ... compromised."

"Meaning when we jump, we may run out of air very fast," Heather said.

"Yes," replied Gopto, "but the moment we appear at the emergency rescue point, rescue ships will reach us very quickly. There should be time for them to save us."

"How are we going to get the ship restarted?" Heather asked.

Gopto was silent.

Heather knew that Gopto was able to respond, but was choosing not to for some reason. "Gopto?" she said.

"I need to ask another favor of you Heather," Gopto said.

"Of course," Heather replied.

"I do not want to ask because I know it is unpleasant to you, but I do not know another way," Gopto began. "Do you remember when we were on The Plain, and I showed you the history of the Mortub and the Japel?"

"Yes," Heather said.

"And that was ... painful," Gopto said.

"Well, yes, I suppose," Heather replied. It was annoying to

Heather to know that she couldn't be diplomatic with Gopto because he could not only hear her, but *feel* her reactions in a way that made it impossible for her to hide the experience ... still she tried. "But really, it was more shocking than painful," she continued, "I just wasn't ready for it. It was *so* much information, *so* fast."

"Your species is fortunate," Gopto continued, "perhaps one of the most fortunate we have ever encountered."

"Why is that?" Heather asked.

"Your minds are largely empty," Gopto said plainly.

"Gee thanks," Heather said, showing mock offense but also genuinely not understanding what Gopto was getting at.

"No," Gopto continued, "This is a very good thing. Your species is currently using only a very small part of your brain's power and storage capacity. You have a lot of room to grow. This is rare."

"Oh," said Heather, "OK."

"When I shared with you, I was able to add all of that information in a very small part of your brain," Gopto said.

Heather thought she had it, "you want to transmit to me all about the ship so I can help fly it."

"I need to do much more than that," Gopto said. "The knowledge of the ship is ... embedded in the life experiences of my Twellock, Neja."

"I know," said Heather, "but she's..."

"Also here," said Gopto. "I saved her."

A very cold chill shot through Heather. "You mean she's alive?!" she said looking over at the body bag.

"No," said Gopto sadly, "her body and spirit are gone, but all that she did, all that she knew, all that she saw, I *saved* her."

"You backed up her brain like a hard drive before she died," Heather said.

There was a pause as Heather again felt Gopto running around in her mind.

"Yes," Gopto said, "that is very like it."

"And you want to transmit all of that to me?" Heather said.

"Yes," said Gopto.

Immediately, Heather could only think of the reasons to say yes. First and most importantly, she needed the knowledge of the ship to help make it work. "It's not like any of the systems will be in English," she thought. And second, holy crap, the things she would learn and know!

"I'll do it," Heather said.

"Understand," Gopto said, "that you will have all of Neja's memories."

"OK?" said Heather.

"You will *feel* them," Gopto continued, "you will not know the difference between them and your own."

That statement gave Heather some real pause. "Will I die?" she asked, "or is she going to be sharing my body or something?"

"No, you will not die," Gopto insisted, "but I do not know what will happen. Your mind has plenty of room for all of you and all of Neja. You will still be you, but you will *not* be the same. Neja's life will be part of yours."

"Wow," said Heather, "that *is* a lot to think about."

"Yes," said Gopto. "I am sorry to have to ask this of you Heather Carson. I should not be alive. Our ship should have been destroyed and you should never have been involved."

"It's not that Gopto," Heather said, "you've already changed my whole life in ways that I couldn't have imagined even ... *yesterday!* And having been through this experience, I would never choose to give it up, even if I could."

"I am grateful to hear you say that," said Gopto. "I am also unable to be sorry we have met. We were never supposed to have met or bonded. We didn't even know that bonding with your species was possible. We weren't supposed to have any contact with humans for a long time. But now I know that, as much potential as we thought you had, we were wrong. You are capable of much more. I need your help Heather Carson, but even if I did not, I would *want* you to come back with me and share with my species. It will be ... amazing."

Heather's mind had a million thoughts racing through it. She was filled with both excitement and apprehension about Gopto's idea. She had to make a decision very fast that was going to completely change her life, permanently. Suddenly the idea of running off into space with Gopto seemed minor by comparison to what he was asking. This wasn't just the possibility of going on an incredible trip outside her body, this was an incredible trip *inside her mind*, and it wasn't one where there was any going back. Who knew what adding God knows how many memories and life experiences of a completely different person would do to her own personality. "My God," she thought, "I don't even know anything about her."

"Can you show me or tell me anything about her first?" Heather asked.

"Yes," Gopto said, "and more. Come with me."

Heather closed her eyes. Immediately the sights and sounds from the inside of the truck faded and she found herself on The

Plain. Walking towards her was a female Japel. She was wearing a tight green and black uniform. She was a few inches taller than Heather, but she otherwise looked just like the other female Japel Gopto had shown her before (aquamarine skin, black eyes, etc.). Heather did notice a couple of things that had gotten past her before though. The alien's fingers were noticeably longer than Heather's, and there were more of them (Japel had seven fingers on each hand and not five). But as Heather looked at her, she was struck by how graceful, elegant and even attractive she was as she approached.

"Klanna, Heather Carson," she said. "It is an informal Japel greeting. Hife du Neja."

"You speak English," Heather said. The alien's voice was a little strange sounding, almost like two voices speaking together with the second one a barely perceptible pitch lower than the other.

"Gopto is translating," she said.

"You're Neja?" Heather asked.

"Not exactly," Neja replied. "The real me is dead, of course, and with you in the truck right now."

"I'm so sorry," Heather said.

"Yes," Neja smiled and said sadly, "so am I. Think of me as ... an echo of Neja. I am all of her knowledge and memories and experiences. My responses to you are based on what Gopto knows of me, which is ... everything."

Heather understood, sort of.

"I want you to know how sorry I am that you are involved in this," Neja began, "I tried to destroy the ship, in fact I thought I had done it ... obviously something went wrong. But I'm not sorry that Gopto survived."

"Neither am I," said Heather quickly, "and I want to help, it's just that, well this is a lot to ask and I, well I wanted to ... meet you."

"I understand," Neja said with a small smile. There was a long pause.

"Tell me ... about ... you," Heather said.

"Well, I am a female Japel, and I..." Neja began.

"No, I'm sorry," Heather interrupted, "I meant, tell me about your personality, your characteristics."

"Oh," said Neja, and she paused for a moment to think. "Curious," she said finally, "I was curious." Heather smiled so Neja continued. "From the time I was very young, I was very interested in the nature of all living things, especially the very small ones and how they affect the very large ones."

"Is that why you traveled with Gopto?" Heather asked.

"It's why I joined the Space Exploration Corps, yes," Neja answered, "I traveled with Gopto because we agreed to after we chose to join."

"Did you like the job?" Heather asked.

"Oh yes," Neja replied. "Loved it. I was a biologist on Japella for several years before joining the corps. That was fun too, but this was way better."

Neja could sense that Heather wanted to know more about her relationship with Gopto, but that was too difficult to think about, so she changed the subject and continued on about herself as a child. "Anyway, I enjoyed school, especially science classes. As a child, I tried to play the Keenar for several years, but I was ... not good ... actually I was kind of terrible at it." Neja laughed a little at the memory and added, "I'm pretty sure my parents let me stop because they couldn't take the noise."

Heather laughed. "What did you do for fun, to relax?" Heather asked.

"I liked to run," said Neja. "On my planet, near my home is a very long, very flat beach. I would run ... what you call east, away from my home in the late afternoon, and then in the evening I would turn and run home towards the setting star."

"That sounds beautiful," said Heather.

"It was," Neja said, "and if you get tired, you can just jump in the water, find a Niphol and hold on." Heather was about to ask but Neja continued. "It's a water creature. They're harmless and fun. Fortunately, they don't mind passengers and they always swim along the shore towards the setting star."

"That sounds like fun," Heather said, smiling.

"Yes," agreed Neja, "of course, you'll get the chance to see all of that yourself, both through my eyes and your own."

"Yes, I suppose I will," said Heather.

After another pause, Neja said, "if it means anything, I would be very ... nervous, about this too."

"Why?" Heather asked.

"Well," said Neja, "you're about to know *everything* about me, including all of the things that are *very* private to me. You'll know me better than anyone except Gopto."

"I know he misses you," Heather said.

"Yes," Neja said softly.

Heather hadn't thought about the incredible intimacy of knowing *everything* about someone, and suddenly realized how she might feel if the roles were reversed. "So were you ever ... married?" she asked. Neja looked confused, so Heather clarified, "umm, married, mated, did you share your life with a single male Japel ... do you even do that?"

"Oh," Neja smiled, "yes, well, obviously we mate, although how long a mating lasts is different for everyone. But I was not, no."

"Were you and Taynar...?" Heather asked.

"No," Neja said, laughing a little. "Taynar was a good man. *Full* of energy, always bouncing around, always ready to go. Impatient, but in a good way ... we were friends and we worked well together as a crew, but no, we were not ... together." Neja looked very sad. "We had one more quick stop scheduled after Septar 3."

"Septar 3?" Heather asked.

"Your planet," Neja said, "after checking in on it we were going to make a quick trip to a moon with some interesting new microbial life forming, and then we were going home. Gopto and I were going to go to Morta for a while to bond and share what we had learned with the Mortub collective, and Taynar was planning to take a vacation on our planet."

"Do you know what happened?" Heather asked.

"Not really," said Neja. "I mean obviously we hit something, something that wasn't on our charts. Whatever it was, it happened very fast and it was devastating." Neja was clearly going through it in her mind and her voice sounded hollow as she spoke. "There wasn't any warning," she continued sadly, clearly looking for meaning or justification or ... *something*, that just wasn't ever going to be there. "We had just finished our survey work on Linto 1." Heather had no idea what that was, so Neja added, "Your species refers to the planet as Kepler 22b." Heather nodded; she remembered reading about that planet in an astronomy class. Neja continued, "Almost all of the life on the planet is microscopic ... but they're incredibly resilient and tough little things that's for sure. Anyway, I was having a great time, but Taynar was not."

"What was his job?" Heather asked.

"Oh, he was a researcher too," Neja continued, "but he wasn't a biologist. Taynar was an anthropologist. And he specialized in the study of higher intelligence species, like yours." Neja paused, sounding sad again. "He was so excited about visiting your planet to see how your species was progressing."

"It's alright," Heather said, "you don't have to..."

"No," Neja said, cutting her off. Telling the story was obviously difficult for her, but she clearly wanted to continue. She took a deep breath in, regrouped and went on. "Anyway, he was bored and I figured I could finish my report later, so we prepared for the jump." Neja again appeared to be going over the events in her mind, looking for a mistake. "It took a little longer than normal, but there weren't any problems." She smiled as another memory came to her. "I remember Taynar making some comment about how Gopto and I were obviously 'chatting' about my work on the planet below as opposed to working on the jump."

"I'll bet it was odd for him to not hear your conversations," Heather said.

"Oh," Neja replied, "I don't think it really bothered him if that's what you mean. He *did* think it was odd that our ability to explore the galaxy was so dependent on this strange relationship between our species. And he *loved* to note how it was hardly the first time intelligent creatures were at the mercy of technology they didn't quite understand or control. That was actually something he loved about studying your planet. He thought it was a perfect example of a species that was constantly battling to understand, control or at least come to terms with its own technological capacities."

"Yeah," said Heather, "that's true."

"Anyway," Neja continued, "the calculations, the jump ... everything went perfectly. We re-entered normal space exactly where we were supposed to be. And then..." Neja's voice trailed off. Then she looked back up at Heather and said, "did you know that I made it to the ground alive?" she asked.

"No," said Heather, "I didn't."

"Yeah," said Neja, obviously deeply saddened as she went through the last moments of her life. "I knew Taynar was probably gone, but I thought that, if I could get the ship down in one piece, we might keep the starboard engine running, and that's all we would need for a ground jump. I knew that the right thing to do was to destroy the ship, but I ... I had to try. I was never that great as a pilot, and I certainly never trained for anything like that, but the closer we got the ground in one piece the more it seemed ... possible ... and then the retro jets actually fired and we got to that lake ... and then ... " Neja's eyes looked away again. Her gaze was totally empty and her voice became very shallow as, in absolute sorrow for herself, she recalled the moment of her own death. She looked at Heather as a black tear fell from her eye, "I almost made it," she said softly. "Stupid way to die."

Heather also had tears running down her cheeks. "I'm so sorry," she said.

Neja nodded, and then, something important came to her mind. "You asked about Taynar?" she said to Heather. "When whatever happened, happened, he didn't hesitate. He risked his life to save us and the ship without any thought for himself at all. His family should know that."

"I will tell them," Heather said quietly but firmly.

"Thank you," said Neja.

"Do you have any relatives?" Heather asked.

Neja nodded. "My parents," she said with another sad smile, "they will be very sad. And my sister." Neja paused again, and seemed to be weighing whether to say something more. "If you do this, and you make it back to my world, you will visit them for me?"

"Of course," Heather said.

"It will be *very* strange for you," Neja said. "You will literally *remember* them. You will have my memories. It will be strange for them too, but you will be able to tell them the things I never got the chance to." Another tear formed and fell from the corner of Neja's eye.

"I don't have any more questions," Heather said. "I'm ready."

"Thank you," Neja said, and then she smiled slightly as she looked at Heather and added, "it is important to me that you continue to live for *yourself* Heather Carson ... but maybe, live just a little for me too."

Heather nodded and, on her own, left The Plain and returned to the truck.

As the sights and sounds of the physical world returned, Gopto said, "Are you sure?"

"Yes," Heather said.

Immediately she felt something like a low hum, like the sound a speaker makes when it's plugged in but has no music playing through it. The hum got louder. Then in a burst her entire implant along her spine felt like it was filled with ice water. Heather gasped, threw her head back and opened her eyes and mouth wide ... and that's when it came. Heather's *entire* mind was invaded on a *massive* scale. As difficult as it had been to absorb everything Gopto had taught her about himself earlier, this was orders of magnitude worse. She felt like her head was literally going to explode off her body. She felt like she could actually *feel* all the neural pathways in her mind, and they were all being flooded with power. And then, in a matter of minutes, Heather lived through decades of Neja's life. Every moment of every day. Every pleasure, every pain, every meal, every activity, every day of every class in every school. She experienced the music lessons, the birth of Neja's sister, helping care for her, family vacations, going on dates, a fall when she broke an ankle. She played outdoors, she ran on that beach, she joined the Space Exploration Corps, she trained, she met Gopto, she *bonded* with Gopto, she experienced trips on The Plain with Gopto *and* the

Mortub collective. She felt the incredible depth of their relationship, far more than either of them had ever told her about. She met Taynar, she lived through a number of missions with him. She arrived at Septar 3, felt the explosion and lived through the terror of the crash. She guided the ship to the ground, and she felt the rod fly through the deck plate and pierce her body ... and finally she felt her life slipping away and the incredible sorrow of death. Memory upon memory, day after day, year after year, and it was all being shoved into her brain at an inconceivable pace.

And then it was over. As her mind fought to return to normal, she realized that she was literally just screaming out. She stopped. She looked around. She felt completely confused and disoriented.

A moment later the walkie-talkie crackled to life. "Heather this is Andy, is everything OK back there?"

She grabbed the walkie-talkie, but as she did she looked at her hands. They were the wrong color! And what the fuck had just happened to her fingers?! They were white! And shorter! And some of them were *missing!* And her whole body was different. A wave of incredible panic swept over her. She grabbed the walkie-talkie and nearly shouted, "Verrata! Non koppa be flanchilay!"

"What the fuck was that?!" she thought, "my voice sounds all wrong!" And then, like a car that had been traveling at very high speed but then suddenly pulled over and slowed to a stop, the world slowed *way* down. She looked around and remembered. "I'm Heather Carson," she thought. "I'm in the truck with Gopto, heading back to the ship."

"Heather! Are you alright?!" Andy asked again. He sounded very worried.

"Umm, yeah!" Heather said. "Sorry about that. I'm fine ... just ... fine."

Her breathing slowed down. She put her hand on her forehead and with her lips close together blew all the air in her lungs out of her mouth. "Holy fuck," she said aloud.

24 HIDING

Time: 9:45 a.m., March 23, 2025
Location: BioSec, Women's Staff Locker Room

It took Colonel Wisener over 20 minutes, much longer than she had anticipated or hoped, to work her way back to Heather's locker. More importantly though, she had made it *without* being noticed by any of General Bradley's guards. There had been one particularly close call, but a fortuitously placed Ladies room had saved the day. She immediately went to Heather's locker and grabbed the car keys and phone off the shelf. She punched in the code and immediately dialed the phone.

"Thank you for calling E.T. Software my name is Jenny how may I direct your call?" the cheerful voice said.

"Research and Development please," the Colonel said.

"Please hold," the voice said.

After several seconds, a series of beeps on the line told the Colonel that they were identifying her phone. Then, as expected, she heard a recorded male voice say, "You are calling from an unrecognized phone, please provide you voice print identification and calling code after the tone." The line beeped.

"Wisener, Jane M.," the Colonel said, "November, Tango, one one, two two, five nine."

There was a series of clicks and ticks as the automated phone system at NORAD did its thing, then about 20 seconds later a voice picked up and said, "NORAD Command Duty Office this is Lt. Colonel Taylor may I help you sir or ma'am?"

"Tom?" Colonel Wisener said.

"Yeah, who's this?" Taylor responded.

"Tom, it's Jane Wisener," the Colonel said, happy to reach someone at NORAD that she knew personally.

"Jane! What are you doing on an outside line, is everything OK?" Tom asked.

"Actually no, Tom, it's not. I need to talk to General Bradley right away ... like now," the Colonel said.

"Jane, it's Sunday morning," Tom said, in a "you can't be serious" voice, "he's ... I don't know where ... home, church, golfing..."

"Tom," Colonel Wisener said slowly, "the Jaguars are in cages."

"Oh shit," Tom said slowly and quietly. His voice and demeanor completely changed thanks to the code he'd just heard. "Alright, sit tight Jane, give me a couple of minutes here."

"Thanks Tom, wilco," the Colonel replied. She had known Tom for almost 10 years, she knew he'd get the job done. While she waited, she sat down in front of Heather's locker, stared at its contents and thought about the incredibly strange series of events over the last few hours.

"Jane?" Tom's voice said on the phone.

"Yeah Tom, I'm here," she replied.

"OK, we've isolated and scrambled your line, so you should be secure now, however, we still recommend following Regulation 46A," he said.

"Will do, thanks Tom," she said.

"No problem, stand by for General Mitchell Bradley, CINC NORAD," he said.

Tick. Tick. Tick. Tick. Click! "Jane?" said General Bradley.

"Brad!" the Colonel said, relieved to reach him.

"What's going on?" the General asked.

"Well, we've had a hell of a morning sir, and we've got a real problem here," the Colonel replied. "Just under two hours ago, at least two dozen armed MPs from Holloman arrived at BioSec, seized control of the property, confined all of my personnel and attempted to take possession of The Immigrant."

"WHAT?!" the General nearly shouted into the phone.

"I'm afraid so sir," the Colonel continued. "Their intention appears to have been to steal The Immigrant and deliver him to Holloman for purposes unknown, but ones we can certainly imagine."

"Shit," the General said.

"Yes sir," Colonel Wisener said, then she continued, "but there is some good news."

"What's that?" the General asked.

"Well sir," she began, "first, and most importantly, with the aid of a civilian here at BioSec, we were able to make contact with

The Immigrant and..."

"How the hell did you do that?" asked the General.

"I'll have to explain that later sir, but we did, and subsequently three of my men, including the young man from Kirtland who I told you about yesterday, managed to hijack the truck that The Immigrant was being transferred in ... and they are all currently returning to Bonito," the Colonel said.

"Why are they headed *there?*" the General asked with no small amount of concern.

"Sir, The Immigrant is convinced that his vehicle is drivable and wishes to use it to return home," the Colonel said.

"And what's your call on that Colonel?" the General asked.

"Sir, I think we should at least allow The Immigrant to attempt to proceed sir," the Colonel said.

"We're giving up a lot of potential there are we not?" the General asked pointedly.

"For the moment, yes sir," the Colonel conceded, "but I believe it will foster strong international relations and better opportunities in the future."

"I understand," the General said.

"And it's the right thing to do sir," the Colonel added.

The General paused, exhaled loudly and then said, "OK, what's your status?"

"I'm holed up in the Ladies locker room right now sir," the Colonel said.

"Safe?" the General asked.

"For the moment," she replied.

"What about your people?" he asked.

"Unknown sir," the Colonel said ... and they both knew *that* fact was eating away at her.

"Can you get out?" the General asked.

"Well sir," she began, "thanks to the civilian who assisted us, I do have access to a vehicle ... assuming I could get out of the building and to it without being stopped by any of the patrolling MPs."

"I don't suppose I could get you to use that vehicle could I?" the General asked, knowing the answer.

"Not without my people sir," the Colonel replied.

General Bradley paused and shook his head. He knew he could order Colonel Wisener to abandon her people, but he preferred to have his orders obeyed, and they both knew what she would say and do if he ordered her out of there. "Yeah, OK Jane, I understand. But I also think it's extremely important for you to get your ass back up to Bonito as quick as you can. Your men en route are going to be facing unknown opposition when they get there."

"I know sir," she replied, and then she took a deep breath and added, "there's more sir."

"Go ahead," the General said.

"Sir, your brother indicated that he may have been in contact with someone at JCS," the Colonel said.

"Well, that's possible," General Bradley said solemnly, "I can check that out." The General sighed. "OK, I want you to stay right where you are and do your best to stay undetected," he said. "I'm going to call my brother, jump all over his shit and see if I can't get him to release your people ASAP. You are NOT to take matters into your own hands without my permission, do you understand?"

"I understand General," the Colonel replied.

"Yeah, I know you do," the General said, both of them knowing that if the Colonel saw a legitimate opportunity to rescue her people that she would take it without hesitation. "I'm on my way in to The Palace right now. I'll call you as soon as I have something, OK?"

"Thank you General," the Colonel said, and the line went dead.

25 WHERE'S THE TRUCK?

Time: 10:12 a.m., March 23, 2025
Location: General Colin Bradley's office, Holloman AFB

General Colin Bradley was just about to inquire again about whether or not the truck from BioSec had arrived when he heard one of his aides on the phone say, "yes sir, right away sir." A moment later, First Lieutenant Pete Morgan stood in his doorway.

"Yes Lieutenant, what is it?" he asked.

"It's CINC NORAD, General Mitchell Bradley on the phone for you sir, line 2," Morgan said.

"Really?" said Colin suspiciously. "Wonder what he wants."

"He sounded pretty upset sir," Morgan added.

"Oh?" Colin said, making it clear he didn't care. "Well, I don't give a fuck about that."

Morgan smiled and laughed a little. "Yes sir," he said, and walked away.

Colin picked up the phone, "General Bradley," he said.

"Colin!" his brother shouted, "Have you lost your *fucking mind?!*"

Colin smiled. Man, was he going to enjoy this. "Mitch!" he said with a voice dripping with fake pleasantry, "how's it goin' bro?"

"Do you have any idea what the punishment is for illegally detaining a dozen or so people who are DoD Personnel?!" Mitch yelled.

"Nope, sure don't," Colin replied, "aaaand I wouldn't really give a fuck even if I did." His voice remained calm and flippant. He was enjoying pissing his brother off, but on the inside he was also fuming because the fact that his brother knew what was going on at BioSec indicated that someone had somehow gotten word out to him.

Mitch had no idea what his brother *thought* he knew about the situation, or if he had just plain gone insane, but he tried to calm down as he continued. "Col, listen, this isn't just a career ending move here, if you don't knock this shit off, and I mean *right now,* you are going to *jail.*"

"Yeaaaahhh, I don't think so," said Colin, warming up to deliver the real news of the day.

"And what in the world makes you think that?" Mitch asked angrily.

"Mitch," Colin said, and he paused because he wanted to enjoy every second of what he was about to say, "did it ever occur to you that there might be other members of the Joint Chiefs who are getting a little tired of the way you and your crew of space cadets are running things with respect to ... oh let's just say the 'out of this world' side of your job?"

Mitch's voice got lower and far more serious, "what?"

"Yeah," Colin continued, "so I had a *really* interesting

conversation yesterday, and in that conversation I learned a lot about how, apparently, you and several other people have known for a long time that we've had access to some really amazing technology that you're ... well, you're kind of hoarding Mitch."

"Colin you have no idea..." Mitch started.

"Fuck off Mitch!" Colin snapped quickly, then he recovered and continued, "So anyway, it turns out that if someone else had control of some of those toys, well, then there'd be another player in the market."

"Colin..." Mitch started again.

"Competition Mitch! It's the American way," Colin said happily. "So we're looking at a whole new world here, a world where you and your little band of eggheads aren't the only ones who get to decide what technology gets used and when. Yes sir, weapons technology is about to take a giant leap. And just think of the lives we'll save, the jobs that will be created, the *money* we'll make ... and we could have been doing it all along if it weren't for a few elitists who wanted all the toys for themselves. And once I have our new guest and his ship inside my gates, the first of which should be arriving literally any minute now, I understand that the power to write my own ticket largely shifts to me, and the fact that I detained a few of your people in a nice, comfortable, air conditioned office for a couple of *hours* on a lazy Sunday morning ... yeah, nobody's going to give a shit about that."

The line was silent. Mitch's mind was moving fast. He was immediately reassured by the fact that Colin didn't seem to know that the truck carrying the alien was currently under UNCLE's control ... and he was amazed by how his brother's animosity for him had once again so blinded him that it led him to essentially tell Mitch his entire plan. After a long silence, Mitch said slowly, "Well, it sounds like you've thought of everything."

Colin's blood ran cold. "His response is *way* off," he thought, "something's *wrong!*" His mind raced to think of what he had overlooked. He had control of the crash site, the truck was on its way ... he couldn't see a hole. "You're gonna lose this time Mitch," he said coldly.

"It's not over yet Colin," Mitch said, and hung up.

"SHIT!" Colin screamed at the phone, then he yelled, "MORGAN!"

First Lieutenant Morgan just about jumped out of his skin, then raced to the doorway. "Yes sir General," he said.

"They here yet?" Colin asked.

"I told them to call us as soon as it arrives sir, but I'll call and ask right now," Morgan replied. He went to his desk to call the Main Gate and, having heard the reply he already knew he was going to get, he exhaled quietly to himself before going back to the doorway of the General's office to report. "I'm sorry sir, the Main Gate reports that the truck has *not* arrived yet."

"Shit," said the General. "How Goddamn long could it be taking them?"

Morgan knew it was a rhetorical question, but he said, "I don't know sir," as respectfully as possible anyway.

"They couldn't have been *that* far behind me," the General said. "Do you have Thorn or Black's cell phone numbers?"

"Uhh, no sir General, I do not," Morgan replied.

"Well find somebody who does, FAST!" the General demanded.

"Yes sir," said Morgan.

"I want to know what the fuck is taking them so long," Bradley said quietly to himself as Morgan quickly walked away to try to reach the missing men. "And Morgan!" the General barked again.

"Yes sir," said Morgan, turning and jogging back to the door yet again.

"Get Franklin on the phone over at BioSec. Tell him to get down the hall and check on that Colonel and her people we've got locked up down there," the General said.

"Yes sir," said Morgan.

"My guess is that one of them somehow got access to a phone," the General said.

"Yes sir," said Morgan.

Colin Bradley went back to his office and stared out his window. His brother had taken the news entirely too calmly. Mitch wasn't anywhere near as hot headed as Colin was, but he hated to lose every bit as much as Colin did, and Colin knew that he had him beaten here. "He should have been furious," Colin thought, "and he wasn't." He went over the plan again in his mind; the conversation he'd had with General West (one of the Joint Chiefs) yesterday, the events of the morning ... he couldn't see a hole, but he knew *something* was up.

He wasn't entirely lost in his thoughts of course. While he was going through everything in his mind and playing and replaying the conflict with his brother, he was also half listening to Lieutenant Morgan in the next room, making an effort to get cell phone numbers of Thorn and Black and then calling First Sergeant Franklin over at BioSec to check on that Colonel and her people. "Where the fuck could they be?" he thought.

Suddenly he heard Morgan's voice change dramatically. "What?!" he heard Morgan say loudly, and then, "oh shit! ... Right ... OK, stand by, I have to tell the General right now!" General Bradley's pulse and blood pressure was already on the way up when Morgan entered the room. His face looked frightened. "Sir, I've got First Sergeant Franklin on the line over at BioSec..."

"Yes?" the General said impatiently.

"The prisoners in B-Wing sir, they're gone," Morgan said.

"What?!" the General said angrily.

"Yes sir," Morgan replied, already knowing that the next thing he was going to say would cause the General to completely lose it, "there's more sir," Morgan said and paused slightly again, preparing for the explosion, "they found Thorn and Black's bodies in the room sir, stripped and unconscious."

"FUCK!" the General shouted and swiped his hand at his desk sending papers flying. "He knew again!" Colin shouted in a nearly uncontrollable rage. "Goddamn it, that sonofabitch lied to me again!"

Pete Morgan knew enough about what was going on. He knew that it was primarily the General's ass that was on the line. But he also knew that if any of the stuff they had now done was illegal ("and let's face it," he thought to himself, "some of it has definitely been illegal"), then it was likely that they were *all* in at least *some* trouble. As a result, they were all married to the General's plan now, whether they wanted to be or not ... and since that was the case, it was important that the General not completely lose it. "What are your orders sir?" he said as directly as possible.

Morgan's question went shooting through Colin Bradley's brain like a bucket of ice water. He immediately reminded himself that his brother was very right; it wasn't over yet. "Right," the General said, gaining control over his own rage. "We need to know where that fucking truck has gone Lieutenant, and I think I know. Tell Franklin to get all of his people the hell out of BioSec now! I want them in their vans and ready to go immediately. Tell them to drop everything, grab their guns and go!"

"Yes sir," Morgan said.

"And then get me whoever we've got on guard up at Bonito Lake," Bradley said.

"You think they're headed back up there sir?" Morgan said.

"Maybe," said the General. "If I'm right, how quickly can we get me up there?"

Morgan's mind raced, "uhh, we've got a bunch of reservists in this weekend using the Pave Hawks," he said, referring to a squadron of HH-60 helicopters on the base.

"I want one of them at my command, standing by," Bradley said.

"Yes sir," Morgan said, turning to leave, "and I'll get you Bonito right now sir."

Colin turned and looked out the window again. "You're right Mitch," he said aloud, "it's not over yet."

26 RESCUE

Time: 10:28 a.m., March 23, 2025
Location: BioSec, Women's Staff Locker Room

Colonel Wisener stood quietly by the door to the locker room. She had been concentrating on the sounds in the hall for about twenty minutes. She was just about to make her move back into the hall when she suddenly heard footsteps approaching. She quickly ran down the aisle of lockers and stood behind them, out of sight. The door opened and she heard two voices entering the room.

"Nice!" a female voice said, "wish we had a locker room like this."

"MPs on patrol," the Colonel thought, "great."

"You can come in you know," the female voice said.

"Yeah whatever Jess," the second, male voice said, obviously preferring to stand by the door. "C'mon, we're supposed to go down and relieve the guys watching the prisoners in like 2 minutes."

"I heard they're DoD," she said.

"So?" he said.

"And you're OK with this?" she asked.

"Hey, I just work here," the male MP said, "I'm just following my orders. It's the General's ass, not mine."

"Yeah I guess," she replied.

"Look, I'm going down to the end of the hall to relieve Harris and take my post," he said.

"Yeah, hang on, I'll be there in a second," she replied.

The Colonel stood silently. She could hear the girl's footsteps only a few feet away. She turned her head to the right and silently raised her right arm and held her hand by her left shoulder, ready to strike. The silence was deafening and the Colonel wondered if she'd been detected. "Hmm," she heard the female MP say, and then she heard a zipper sound and the sound of cash being removed from a small wallet or purse.

"Let's go Martin!" the voice in the hall said impatiently.

The Colonel heard the girl stuff the money in her pocket and say, "coming!" as she turned and hurried out. The Colonel exhaled after she heard the door close.

"Well that's good news," the Colonel thought. Now she knew where her people were being held. She had no idea how to get to them or how to get past two armed guards, but she knew she had to try. She was in the process of trying to think up a plan when she suddenly heard shouting in the hall, and a lot of it. She went to the door and slowly, carefully opened it the tiniest crack to listen.

"Everybody out!" a booming voice was shouting, "let's go!! NOW!!"

"What's up First Sergeant?" she heard a female voice ask

(probably the one that had just been in there a few minutes ago).

"We're buggin' out, right now!" he replied authoritatively.

"What about the prisoners," another voice said.

"Leave 'em!" the First Sergeant shouted. "Grab your gear, grab your weapons, and get outside, NOW!!"

The Colonel waited for several more minutes. There was a lot of shouting, a lot of running footsteps, and then nothing. After several minutes of complete silence, the Colonel opened the door and peered out in to the hall. Nothing. She ran down to the end of the hall. It was a large conference room and it was crammed with people from both her team and BioSec. Several of her people saw her approach and jumped up.

"It's good to see you Colonel!" said Staff Sergeant Tammy Miller, "are they gone?"

The Colonel nodded, "I think so, but I'm worried about why," she replied. "We need to get out of here too, right away."

A BioSec employee nudged his way to the door and said, "The emergency code for the door is 4215."

The Colonel punched the code in. The door made a beep and click sound and they pushed it open. As everyone streamed out of the room into the hall, the Colonel said to Miller "run down to the main entrance, I want to know where those MPs are going."

"Yes, ma'am," Miller said, and she ran down the hall.

The Colonel raised her voice and shouted out to the emerging group, "Doctor Schneider?"

"Here!" said the Doctor. He was several people back and still making his way to the door. Doctor Tim Schneider was one of the managers at BioSec and had been in charge that morning.

"Doctor," the Colonel began, "are all of your people OK and accounted for?"

"All accept Miss Carson," Schneider replied.

"We've got her," the Colonel replied as they finally got to a position where they were face to face. "Doctor, obviously we're very sorry about all of this..."

"Clearly not your fault," Schneider said, accepting the apology.

"Thank you, and I hate to leave you right now, but obviously we have a much bigger problem on our hands," the Colonel said.

"I understand completely Colonel, good luck," Schneider said.

"Thank you," the Colonel said, and then in a much louder voice, "alright! All UNCLE personnel form up over by this wall behind me."

The groups separated quickly as they finished emerging from the room. As the Colonel got her people together and was about to speak, Staff Sergeant Miller came running back down the hall.

"Report," the Colonel said.

Miller was a little out of breath but quickly said, "They're bugging out ma'am. They're in vehicles and headed for the main gate, picking up people as they go."

"Meaning we can get to our vehicles?" the Colonel said incredulously.

"I think so ma'am," Miller said.

The Colonel smiled, "well shit, let's do that."

27 ONE MORE BLUFF

Time: 10:35 a.m., March 23, 2025
Location: General Colin Bradley's Security Checkpoint, Bonito Lake

Andy slowed the truck as they started up the last road to the entrance at Bonito Lake. General Bradley had already told them that he had some people up here, but they had no idea what to expect. As they came around the last corner towards the dam, a roadblock was set up. There were two MPs.

"That's a good sign," said Jim as they approached.

Andy was encouraged by Jim's optimism, but he also noticed that Jim had reached down and pulled one of the pulse guns up on his lap, and he knew what that meant; if necessary, they were going to use force at this point. There were no other options now, this *had* to work. As the truck approached, one of the MPs held up his hand, signaling them to stop. "Morning Staff Sergeant," Andy said in what he hoped was a pleasant, but not too pleasant, tone.

"Good morning sir," Staff Sergeant Matt Foster responded, "what can we do for you?"

"We're here on General Bradley's orders to take this truck over to the ... ship and prepare it for loading," Andy said.

"Loading what, sir?" Foster asked.

Andy looked at him and, without hesitation said, "I'm a Second Lieutenant, Staff Sergeant, do you really think they'd tell me?"

Foster stared at Andy for a moment, then nodded, half smiled and looked down at his clipboard. "We weren't told to expect any traffic up here for hours sir," Foster said.

"Well, the General wanted us here early for some reason," Andy replied.

"And who's with you Lieutenant...?" Foster asked.

"Newton," Andy answered, "Lieutenant Andrew Newton. Just the three of us; myself, Staff Sergeant Thorn and Sergeant Black."

"And the truck?" Foster said.

"Empty," said Andy, "we're supposed to deliver the truck and then wait for instructions."

Foster looked nervous, not sure what to do, finally he said, "err, yeah, umm, hang on Lieutenant." He grabbed his walkie talkie and said, "hey Charlie, it's Matt."

"Go ahead," said Staff Sergeant Charlie Wilkins over the walkie-talkie.

"I got a Lieutenant Newton here with a Staff Sergeant Thorn and Sergeant Black," Foster said, "they said that General Bradley sent them up here, but their names aren't on my list and I was told that no one was going to be here until this afternoon. Do I let them through?"

Andy swallowed very slightly and Jim moved his pulse gun ever so slightly. The pause seemed to take forever.

The walkie-talkie crackled. "Yeah," said Charlie. "I know Thorn, if the General sent him up here it's gotta be legit. I'd let 'em through."

"Roger that," Foster said, then he looked up at Andy, "OK sir, if you guys need a hand, just wave or something. There's only six of us up here right now, but as you can see there's nothin' going on so..."

"Thanks Staff Sergeant," Andy replied, "we'll holler if we need anything."

"Yes sir," Foster said and waved them through.

As they began to drive around the lake on the Forest Service Road, Andy looked across the dam at the area where Jim had shot him. "That was yesterday morning," he said to himself in complete disbelief.

All three men were still a bit tense as they drove by a couple of the other MPs on patrol. Each of the MPs acknowledged the truck as it passed. Finally Jim quietly said, "you, young man, are a *Class A* bullshit artist. *Nice* work!" He glanced over at Mike. "Mike?"

"Yeah," echoed Mike, "hell, that was so good even *I'm* not sure who I work for."

"Thanks guys," Andy said. He looked across the lake at the ship. It was in shadows underneath the giant tarp that UNCLE had set up the morning before (although that was unnecessary at the moment since the weather had clouded over on their ride up and there was no way any satellite was getting *any* look at the area now), but Andy was more worried about getting to it with the truck. As he looked down towards the end of the lake, he asked, "How did you guys...?"

"Go past the lake," Mike quickly began to explain. "Take your next left, then the one after that, then stick to your right. The road dumps you off right over there," he said pointing to the far shore.

"You'll see where we pulled off. You'll turn around there and just back it down the shoreline to the ship. The ground was pretty dry yesterday. We got in and out with no problems. Just stick close to the trees as you back down."

"Got it," Andy said.

They passed one last MP as they got to the west end of the lake. He looked up at them and waved as they drove by, but Andy noticed, at the very last second, the MP had a strange expression on his face.

Sergeant Miles Lannert grabbed his walkie-talkie. "Hey guys," he said, "Charlie, Matt?"

"Yeah Miles, what's up?" Charlie replied.

"Who did you say was coming through with that Lieutenant?" Miles asked.

"Black and Thorn," Matt Foster replied, "why?"

"And did you see them Charlie?" Miles asked.

"I saw the truck as it went by, and I saw the L-T driving it, but no. Why, what's up Miles?" Charlie asked.

"Well, I don't know Thorn that well," Miles replied, "and I didn't exactly get a great look at them either, but ... well, the guy in the middle *could* have been Thorn, but Black and I play pool together all the time, and I'm telling you, that guy on the end was absolutely *not* Black."

Everyone was silent.

"Couldn't there be another Sergeant Black at the Base?" Foster asked.

"I suppose," said Miles.

"Yeah could be," said Charlie, "but we'd better check it out. Matt, call down to the Base and find out what's going on. Good call Miles."

"Thanks," said Miles.

Matt Foster walked over to the duty truck, opened the door and reached for the phone, but as his hand was reaching for it, the phone rang.

"Staff Sergeant Foster, may I help you sir or ma'am," he said.

"Foster, this is Lieutenant Morgan, General Bradley's aide," Morgan said over the phone.

"Yes sir, what can I do for you sir?" Foster asked.

"Staff Sergeant, you haven't seen a truck come through your check point by any chance have you?" Morgan asked.

"Yes sir, just a couple of minutes ago sir," Foster answered.

"Shit!" Morgan said, "Stand by." Foster could hear Morgan cup the phone and say, "we found them General, you were right, they're up at Bonito."

In the background Foster then heard the General's voice. There was a curse he couldn't quite make out, but then he heard, "I'm on my way, make sure that Goddamn chopper is waiting for me when I get over there Morgan."

"Yes sir," Morgan replied.

"And tell our people up at Bonito to stop and arrest those people in that truck. They are authorized to use *any means necessary* to apprehend them is that clear?" the General said.

"Yes sir," Morgan replied.

"The use of force is absolutely authorized, am I clear

Lieutenant?" the General asked.

"Very clear sir," Morgan said. Foster heard what sounded like a door and then Morgan's voice, obviously talking to him, "Did you get that Staff Sergeant?" Morgan asked.

Foster was already sweating. He was in a panic because he felt like he was going to be in big trouble for letting the truck through, but he was also just plain freaked out that he'd just been given an order to use force if necessary to arrest the people in that truck. "Yes sir, I did sir," Foster replied. "We're on it sir."

"See to it Staff Sergeant," Morgan said, "All of our asses are in your hands, got it?"

"Got it sir," Foster said, and hung up. "Shit!" he said to himself. He grabbed his walkie-talkie and said, "guys! Everybody! Listen up! That truck that just went past us was *not* I repeat *not* authorized."

"Shit," he heard Charlie say.

"Yeah, it gets worse," Foster went on, "we're supposed to stop and arrest them, and the use of force has been authorized."

"What?!" said Miles in disbelief.

"You heard me," Foster replied, "I heard the General himself say it, and he's probably on his way ... by chopper."

"Shit," said Charlie. "Alright, everybody form up over by me except you Matt. I want you to cross the dam and come at them from the other side."

"What about the locks on the gates?" Foster asked.

"Shoot the fucking locks off the fucking gates Matt," Charlie said angrily, "and hold position by that big rock on the other side."

Andy had driven a truck before, but not very often, and he was understandably nervous about backing down the shore in this one to the spaceship. He had lowered the windows and was checking his side mirrors constantly as he slowly backed down the shore. Mike was looking out his window across the lake when he saw several of the MPs coming together. They were talking in an animated way, one of them pointed over towards them. And then all of them drew their weapons.

"Uhh, Jim!" Mike said rather urgently.

Jim quickly took his eyes off of Andy's driving job and focused across the lake. "Well shit," he said quietly, "we're made guys."

Andy stopped paying attention to his driving and looked across the lake. Three of the MPs looked to be taking up position together. Two others were running to other spots. All of them had weapons in their hands. "Oh that's not good," he said.

"Don't panic," said Jim right away in a calm voice. He picked the second pulse gun off the floor of the cab and handed it to Mike. "Here, now there's only six of them, probably led by an E-5 or E-6. They're trained as MPs, but it's not likely that any of them has any combat experience."

"Yeah, Jim," Mike started, "I know you know this, but ... *I* don't have any combat experience either."

"Yeah, me neither," said Andy.

"Well, today's your lucky day, guys," Jim said. "The bad news is that the course is pass/fail, the good news is that you've got me."

"They're shouting at us," Mike said, unable to make out what they were saying across the lake and over the truck noise.

"Put the window up," Jim said.

"What? Is the glass bulletproof?!" Andy asked.

"Actually, yes, it is," said Jim.

"Well *that's* cool," Andy thought. As he was putting the window up he thought he heard a sound on his side of the truck that sounded like a "sss" sound. Then another. Then *PLINK*! A bullet hit the truck!

"Alright, well that pisses me off a bit," said Jim. "How close are we?" he asked Andy.

"About 50 more feet," Andy said.

"OK, when you get about 15 feet away from the ship, I want you to stop," Jim said, "We'll need a little bit of room." Andy continued backing up. "Now we're all going to get out on Andy's side. Mike you and I are going to go under the truck and we're going to pick these guys off one at a time."

"Yeah OK," said Mike, thinking that really meant that *Jim* was going to pick these guys off one at a time.

"What am I going to do?" Andy asked.

"You need to get Heather and Gopto on that ship Andy," Jim said seriously.

Andy looked straight at Jim for a moment. He could see in Jim's eyes that this was a "you will give your life to accomplish this task if necessary" order. "Yes sir," he said.

Jim could tell from Andy's face and voice that he understood. "This kid really is UNCLE material," he thought, but he also knew that one of the easiest ways to die in a potentially lethal situation was to assume that you're going to. He needed to clean that up in Andy's head right away. Jim smiled at him. "Yeah, uhh, *alive* Andy," he said, "and that means you too."

Andy understood. He had total confidence in Jim as a leader, and clearly Jim was trying to make sure he didn't do something stupid in the process of trying to do something brave. He smiled back. "Right. Important tip. Got it," he said.

Pow! Sssssssss! A bullet hit and penetrated the right front tire of the truck.

"All right. Now I'm really getting annoyed," Jim said, "let's go."

Andy jumped out of the truck and ran to the rear axle and stopped. Jim hopped out behind him, then Mike. Both men immediately crawled under the truck. Their mostly black uniforms in the shadows and the dirty shore made them very hard to see. Jim had his pulse gun out in front of him and laid very still for a moment. Then he suddenly said, "found one," and fired. In the distance, Jim watched one of the MPs fly backwards several feet through the tall grass he had been crouching in. "One down, five to go," he said ... and then, without looking back, "get moving Andy!"

The order shook the fear out of Andy's head for an instant and he flew around to the back of the truck, threw open the door, jumped up and rolled into the back of the truck. Heather was right there. "Hi," he said. He looked in her eyes. "Wow," he thought, "she really is ... perfect."

It was pretty obvious to Heather that Andy really liked her. Heather almost blushed as she smiled and said, "hi."

Pop! Pop pop pop!

"What is that?!" Heather asked.

"Yeah umm," Andy started.

"Is someone *shooting* at us?!" Heather asked, suddenly very concerned.

"Uhh, kinda yeah," Andy said, "but, don't worry, Jim's got it under control."

"Scratch two!" Jim yelled from under the truck.

"Listen, we gotta get you and Gopto into the ship," Andy said, "Do you have any idea how to do that?"

Heather looked out. The right side of the spaceship was only about 20 feet from the back of the truck. There were markings. She had no idea what the markings meant, and then suddenly she did. "That's the lower starboard access hatch," she thought.

"Otni!" she said. Without warning Heather jumped out of the truck ran over to the side of the ship and slapped her palm on a particular spot on the side of the ship. Andy was startled but immediately followed her. When he reached the ship he tried to position himself between her and where he thought the shots were coming from. Heather was confused. Again she slapped her palm on the access panel, "Kof!" she said angrily. It wasn't working, why wasn't it working?! She looked at her hand and was momentarily very startled. "Holy crap, what happened to my hand?!" she thought. Then her brain caught up. "Right, I'm Heather, I'm human," she said aloud. "Come on!" she said and raced to the front of the ship. Andy was confused but quickly followed her. As they started to run up to the front of the ship (away from the lake), he heard a whizzing bullet nearby.

"Got him," he heard Jim say, then he heard the pulse gun fire. "Scratch three!" he shouted.

Andy and Heather got around the front of the ship and ran down the port side until they reached the lower port access hatch. "It's OPEN," Andy thought.

And right then he heard "freeze!"

Andy froze. So did Heather. Andy put his hands up and turned towards the voice. It was Staff Sergeant Foster. He was standing very near where Andy had been the previous morning when Jim shot him and Andy took a moment to appreciate the irony.

"Put your hands on your head!" Foster shouted, "and walk slowly away from that thing and towards me!"

"We got it Staff Sergeant," Andy said, trying to make sure Foster stayed calm.

An instant later, Staff Sergeant Matt Foster flew into the air. It looked like someone had tied a rope around his chest and had suddenly yanked him backwards. His rifle went sailing off into the lake, and he hit the ground hard, unconscious.

"Scratch five!" shouted Mike Powell from the rear of the ship.

Andy exhaled loudly. He wasn't sure how much more of this his heart could take, but he sure was grateful to Mike.

"Thank you!" Andy said loudly to Mike.

"Well that was fun!" Mike said, making it clear that shooting a pulse gun was *not* a normal activity for him. He walked up to Andy and Heather, "don't worry about number six, he's off to the far side trying to get position. Jim's got him. Shall we go in?"

28 RACE TO BONITO

Time: 10:55 a.m., March 23, 2025
Location: UNCLE Command Vehicle, Highway 70, northeast of Tularosa, New Mexico

Colonel Wisener was the last one into the command vehicle. All of her people were loaded up and ready to roll. The door closed behind her and the mobile command center began rolling towards the front gate. Within minutes they were on the road to Bonito. "Lieutenant Chang, Get me CINC NORAD on comms right now," the Colonel ordered.

"Yes ma'am, Lieutenant Chang replied.

The Colonel moved to her chair and sat down. There was no doubt in her mind about why the MPs from Holloman had bugged out of BioSec so quickly, and no doubt about where they were going. Clearly they had figured out that her people had control of the truck and were returning it, with Gopto, to Bonito Lake. But beyond that, there were a bunch of unknowns. Had her people been successful in getting Gopto back to the ship? If they had, was Gopto right about it being usable in any way? How many men from Holloman were already at Bonito? She assumed it was just a few men, but now there were at least two dozen, armed MPs on their way to assist. She figured that the MPs that had been at

BioSec were about 10 minutes ahead of them, but she had no idea whether or not that fact would be significant.

"Roger that." she heard Chang say. "Colonel, CINC NORAD is on the line for you ma'am."

"Thank you Lieutenant," the Colonel replied. She picked up the handset by her desk, "General?"

"Jane!" Mitch Bradley said, "Sounds like you have some good news."

"Yes sir, a little," Wisener began. "Shortly after our last conversation, the troops your brother sent from Holloman suddenly bugged out. No warning, no explanation."

"He figured out we have the truck," the General said.

"And where it's heading," the Colonel added.

"So you got all your people?" the General asked.

"Yes sir," she replied.

"Good," he said, "and where are you?"

"We're on highway 70 headed for Bonito sir," the Colonel answered. "We figure we're about 10 minutes behind the troops from Holloman."

"That's a lot of time for things to go wrong Jane," the General said.

"Yes sir," the Colonel acknowledged, "we're burning all the gas we have sir."

"Colonel!" a voice in the command center said. It was First Lieutenant Emily Hernandez. "Sorry to interrupt ma'am, but I've got something on the Spook."

"Stand by General," the Colonel said. She laid her handset on the desk and moved over to Lieutenant Hernandez.

Lieutenant Hernandez was one of the Electronic Systems Officers for the mobile command center. "The Spook" was shorthand for the short range air search radar system that was housed in a small dome on top of the vehicle. As the Colonel got closer, Hernandez pointed to her screen, "right there ma'am."

"Do you know what it is?" the Colonel asked.

"Yes ma'am," Hernandez replied, "it's an HH-60 Pave Hawk ma'am ... and it's headed for..."

"I know where it's headed Lieutenant," the Colonel interrupted. She quickly went back to her chair to pick up the headset. "General, we've got a helo running like a bat out of hell from Holloman on a straight line for Bonito ... and it's a good bet we know who's on it sir."

General Mitch Bradley closed his eyes and pinched the space on his nose between them. "Yes, well, that brings me to the news I have for you Colonel," he began. "I just got off the phone with two members of the JCS, and it turns out that my brother has in fact had conversations with at least one other member. And the consensus there is that, well, that there is no consensus there."

"Uh oh," said the Colonel gravely.

"Yeah, uh oh," the General echoed. "So basically what that means is that if he gets control of the alien and or its technology, they are in fact going to cut a deal with him and our whole world changes."

"Wow," the Colonel said.

"Colonel," General Bradley said plainly, "I can't over-state how important it is to make sure that doesn't happen."

"I understand sir," Colonel Wisener replied. The situation was clear. Everything that she and General Bradley and all of their predecessors had worked for, everything that UNCLE had ever stood for, was now on the line.

"Good luck Colonel," General Bradley said.

"Thank you sir," she replied, "Wisener out."

29 INTERFERENCE

Time: 11:05 a.m., March 23, 2025
Location: South shoreline of Bonito Lake

Jim Landrum moved quickly and quietly among the trees just uphill along the south shore of the lake. There was one last MP to track down and neutralize, and he pretty much knew where the guy was. Jim knew that he had years of experience, combat experience and lots of training as advantages over this young man, but he also knew that complacency and overconfidence were keys to getting yourself killed, so he took the situation very seriously. Finally, almost all the way down the south shore of the lake, he saw movement. "Gotcha," he thought. His target had gotten surprisingly close to him, but Jim could see him and it was obvious that the young man could not see Jim. He trained the pulse gun on the target and fired. The man flew backwards and down into some tall grass and brush. Jim exhaled and walked from the trees on to the shore. The man was motionless. "Scratch six," he said quietly to himself with satisfaction. He turned to walk back down the shore towards Gopto's ship. He got about fifteen paces down the shore.

"FREEZE!!!" he heard the man shout.

Jim stopped.

"Place your weapon on the ground and put your hands up over your head!" the man shouted.

Jim slowly placed his weapon on the ground, then stood back up with his hands over his head.

"Turn around!" he shouted, clearly getting closer to Jim.

Jim turned around, and was very confused to see the man he had just stunned walking towards him. "That's impossible," he thought.

"My name is Sergeant Miles Lannert, and you are under arrest you son of a bitch!" Lannert said.

Jim could see his face clearly now. His eyes were wild, uncontrolled. He had tears on his face. He was angry, freaking out, irrational. He started to speak, "OK, stay calm..."

"Shut up!" Lannert shouted. "You'll talk when I say. Who are you?"

"My name is Captain Jim Landrum," Jim began calmly, "and I can explain."

"You killed my friends Captain," Lannert said with barely controlled rage.

"No! No I did not!" Jim said quickly, "Your friends are merely stunned."

"Bullshit!" Lannert nearly screamed.

"No," Jim said, trying to be reassuring, "not bullshit, they're just unconscious." Then he added quietly and confused, "just like you should be right now."

"I know what's going on, I know what you're here to do," Lannert said.

Jim looked confused, "what ... do you think I'm here to do?" he asked.

"You're here to change history," Lannert said.

"What?! No!" Jim said.

"Yeah, he said you'd say that," Lannert went on. "He told me exactly who you are, what you're doing here. He told me you were going to kill my friends and try to kill me. And that's when he gave me this." Lannert reached down and revealed a small purple device on his belt. It looked like a flashlight. "It kept your gun from killing me like you killed the others."

Jim was confused and starting to get very worried. This kid was obviously out of his depth, probably suffering from traumatic stress, and he had a rifle pointed right at Jim ... but more importantly, he had some kind of device that had rendered his pulse gun ineffective. Jim was *very* worried about who the hell Lannert was referring to and *how* he got that device. "Sergeant," Jim started again.

"Shut up!" Lannert nearly screamed. "I have to kill you now Captain," he said. His voice was shaking. "It's the only way." Lannert raised his weapon and prepared to kill Jim.

"Listen, I don't..." Jim started to say, and then, behind the Sergeant, he saw something that made even him nearly pass out. "Holy....." Jim whispered.

Lannert saw Jim's eyes move. He scoffed and said, "do you really think I'm *that* stupid?!" he said.

"Well," said the voice behind him.

Lannert spun around just in time to get a glimpse of a man pointing a pulse rifle right at him. Lannert sneered and pointed to the deflector on his belt. The man smiled, gave him a slight shrug and fired. Lannert's body went flying and he landed on the beach, unconscious.

"Yes," the man said.

Jim stared in total shock and disbelief. He guessed that the man was in his mid-40s, but the face was unmistakable.

It was Andy Newton.

30 REPAIRS

Time: 11:00 a.m., March 23, 2025
Location: Gopto's ship

Heather, Andy and Mike stepped in to the ship. It was very dark and it took their eyes several moments to adjust.

"Fee-tanna ep," Heather said.

"What?" said Mike.

"Sorry," said Heather, "it means welcome aboard."

As Heather moved into the passageway Mike looked at Andy with a concerned look. Andy said, "Yeah, she's been doing that."

They walked from the hatch towards the stairs in the middle of the ship. Heather pointed to her right (towards the back of the ship) and said to Mike, "That's the engineering section."

"Yeah, we kind of gathered that when we were here yesterday," Mike replied. "I've got a million questions about it though."

Heather started up the stairs.

"Hey, where are you going?" Mike asked.

"The bridge," Heather replied. "We've got to get at least partial main power back online in order to jump start the starboard engine."

The three of them walked up and then along the passageway to the Bridge. Heather was focused on the task at hand, but her mind was also a very confused mix of herself and Neja. It was getting easier by the minute to translate between Japel and English, and to separate the parts of her brain that contained Neja's memories from her own, but emotionally it was still a confusing and overwhelming experience. As they walked into the Bridge area, Heather saw Neja's chair and gasped slightly at the sight. The rod that had killed her was still there, still covered in her blood. She instantly felt sick to her stomach.

"That's where..." Mike said.

"I know," Heather interrupted. She decided that it was time to tell them. "I know everything she knew." They looked puzzled. "Gopto ... saved all of her memories, like backing up a hard drive, and he downloaded them all to me."

Mike couldn't help himself, he whistled softly. "So you know everything she knew?"

Heather stared at the rod, still feeling very queasy. "Yeah," she said. She walked up to the panels of her old station. "The self destruct sequence is still active," she said, "the power ran out after I ... that is after she ... or after we, died." Heather counter rotated the auto destruct switch and closed the cover. "There," she said. She then looked over to the far left of the panels in front of her station. She walked around the chair carefully, bent down and opened a panel underneath the desk level of all of her controls. There was a large switch. With no small amount of effort, she flipped the switch up.

Immediately there was a series of tones that sounded like "Beedee booboop beedee booboop beedee booboop." Andy looked at Heather. She appeared relieved. Another sound, "Blink blink, blink blink," and then suddenly several LED like lights came to life all over the Bridge.

Heather exhaled loudly. "Emergency lights," she said, with significant relief in her voice, "that's a good sign." Several lights on panels in front of them started to blink to life and then illuminate. Heather's eyes moved quickly until she saw one in particular that was obviously significant. "Yes!" she said, "the Emergency Power Supply has recharged enough to restart one of the auxiliary generators." She smiled, "watch this."

She began typing on one of the screens in front of them. She stopped and looked at her hands, clearly annoyed. "Five fingers," she muttered to herself, "definitely gonna have to get used to this."

Whoom! A sound went through the ship like a giant rubber mallet had just hit it, and then ... lights! A very low hum began and the vent system turned on.

"Sheesa!" Heather said, then she looked at Mike and Andy and added, "it means, umm, bingo!" With the lights on, Neja's blood all over the floor and chair became very obvious. Heather's nausea became significantly worse. She physically shivered as she looked at it and put her hand up to her mouth. "Listen," she said, "this is going to take a couple of minutes ... I need to, uhh ... I'll be right back."

"Sure," said Andy, "we'll wait right here."

Heather left the Bridge and headed aft. Instinctively, she walked to the second door on her right and punched in the code. It was Neja's quarters. Heather was overwhelmed by the sense of loss that she felt for Neja ... or rather for herself ... or ... it was still *very* confusing. She was definitely still Heather Carson, but it was also as if she had at least *been* Neja. Her mind was still sliding back and forth a bit, looking for the "new normal." She walked around the small compartment, touching a few things here and there. She opened the closet door and stared at a row of Neja's uniforms. Suddenly she realized that she'd only been wearing a lab coat this entire time. Gopto had been keeping her warm when they were physically connected, literally helping heat her blood so that she would be comfortable in the truck, but now that she was on her own again (disconnected physically), she was acutely aware of the fact that she was feeling cold. She pulled one of Neja's uniforms off the hangar, took off the lab coat and put the uniform on. It was a little big, but it would do. Neja had indeed been several inches taller than Heather (as she had appeared on The Plain) and she had slightly longer limbs. "And bigger boobs," Heather thought as she looked at herself in uniform in the mirror, "like that's so unusual." She pulled up the sleeves a bit and then looked in the mirror. It felt good to be back in uniform ... sort of. "Clearly this is going to be difficult," she told herself. Gopto and Neja had been correct; she was still very much Heather Carson, but she was now also Heather *and* Neja, and that was going to take some real getting used to. Suddenly her brain rushed back to their present situation and the fact that Gopto was still out in the truck. She jumped up and ran back to the Bridge. As she came back she could hear a "bang, bang, bang" sound, like someone was hitting something. She was alarmed, but when she got through the door to the Bridge she saw that Andy had found a tool and was beating the rod that had killed her backwards out of the chair. Mike had found some pads over on the emergency medical table and had been trying to wipe up some of the remaining blood.

"Yeah I don't know either," said Andy, taking a break after having finally gotten the rod back through the chair.

They both stopped and looked at her. Andy in particular looked, well, smitten. "Thanks guys," she said with a slightly blushing smile.

Andy recovered. "Nice uniform," he said.

"It'll do for now," she replied, then asked "you don't know *what* either?"

"How the hell are we going to get Gopto back in here?" Andy asked.

Heather smiled, "that's easy, and it's the next thing we need to do. Mike, I need you to go back to the truck and use that lifter thing and get him out of it."

"Sure," Mike said, and he left down the passageway.

"But how are we going to..." Andy started to ask.

"Just trust me, you'll see," she said.

Heather led Andy off the Bridge and down to the only door on their left as they moved aft down the main passageway; Gopto's space. As they entered, a low level light automatically turned on. Heather walked over to a panel on the wall and began typing.

"Bod nok, to pi, Bod nok, to pi," the ship's computer said.

Heather tapped a button. An alarm sounded, and suddenly a large hatch on the far bulkhead began to swing outward and open. As it did, a rail appeared from the ceiling. It dropped down slightly and then began extending out the hatch. The rail sections seemed to self-assemble as the system moved. Once the end section was several feet away from the hull outside, it rotated so that it was perpendicular to the other rail and parallel with the side of the ship. Four sections built out along this perpendicular. Strands of cable began dropping out of holes in the rails. When they reached the ground, several more feet came out and then the system stopped. Andy walked over to the hatch to look down. He saw Mike already in the back of the truck getting Gopto ready on the lifter. Heather walked to the edge as well, stared out and made sure that Gopto was reading her thoughts and seeing through her eyes. Within moments, Gopto was out of the truck, attached to the lift, and being hoisted into the ship.

Mike was fascinated as the lift mechanism brought Gopto up and into the ship and he ran back in so he could watch the operation from the other side. He arrived just as the vast bulk of Gopto's body was in the ship and on the deck. The cables disconnected and the entire apparatus collapsed and receded into the ceiling. Gopto made his way in a series of inchworm like movements onto a large pad along the far bulkhead. The hatch closed and sealed. Mike's eyes had to adjust to the decreased light, but he definitely wanted to see this part. There were a series of cables and tubes and things along the bulkhead that were extending down from the ceiling. A large, translucent, gel like pad that was about as large as a horse blanket, descended from the ceiling. It had a *lot* of electronic looking devices on it, and Mike assumed that it was a significant part of the mind/machine interface that would be necessary for Gopto to communicate with the ship. It gently laid on top of him, centered on the tallest part of his body (where Mike understood Gopto's brain was located) and almost immediately the devices began lighting up.

Heather looked relieved and then smiled, "it's working," she said.

A couple of tubes descended near the front of Gopto's body. His mouth opened and the tubes went in several feet. "Food and air?" Mike asked.

"Exactly," replied Heather. "He should feel better relatively quickly, but the air is going to get pretty thick in here for us."

Mike and Andy were both already noticing that the pressure and thickness of the air was increasing, it was a little more work to breathe, but not difficult.

"Now what?" asked Andy.

"Now we need at least one other auxiliary power unit to come back online," Heather said. "If we can do that, then we have a decent chance of starting the engine."

"How long will it take Gopto to do the calculations for the jump?" Mike asked.

Heather looked blank for a moment. It was clear to both of them that she was conversing with Gopto on the subject. "Not long," she answered. "Every ship has its own emergency jump location in orbit around Japella, our home world. It is, relatively speaking, a fixed point, and Gopto already knows it. Once we know our *exact* location in space, Gopto can do the calculations for folding the space between the two points relatively quickly. Fixing our location on the planet is difficult, but it's not impossible. The bigger deal is the power though. If we don't get that engine going, none of this will matter."

31 IT'S ABOUT TIME

Time: 11:15 a.m., March 23, 2025
Location: South shoreline of Bonito Lake

"I got it right didn't I?" Andy said.

Jim was rarely at a loss for words, but this was way beyond anything he had ever prepared himself for. "Huh?" was all he could say.

"The 'well' and then 'yes' thing, that was what you said earlier," Andy said, pointing to the ground, "... today ... when you saved my life, right?"

"Umm, yeah," Jim replied.

"I thought it would be funny," Andy said with a smile, "kinda funnier in my head actually but..."

This wasn't getting any easier for Jim. The man in front of him absolutely *was* Andy Newton, and yet it *couldn't* be. "Do you want to explain this to me?" Jim asked.

Andy laughed. "No!" he replied, "no, I *really* don't. But it's good to see you again old friend."

"Yeah ... well ... thank you, for saving *my* ass this time," Jim said. His brain was beginning to accept the unacceptable and simply move on. "How'd you get through his magic shield there?"

"Ahh," Andy said, "I have a 'magic shield' disabler."

"Of course you do," Jim said dryly. "Any chance you'd like to share that toy with me?"

"Actually, this one *is* yours, but not yet, so ... no, sorry," Andy said.

Jim rolled Lannert's body over and pulled the purple device off his belt. "So who gave this to him?"

"I can't answer that," Andy said, "but don't worry, I've got him, right over there," he added, gesturing just out of sight behind him. "He's taking a little nap right now, but he's going back with me in just a minute." Andy gestured to Jim to toss him the shield generator. Jim stared at it, then frowned and tossed it to Andy.

"Any chance I can see him first?" Jim asked

"Noooo," Andy answered. "Sorry, I have my orders."

"Wisener?" Jim asked.

"Oh no," Andy said, "*General* Wisener, who retired ... a long time ago actually, is enjoying life on the Kona side of the Big Island."

"Oh. Well that's nice. So who gave you those orders?" Jim asked. Andy looked at him with no expression on his face, and yet that lack of expression told him everything he needed to know. "Oh," he said, suddenly knowing the answer, "I did."

"Yeah," Andy said, looking down.

Both men were silent for a moment. Jim's mind was still trying to cope with the implications of Andy's sudden dual presence and the information he now had about himself. "So," he said hopefully with a smile, "I do come back some day. That's good." Andy pursed his lips and looked down. When he looked up at Jim again he looked pained. Jim's heart fell into his stomach. He felt like someone had just taken his birthday *and* punched him in the gut. "I don't go at all do I?"

"I'm afraid not Jim," Andy said quietly.

"And Mike?" Jim asked. Andy shook his head.

"But how?" Jim asked in a voice that sounded genuinely hurt.

"More bad guys are coming Jim," Andy answered, "right now. And they'll be here in just a few more minutes."

"I see," said Jim. "But you go," he added, as much a question as a statement, and with no attempt to hide his jealousy.

"Yeah ... I do," Andy replied. Andy could see the pain in his friend's eyes, and he almost choked up as he tried to make it better. "If it helps at all Jim, you're needed here ... really badly."

"Yeah," Jim said. His voice was resigned, dejected.

"Jim, you don't know..." Andy continued as a tear actually came to one of his eyes. "The things I *can't* tell you ... but ... you really are ... what Mike said in the truck this morning ... I still remember that like it was yesterday ... you really *are* a true to life God damn American hero. And they're gonna *need* you."

Jim had never felt this level of disappointment in his entire life. He felt numb. He heard everything that Andy said. He knew that he had an important job to do and he knew that he'd do it, but he couldn't help feeling that fate was about to cheat him in a way that he wouldn't ever recover from. This was the sort of disappointment that could gnaw at a man's soul. It would be completely normal to be bitter and angry about this for the rest of his life.

But Jim Landrum was not normal.

Immediately, from *way* deep down inside him, a thought came to Jim. From the time he was a little boy, he had always believed that people are, and should be, measured in no small part by the way they handle their worst moments. And those measurements weren't just about how you faced things like death on the battlefield. He already knew that he had the honor and courage he demanded of himself for moments like that. No, the measure of a man was also about moments exactly like this one. Jim's mind suddenly framed the events of this moment as a defining one for his life. And it wasn't so much about how others might judge him for how he handled it; it was about how he would judge *himself*. And that, was all it took. He fixed his posture a bit, stood straight, blinked a couple of times, and somehow, completely, let it go.

"So!" Jim said, "Time travel."

Andy couldn't believe it. He couldn't know exactly what Jim was going through, but he could imagine it. He had always admired Jim, but to witness the strength of his character and resolve in a situation like this was really amazing and inspiring. "Jesus Christ," Andy thought, "this guy really is a hero." And Andy knew that the only way to respect and honor his friend was to reflect that honor and courage right back at him. He looked right back at Jim and smiled and said, "yep." Then he added, "yeah if you think what UNCLE does *now* is challenging, just wait."

"I'll bet," said Jim. Then he thought about the events he'd just been a part of and added, "wait a minute ... so how many rules are you breaking by showing up here and saving my life?"

"By saving your life?" Andy said, "none, actually. In fact, what I just did here was to *restore* the correct timeline, not interfere with it. Jim Landrum survived the events at Bonito Lake today, that's a historical fact."

"One I'm sure I'm not supposed to know," Jim said.

Andy smiled and laughed a little to himself. "My God," he

thought, "he really is going to be the perfect man to stand guard over history isn't he? He's been on he job for less than a minute and he already knows we shouldn't be talking." He nodded broadly and added, "Well, yes. And to answer your question more completely, I'm not breaking any rules by saving your life, but by letting you see me and talk to me ... yeah, there's ... *several* ... actually."

"Alright," Jim nodded, "well, you should go."

"Yes," Andy agreed, "and you need to get back to your friends." Then he looked at his watch and his eyes got just a little wider before he added, "uhh, right now!"

"Including you," Jim said, making a statement about their relationship.

Andy was touched. "Yes, including me," he said, agreeing. "You have to make sure that ship gets away, Jim. Understand?"

"Yeah, I understand," Jim said.

Andy was again just blown away by how Jim was taking the situation. He seemed to be improving every moment. "It was really good to see you again," Andy said.

"Thanks, you too." Jim said. "Goodbye Andy."

"Goodbye," Andy said.

Jim turned and walked away.

Andy stood there for a long moment. When he was sure Jim could no longer hear him, he quiet added, "... Goodbye Colonel. See you in a minute."

32 JUMP!

Time: 11:26 a.m., March 23, 2025
Location: South shoreline of Bonito Lake

As Jim was jogging back to Gopto's ship, he thought about what the older Andy had just told him. Part of him was still devastated by the news. Something was about to happen that would keep him off the ship when it left. He wanted to fight it, to try to change history, but Andy had also made it clear that he was going to play an important role in future events ... and it certainly sounded like those events were going to be interesting. By the time he got back to the ship, he decided that focusing on all the "ifs" was dangerous and distracting. The best thing to do was to do all he could to forget what he had heard and proceed as normally as possible. He stepped through the port side hatch of the ship for the second time in two days, but this time he could hear the hum of equipment running, and there were lights. "That's a good sign," he thought. He heard voices from deeper inside the ship. "Helloooo," he called out.

"Jim!" Mike said from somewhere inside the ship. Jim heard footsteps and then a moment later Mike appeared at the top of the stairs between decks.

"Hey," said Jim, "how are we doin'?"

"OK," said Mike, "Gopto's safely back on board, feeling better and doing whatever work he needs to do to get the ship out of here."

"Well, that's good," Jim said.

"Yeah," Mike replied, "but the bad news is that it isn't going to mean squat if we can't get one of the engines online."

"OK?" said Jim, knowing there was more.

"Yeah, well that's the issue," Mike went on. "Heather says she's got to get two of these auxiliary generators going to jump start one of the engines. She got the first one going no problem, and that's what has gotten us lights and some power, but the second unit was apparently completely dead stick."

"How many are there?" Jim asked.

"Four," Mike answered, "Heather and Andy are gonna come down here in just a second. We're going to the engine room so she can show us a couple of things. Apparently at least one of us may need to be down here while she tries to get the third or fourth aux unit online."

"Hey! Jim!" Andy said as he appeared at the stairs.

Jim did his absolute best to handle his reaction to seeing the younger Andy again, but he couldn't help thinking, "wow, *this* is bizarre."

Andy saw Jim's face and immediately said, "everything OK?"

Andy's comment shocked Jim's mind sharply back to reality, and he reminded himself of the importance of preserving events as they had to play out. He smiled, "yeah, you're lookin' good kid."

Andy smiled, "thanks. I guess Mike told you what's up?"

"Yeah," said Jim.

"Hello Captain," Heather said as she appeared at the stairs and started down.

"Hi," said Jim, immediately noticing the Japel uniform. "Nice uni," he said.

Heather smirked. "Thanks," she replied without stopping. "Come on," she said to all of them as she walked in to the engineering section.

"Yeah, umm, give us a second," said Jim, "Mike can you step outside with me for...?"

Mike looked at Jim's face and immediately knew something was up, but he did his best to not show it. "Uhh, yeah, sure," he said.

The two men stepped outside, and Jim wasted no time coming straight to the point. "Listen," Jim started, "I don't have time to explain this right now, but ... we're not going."

"What?!" Mike said, "Jim we have *orders*."

"I know," said Jim earnestly, "but I also know that we're not going to be on this ship when it leaves."

Mike looked hard at his friend. He trusted Jim more than any other person he had ever known. Mike had never been that crazy about the mission to begin with, but he knew Jim was. Whatever had happened to suddenly change that, whatever that thing was, Mike knew it must be really important. He inhaled and exhaled loudly, pursed his lips, and then he looked at Jim again and said, "OK."

Jim smiled and allowed himself a moment to appreciate how cool it was to have a friend like Mike.

"So," Mike asked, "what do we do?"

"Well," Jim started, "we need to make sure the ship gets out of here."

"OK," said Mike, "well let's get back in there then."

"No," said Jim. "We're about to have company."

Mike knew what that meant. He again looked at his friend for a long moment, and then he said, "you remember that I'm a science nerd right?"

"You can shoot," Jim said with confidence. "Two of us can do a lot."

"Yeah well," Mike said, and then both of them heard vehicles approaching. "Shit! Is that?"

"Probably, yeah. No time like the present," Jim said, and both men took off towards a couple of rocks that would protect them from the most likely direction of assault (across the dam).

"Andy!!" Jim shouted once he was safely up against one of the large rocks.

Jim and Mike could now see them. Three white government vans came up the road. They came to a stop just past the far side of the dam. Mike and Jim knew that they had probably been seen running for cover. The men in the trucks all exited on the far side of their vehicles. Andy appeared at the hatch.

"Yeah?!" Andy shouted back.

"We got company!" Jim shouted.

"Oh shit," Andy said quietly.

"We're going to hold them off for as long as we can, but you need to get that ship out of here! Understand?!" Jim shouted.

"Not without you," Andy shouted back. He couldn't see how many men were coming but he could see in Jim's face that the situation was not good. But this was Jim's mission, and Andy knew it. "We gotta switch!" Andy shouted.

"No!" Jim shouted. "No time and no way."

"Inbound," Mike said quickly and softly to Jim as two men with rifles suddenly started running across the dam.

"Take 'em" Jim said quickly. The two men raised as little of their heads and bodies over the rocks as possible and fired their pulse guns. The two men both fell backwards.

"Open fire!!!" they heard a voice shout from behind the truck, and immediately the area erupted in a hail of gunfire.

Mike and Jim were safely behind rocks, but relatively speaking they were pinned down. Andy noticed that Mike had put down his weapon and was frantically doing something on his mini-tablet. It took several moments.

"Cease fire!!!" the voice on the other side of the dam shouted. The bullets stopped.

Jim knew it was just a matter of time. Six against two was one thing, especially when you had a position advantage, but there were at least two dozen men on the other side of those trucks. Those weren't odds they were going to survive, especially if any of them had any brains about how to flank them. He saw what Mike was doing and was curious. "What are you doing?" he asked.

"Our instructions," Mike said, "the file the Colonel wanted us to have. If he's going and we're not..."

"Got it," Jim said, "good idea."

"Hey Andy!" Mike shouted.

Andy peeked out from behind the door, "yeah!"

Mike gestured to his mini-tablet. Andy saw it and nodded. Mike threw it like a Frisbee in Andy's direction. It landed, then skipped and skidded and finally stopped about 10 feet from the hatch. Andy looked out and then at Jim. Jim nodded, and then quickly stuck his head and weapon out over the rock. Andy knew he was covered as well as he was going to be and, as quickly as he could, ran to the tablet, picked it up and dove back in.

"You got it?!" Mike shouted.

Andy got up and again poked his head out. "Yeah!" he shouted back.

"Do you see it?!" Mike shouted, trying to make sure that Andy was looking at the file and understood.

"Yeah! I see it!" Andy said.

Gunfire began again.

"GO!" Jim shouted. Andy disappeared, and he closed the hatch behind him.

Andy ran back in to the Engine room.

Heather was still working frantically, but when she saw Andy re-enter the room she anxiously asked "Is that shooting I hear?"

"I'm afraid so," Andy answered, "how close are we?"

"There's no way I can get generator number three functional in time," Heather replied. "If we had a day, maybe, but we don't. So we're down to number four or nothing, and I can get it started OK, but it keeps tripping offline."

"What can I do?" Andy asked.

"You followed everything I was saying about how to keep these breakers online?" Heather asked.

"I, yeah, I think so," Andy replied hesitantly. He didn't really understand most of the controls or what they were necessarily doing at all, but he had grasped which switches had to do with which systems, especially the generators and how to reset them.

"OK, I'm going back to the bridge," Heather said. "We'll talk through this panel here, got it?"

"Got it," Andy said. "Hey, once we have both generators running, how long will it take to start the engine?"

"It shouldn't take long, a few moments," Heather answered.

"And then how long to jump? Is Gopto ready?" Andy asked.

Heather suddenly realized she hadn't heard from Gopto at all for some time. She paused, closed her eyes and thought to him, "Gopto."

Nothing. Heather panicked, and thought more strongly, "Gopto!" and this time she felt immediately as if she was on The Plain, but all she could see, everywhere, in all directions, all around, were equations. Everywhere she looked, every space was filled with an absolutely unbelievable number of numbers and symbols, all moving at incredible speeds. "Whoa," she said.

She opened her eyes, looked at Andy and said, "He's busy," and quickly headed off to the bridge.

Outside, Jim and Mike heard the men behind the trucks talking. They couldn't make out what the men were saying but they could guess, and it wasn't good. Suddenly they heard one of the trucks start. Jim peered over the rock in time to see the truck pull away and start its way around the lake. "Damn," he said.

Mike peered over as well. On the other side of the dam he saw several men run off down the road away from them. "They're going around," Mike said.

"Yeah, I knew they couldn't be that stupid," Jim said. "OK, this is a matter of time now." He pointed to the van driving around the lake. "Those guys over there are going to drive around the lake and then all they have to do is run down the shore and they've got us from the west. Those guys down there are going to go down under the dam and then up and over this hill, and they'll have us from the south. And that's it. All the guys in front have to do is..." and as the words were leaving his mouth, several shots were fired over their heads. They heard the bullets whiz by.

"All they have to do is keep us here," Mike said.

"Exactly," Jim said.

Heather was back at her station on the Bridge moving as fast as her mind would allow. The parts of her mind that were Heather and Neja were now working together seamlessly, but both knew time was running out. She went through the start up sequence for generator number four one more time.

Down in engineering, Andy saw the generator indicator light come on, and then the switch flipped. Andy flipped it back. It flipped off again. Andy flipped it again and this time held it in place. Immediately there was an alarm like noise. Andy figured that there was some kind of overload or something in progress, but he also knew the generator *had* to stay online to start the engine.

Heather couldn't believe it; Generator 4 showed online! She immediately started the sequence to restart the starboard engine. The control responded immediately.

In engineering, Andy nearly jumped out of his skin as the engine fired up.

Outside, the men who had driven around the lake were now running down the shore. When they heard the engine, they slowed and stopped.

Jim and Mike were trapped, but when they heard the engine

start, Jim smiled. "How long?" he asked Mike.

"Dunno," Mike replied. "The engine powers a wormhole generator of some kind. Once they have enough energy, they project it somewhere next to the ship and they essentially get sucked through to wherever they're going instantaneously, then the thing collapses." Mike paused as he considered the implications of being next to a collapsing wormhole and then added, "that'll be interesting."

The men on the shore began running towards them again.

To the southwest, General Colin Bradley's helicopter appeared over the hill. Bradley was shouting orders into his headset.

Colonel Wisener's command vehicle made the final turn and headed up the last road to Bonito Lake. The Colonel was telling her people to grab weapons and be prepared for a fight.

A second alarm began sounding in engineering, immediately followed by crackling and popping. Sparks began to fly from around the panel Andy was touching. He felt a shocking sensation, but he kept his hand on the switch.

Heather finished the sequence. "Ready," she thought to Gopto.

Jim looked at the ship. "C'mon," he said.

And then, in Heather's mind, it felt like the entire universe slowed down. Everything around her suddenly felt like an incredibly slow motion dream.

In engineering, Andy felt the same thing. The Engine Room was suddenly and completely silent. Andy felt like the walls were moving in on him. But that wasn't all; it was like he and the room and everything in it were shrinking somehow.

Outside, Jim and Mike felt a physical sensation on their skin, like a dull electric current with a very slight tingle over every inch of their bodies.

In Heather's mind, everything completely stopped. There was nothing. No space. No time. Just a voice. It was a voice that was like Gopto's, but like a thousand of his voices, all incredibly calm and beautiful, all speaking as one. The voice said just one word.

"Jump!"

33 THAT WAS *NOT* THE SAFETY

Time: 12:02 p.m., March 23, 2025
Location: South shoreline of Bonito Lake

Neither Jim nor Mike would be able to recall exactly what happened next. In a single, instantaneous moment, the ship completely vanished. And in its place ... was nothing. Literally. Not a single atomic particle of any kind. There was a perfect vacuum in the shape of the ship that had been there an instant before. What happened next was only logical. The vacuum collapsed with incredible and violent force. Jim and Mike, and the tarp that had been covering the ship, and the truck, and the men coming from down the beach, and the nearby trees, and every other atom of matter in the area; *everything* was pulled towards the space where the ship had been. Air from the Earth's atmosphere rushed in to fill the void, creating an eardrum-pulverizing BANG in the process. Jim and Mike's bodies were picked up like scraps of paper and hurled towards the center of the hole as it collapsed. As Mike landed, his head struck one of the poles that had been holding the tarp in place. The truck was pulled several feet from where it had previously been. Even the men down the beach and on the dam were pulled off their feet. General Colin Bradley's helicopter experienced a wind shear like effect, but quickly righted itself and set down on the road at the north end of Bonito Lake. As he ran towards his men, it was quickly obvious that many of them had been rendered briefly unconscious.

As General Bradley continued to run towards his men, Colonel Wisener's Command vehicle came up the hill by the dam and stopped. Moments later, several of her people jumped out. All of them were armed with pulse guns. As the Colonel exited, she quickly directed Staff Sergeant Miller to run across the dam and report. Miller took another man with her and took off running.

When she reached the other side of the dam and got around the rocks to the crash site, Miller stopped cold. "Holy hell," she said.

"Report," the Colonel said anxiously into her headset.

"Yes ma'am, the ship is *gone!*" Miller replied. Then she saw the two bodies in the crater. "We have men down Colonel!" she began, "Captain Landrum and Doctor Powell." She dropped to her knees as she reached them and immediately felt for a pulse. "They're alive ma'am!" she said gratefully.

Captain Landrum opened his eyes and looked around. All he could see was sky and trees and Staff Sergeant Miller. She was smiling at him.

"You OK sir?" she asked.

He could barely hear her. Or anything, but he was definitely alive. "I think so," Landrum replied. His brain was trying to stitch together the last thing he remembered.

"Here, let me help you up," Miller said as she helped Landrum sit up.

Landrum blinked several times, then tried to yawn, moving his jaw from side to side. The world sounded really muffled. He looked at Miller and said, "well you don't see that every day."

Miller laughed and said, "no sir."

Landrum looked at her quizzically and said loudly, "what?!"

Miller said loudly, "No sir! You don't!" Landrum smiled. Miller and the other man with her helped Landrum to his feet just as Mike Powell also began to stir. He had a small cut by his left temple with a little blood coming from it. Immediately, he moved his hand up to the cut and moaned slightly. He started to roll over and, as he opened his eyes, he was looking at the dirt. Miller bent down again and grabbed Powell's shoulder gently. "Are you alright Doctor?" she asked.

As he got onto his knees and elbows, he looked at the small amount of blood from his head that was now on his hand. "Well *that* hurt," Powell said absentmindedly. He rolled over and sat on the ground, looked at Miller, and said rather loudly, "what?!"

"Are you alright Doctor?" Miller asked slowly and loudly.

"My head hurts!" Mike said loudly, "but I think so."

They helped Powell to his feet, and he and Landrum looked at each other and smiled.

"C'mon," Miller said to them loudly, "let's get you back to the truck!"

As they walked back, Miller told the Colonel that the men were up and walking. She added that they appeared to be a bit hard of hearing for the moment but otherwise seemed OK. The troops from Holloman were all quickly regaining consciousness (except for the ones who had been shot with pulse guns). They were groggy and disoriented for a moment, but they too were otherwise OK. The men who had been approaching from the far side of the lake got up, dusted themselves off, and started walking towards the dam. They too looked slightly dazed and definitely confused by the disappearance of the ship and by having been knocked temporarily senseless.

General Colin Bradley arrived at the main group of people on the far side of the dam. He was yelling nearly incoherently. He ordered his men to pick up their weapons and begin arresting the UNCLE people. A few did pick up their weapons as they got up, but as they turned they faced a nearly equal number of UNCLE troops, all with pulse guns and all already pointed at them. They quickly lowered their weapons. General Bradley approached Colonel Wisener in an absolute rage.

"Are you and your people out of your God damned minds?!" he screamed at her. "Do you have any idea what I will do to you for this?"

Colonel Wisener stared directly at the General but said nothing.

Jim and Mike walked up to the group. As he arrived, the Colonel looked at him, smiled slightly, and said, "You OK?"

Jim nodded but then pointed to his ear and tapped a couple of times.

"And you!" the General said, now towards Jim and Mike, "Do you have any idea what you've done to weaken our nation here today?"

Jim and Mike also looked stone faced at the General. No one spoke, which just made the General that much more angry.

"You think this is over?!" the General yelled on. "You think I'm going to just walk away now?! You think for one minute I'm going to let you and your super secret, roving geek squad just run off and disappear again?! If you think I'm not going to take this directly to the Joint Chiefs then you are all out of your *fucking* minds! Do you hear me?! And they *will* listen to me and you *will* be screwed."

The Colonel finally spoke. "General," she said quietly and calmly, "I'm pretty certain that your influence with the Joint Chiefs on this issue was predicated on your being able to possess certain ... assets, and that, without them, well, I don't think we're the ones who will be screwed ... sir."

The General's eyes were wild. His head moved quickly back and forth. Suddenly he dove at Mike's pulse gun and tried to yank it out of Mike's hands. "I am going to fucking..." he started to shout ... and then the gun fired.

General Bradley flew back several feet and collapsed on the road, unconscious.

Everyone was silent.

Mike was shaking just a little. After a long moment, he very quietly said, "oops."

The Colonel pursed her lips and shook her head, suppressing a laugh.

Jim reached over to Mike's gun and flipped the safety switch. "It's that one," he said.

"What?!" Mike said loudly.

"That was *not* the safety switch!" Jim shouted, "*that* is the one."

"Oh!" said Mike, still shouting, "thank you!" He looked around. It was clear that a number of people were suppressing laughter. He looked back at Jim and said, "This is kinda awkward!"

Jim couldn't take it anymore and burst out laughing.

Several UNCLE people converged on Mike to pat him on the back.

The Colonel looked at First Sergeant Franklin from Holloman and said, "First Sergeant, we're very sorry about this incident with the General. Can we count on you to assist us and help handle this with your men?"

Franklin looked at her for a moment, then at the General, then back at her and said, "Yes ma'am Colonel." And then under his breath she was pretty sure she heard him say something like "I've been wanting to do that for over three years now."

Colonel Wisener smiled, then she turned to face Captain Landrum again. Her face turned serious as she said, "I assume you have an good explanation as to what the hell you're still doing here?"

Jim looked at the Colonel, and in his eyes she could see that it wasn't his choice. "Yes ma'am I do," he said directly.

The Colonel smiled a little and said, "Well then, I look forward to reading your report."

"Yes ma'am," Jim replied.

The Colonel nodded. She knew that, whatever Jim had done, it was the right thing. She looked at him and said, "OK, well, why don't you two get your asses over to the Medic and get checked out."

Jim smiled. "Yes ma'am," he said. He turned around and worked his way through several people who were still congratulating Mike on his accidental and yet welcome shooting of the General. As he got to Mike, their eyes met, and Mike knew immediately it was time to go. "Come on hero," he said to Mike loudly, "we've got a shitload of paperwork to do."

34 AFTER ACTION REPORT

Time: 2:27 p.m., April 2, 2025
Location: NORAD, Office of General Mitchell Bradley

General Bradley was sitting at his desk, going over Colonel Wisener's After Action Report for about the third time when his assistant knocked on his door.

"Yes?" the General said loudly.

Amy Taylor opened the door and said, "Colonel Wisener is here for your 1430 appointment, sir."

"Send her in," the General said as he stood up and moved around his desk.

"Yes sir," Amy said and moved out of the way. Colonel Wisener walked in behind her.

"Jane!" the General said as he shook her hand warmly, "c'mon in, have a seat."

"Thank you sir," Colonel Wisener said with a smile.

"Amy," the General said, "would you please close the door and hold my calls while I'm meeting with the Colonel here."

"Yes sir," Amy said as she closed the door.

The General sat down and picked her report up off the desk. "So," he began, "I got the report you sent to the JCS and the White House last week."

"Anything you want to go over sir?" the Colonel asked.

"Yeah, a couple of things," the General replied, opening it up and thumbing through it. "Uhhh, yes, here we are; where are we with the CRU?" he asked, referring to the US Army Corps of Engineers' Contingency Response Unit.

"Clean up work is done sir," the Colonel reported. "We returned command and control of the whole area back to New Mexico authorities on Monday evening."

"Any issues?" the General asked.

"Not really," the Colonel replied. "The Mayor's office in Alamogordo has asked that DoD reimburse the city for water quality testing and a couple of other costs."

"You told them no problem?" the General asked.

"Yes sir," she replied.

"Good," said the General, "and they're happy and quiet?"

"Yes sir," the Colonel replied.

"Excellent," said the General. "OK, where are we with people?"

"Well," the Colonel began, "the list you requested is in the report. It's one of the attachments."

"Yeah, I saw that," the General said, flipping to the back of the report and glancing at it. "And this is everybody?"

"Everyone we're aware of who had any knowledge of or information about the event sir," the Colonel replied.

"Let's see," the General said, "you've got the flight crew of the helicopter that my brother used to fly up there ... and all of his MPs and other personnel that were either at BioSec or Bonito Lake ... good."

"All of the other people at Holloman who were involved," the Colonel volunteered.

"Right, see that," the General said.

"And of course everyone at BioSec who was there on either day," the Colonel finished.

The General stared at the list for another moment, then looked at the Colonel, "OK. Good work. We'll take that one from here." He paused, closed the report and said, "OK, let's talk about the people affected who are *not* in the report."

"Yes sir," the Colonel said. "As you know, I flew to Chicago last Thursday and had a private meeting with the parents of Lieutenant Newton."

"Yeah," the General said slowly. "How'd that go?" he asked, already knowing the answer.

"Well, they're pretty upset," the Colonel responded flatly. "Upset about the situation, upset that they can't talk to their son, *really* upset about the cover story of his death in a car accident." The General was nodding understandingly as the Colonel spoke. "But..." the Colonel finished, "ultimately they seemed to understand. And in any case they did accept the terms of the standard agreement for these circumstances. Bottom line is that I don't think there's gonna be a problem there."

"Good," said the General. "We'll make sure we get them their agreement paperwork and some money as quickly as we can," he said. "What about Newton's 'car accident'?"

"The New Mexico State Police were extremely cooperative," the Colonel said. "Gave us everything we needed. Might want to give their Chief a thank you call this week."

"Get the contact info to Amy, I'll make sure I do it," the General said.

"Will do," she said.

"What else?" the General asked.

"From Chicago I flew back to New Mexico," the Colonel continued, "where I met with Ms. Helen Carson."

"And she is...?" the General asked.

"The paternal grandmother of Miss Heather Carson," the Colonel replied, "and her only living relative."

"Really?" the General said, "well that's handy."

"Yes sir," the Colonel continued. "Ms. Carson is quite elderly. Frankly, I'm not entirely clear on how much she actually understood about the situation."

"Also handy," the General interjected.

"Yes," the Colonel agreed. "In any case, we offered, and she accepted our offer, to provide assisted care for her, indefinitely, at no cost to her."

"Well, that's probably the least we can do for her," the General agreed. "OK, paperwork?"

"Already initiated sir," the Colonel replied.

"You're amazing Jane," the General said. "OK, what about *our* people?"

"Well sir, *Major* Landrum, and we did get his promotion paperwork already, so thank you," the Colonel said.

"Well hell, that's really the least we can do for him under the circumstances," the General said.

"Yes sir," the Colonel agreed, "I agree. In fact, in addition to his promotion and a couple of special recognitions we have planned for him internally, I'm going to be forwarding specific, separate Letters of Commendation for Major Landrum and Doctor Powell. You should have them by the end of next week."

"I will sign them the moment they hit my desk," the General said.

"Thank you sir," the Colonel said. "Now, to answer your question, Major Landrum was released from the hospital several days ago and is resting at home. Our CMO says he'll be cleared to return to duty on 7 April, next Monday."

"Any side effects?" the General asked.

"None," said the Colonel in a genuinely relieved tone. "The damage to his hearing was, as we hoped, temporary."

"Good," said the General, "what about Powell?"

"Doctor Powell is still in the hospital sir," the Colonel said, and then quickly added, "but that's really just for observation at this point. He sustained a minor concussion and has had a few headache issues, but the CMO said that he should also make a full recovery."

"And when do we see him again?" the General asked.

"CMO says not later than 21 April," the Colonel replied, "so a couple more weeks."

"That puts him back after the next update regarding Project

Abby does it not?" the General asked.

"Yes sir it does," the Colonel replied, "and I'll be asking for a delay in that meeting so that Doctor Powell can be part of it."

"How long?" asked the General.

"Two weeks?" asked the Colonel hopefully.

"Anything else in that timeframe?" the General asked.

"We have a scheduled contact meeting with Species 5 the week before," the Colonel said, "that's it."

"Bring your nose plugs," the General said dryly.

"Brad..." the Colonel with a bit of an embarrassed laugh.

The General smiled, "I'm sorry, they ... smell." He paused and then returned to business. "OK, two weeks, done," said the General, "make sure everyone knows."

"Will do sir," the Colonel said.

"I assume it's safe to say that the Project is basically on autopilot at this point?" the General asked.

"It certainly appears that way sir," the Colonel replied. She looked at the General's face and could tell that he wanted a bit more information, so she continued. "At this point, we've deployed all of the major pieces necessary at both the Eden Corporation and their subsidiaries and partners. Further, there is no evidence that *anyone* involved questions or suspects any outside influence."

The General nodded in approval. "Timeframe still in tact?" he asked.

"We believe so sir," the Colonel replied. "We think that 2030 to 2035 is still viable."

The General made a small hand gesture indicating that he was satisfied. "OK. Any questions for me?"

"Well, I still haven't heard what's going to happen to your brother sir," the Colonel said plainly.

"Yeah," said the General slowly. They both knew it was a sensitive subject, but Colonel Wisener had a right to be upset and the General felt that she was owed an update. "That's a bit of a sore subject actually," he said.

"Well, I noticed that he hasn't been relieved of his command yet," she said.

"No, he hasn't," the General replied, "and unfortunately he's probably not going to be either."

"What's up Brad?" the Colonel asked, pressing the issue.

"Well," the General began, "as you know, there is one member of the JCS, and I think we both know who that is, who was giving Colin a bit of ... latitude."

"Yeah, I know who," the Colonel said in an annoyed tone.

"Well, it's become a political thing at the top," the General said. "The bottom line is that they're taking a kind of no autopsy/no foul approach to what he did."

"So that's it?!" the Colonel said incredulously.

"Well, no," the General said. "I mean ... his career is ... *over*."

"Ahh," said the Colonel, feeling a bit better about the situation.

"Oh yeah," the General continued, "a couple months will go by, he'll 'decide' to step down and retire. He'll be playing golf in Palm Springs by the end of the year."

"And that'll be the end of it?" the Colonel asked.

"Oh, I doubt it," the General said sadly. "Unfortunately, there's never any 'end of it' with Colin, but he won't be in a position to do something like *this* ever again." The General looked at the Colonel. He could see that she understood the situation, so he prepared to move on. There was a long, almost uncomfortable pause. "OK," he finally said, "so let's talk about the one really *big* thing that's not in your report,"

"Yes sir," said the Colonel, knowing what was coming.

"I saw Cap ... sorry, *Major* Landrum's private report about what happened to him at Bonito Lake," the General began.

"Yes sir," the Colonel nodded.

"That's kind of a big deal," the General said.

"Yes sir," the Colonel agreed. "What are you thinking?"

"What am I thinking?" the General said, almost incredulously, "I'm thinking we'd better start preparing for your job to get a *lot* more interesting ... and a *lot* more important."

"Yes," the Colonel said, "well, that brings us to the one thing I wanted to talk to you about."

The General immediately looked annoyed. He knew what was coming, "Oh come on Jane, let's not do this again."

Colonel Wisener looked at him and said, "Brad, I'm running out of gas for this stuff."

"What?" the General implored. "What do you need here, some extra time off?"

"Yes," the Colonel said seriously, "I'm thinking the next 20 to 30 years."

"Jane, you can't be serious," the General complained. There

was an uncomfortable silence for several seconds. "Well shit," General Bradley thought, "she is serious." But he wasn't going to give up without a fight. "You would leave right now?" he asked demandingly, "right when the role of the organization is about to involve something as gigantic and complex as guarding *human history itself*?"

"Can you think of a better time?" she asked.

"Jane, I can't think of a worse time," the General argued. "Plus, exactly who the hell do you think could possibly replace you right now?"

"Well I've been thinking about that," the Colonel said.

"Apparently," the General said, trying to sound a little hurt.

The Colonel ignored her friend's emotional protest and went on. "Brad, I'm pretty sure that it would be impossible to overstate the level of courage and character that Jim Landrum displayed during this encounter. He was under the highest levels of stress imaginable. Levels of stress that only you and me and an *unbelievably* small number of people on the *planet* can possibly understand. And in that moment he did it! He held up the highest traditions of our services, our nation ... of all of freaking mankind in his efforts and actions."

"He's a great soldier Jane," the General said readily.

"He's more than just a great soldier Brad," the Colonel continued, "he's a *leader*; an honest to God, natural born, leader of men. And without his efforts, the outcome you and I could be living with today could have been *very* different. The future mission and success of UNCLE itself would have been profoundly, negatively impacted."

"All the more reason for him to stay right where he is," the General said.

There was another long, awkward silence between the two.

The Colonel softened and lowered her tone. "Brad, we both know I can't do this forever, and I really do feel strongly that the United States could choose no better individual to replace me than Major Landrum."

General Bradley stared at his desk. He'd won this fight with Colonel Wisener before, but she was right; it wasn't a fight he could win forever. He couldn't think of another person he had served with who had done more or done it nearly as well as she had. She had long since earned the right to go home. The truth was that he was fighting to hold on to her because he hated to lose such a good officer and a good friend in such a critical role. And when he faced that reality, he knew what he had to do. "OK," he said solemnly. Then he looked up at her and said it again. "OK, but you've got to do two things for me."

Colonel Wisener had an excellent poker face, and she needed it to contain her shock. She had assumed that she would be fighting with General Bradley about her retirement date for at least another year or so. The truth was that she didn't particularly want to leave *right now* any more than he wanted her to go, but he had just given her a permission slip to negotiate what she did want to do, and when ... and that gave her the opportunity to make her goal look like his idea. "I'm listening," she said flatly.

"First, I need you to get at least the infrastructure of this whole time policing thing going," he said.

"A Temporal Protection Agency?" she said.

"See!" Bradley said in genuine exasperation, "that's perfect, and one of a thousand reasons we still need you."

Wisener passed on the compliment. "What's the second thing?" she asked.

Bradley stared her straight in the eye and said, "I want you to train that young man until he is every bit as good at your job as you are."

Colonel Wisener smiled and said, "and how long are you figuring that will take?"

General Bradley also knew that this was a negotiation, and so he went high. "Five years," he said.

"Five years?!" Wisener nearly shouted in reply. "One!" she said defiantly.

"Three," the General said.

"Two," the Colonel said.

The General paused. "Done."

"From today Brad," the Colonel said, "two years from today."

General Bradley smiled, "OK Jane, two years from today." Again, there was a silence, but this one was a lot more comfortable. They were both a little stunned as they realized that they had just agreed to an end date to their working relationship, a relationship that had accomplished a great deal for their country and for humanity itself. They had much to be proud of. After a long silence, he said quietly, "thank you Jane."

"It was my honor Brad," she replied, "thank *you*."

The General smiled, put his hands on his desk and stood up, indicating to both of them that the meeting was over. As he walked Colonel Wisener to the door, he said, "I assume you're staying the night. Can Jenny and I take you to dinner?"

As they reached the door, Colonel Wisener smiled and said, "Brad, do you have *any* idea how far ahead of you your wife is?"

"Jane, *UNCLE* doesn't have the ability to measure distances like that," the General replied. "She's already done everything and talked to you, hasn't she?"

The Colonel nodded. "Eidelweiss," she said. "Reservations are for 1900 hours. You're buying ... and just so you know in advance, we're ordering whatever desserts we like."

The General smiled. "I'll be there," he said.

EPILOGUE: COME WITH ME

Time: Tarful 084672 (approximately June 26, 2025)
Location: Planet Morta; Japel Horticultural Research Station #117

It was an unusually sun filled morning for this part of Morta. Usually it rained well into the mid-morning hours, but today the rain had stopped just before dawn. The air was warm, wet and heavy, but there was a very pleasant breeze rustling the leaves on the nearby trees. Andy looked up from his microscope, took a deep breath and looked around at his surroundings. In some ways, he had adapted incredibly quickly to his new life, but there were still moments like this one, when he had to stop, look around and *again* try to wrap his brain around the fact that he was standing on another planet.

For the moment, being on Morta suited Andy just fine. Due to the very slight size difference, he was about 7 pounds heavier on Morta than on Earth, but that didn't really didn't bother him at all. He had gotten used to the higher oxygen content very quickly as well. In fact, the only thing that rather constantly reminded him that he wasn't simply in some Central or South American Rainforest (other than the aliens all over the place, of course) was the sky. The sky on Morta was a deep, emerald green. Andy thought it was beautiful, but it had definitely taken some getting used to.

Andy was sitting and working at an outdoor table in a small, grassy clearing on the edge of a huge, dense forest. He was taking some notes on yet another fascinating plant species on the planet, but the sound of the wind in the leaves was so pleasant and peaceful that he felt obligated to stop, look up and appreciate it for a moment. The events at Bonito Lake felt like a lifetime ago.

He vividly remembered the instant after the Jump. The panel for Generator #4 basically blew up in his face, which threw him across the compartment because the artificial gravity system was offline. Fortunately, he never reached the bulkhead that he was being blasted towards because, simultaneously, the air in the compartment began rapidly sucking out from the other side due to a breach in the opposite bulkhead that was exposed to space. The air ran out in just a few seconds, and for a terrifying moment (as he lost consciousness), Andy was reasonably sure that he was going to die.

He woke up in a hospital on the planet Japella two days later. The instant their ship completed the jump to its emergency landing zone, Gopto burst transmitted all the data about the ship, its condition, and, of course, about Heather and Andy. As Gopto had promised, the rescue ships were indeed standing by, and they rushed in to assist. The ship, not surprisingly, was deemed a total loss. In fact, both the Japel and the Mortubs were amazed that the ship had made it back at all. It was stripped and destroyed within days.

Andy did his best to follow the instructions that Mike Powell had thrown to him just a few minutes before the Jump. Heather immediately made it clear to the Japel that Andy should be considered the official representative of Earth. As a result, the Japel appointed him as the Ghalla (the most direct translation is special Ambassador). They were very interested in learning all they could about Earth and humanity from Andy and Heather, but they were also very generous in sharing everything about their planets and culture as well. Fortunately, everyone also understood and agreed right away that a larger scale relationship between their two species was not in humanity's interests, at least not yet.

After waking up, Andy spent the next 10 days in the hospital on Japella. Heather was there with him, by his side, every day. Initially, she was constantly needed as a translator, but within days, other Japel who were Twellocks of other Mortubs arrived and, thanks to the unique ability of the Mortubs to share so much information instantly, the number of Japel who could speak English increased significantly.

Heather stayed close to Andy until she was sure that he was able to get around and handle things on his own, but after two weeks she told him that she needed to go and visit Neja's family and home. Neither of them wanted to be separated from the other, but Andy understood Heather's responsibility to Neja, and Heather respected Andy's responsibilities as Ghalla. They agreed to speak by videocom at least once every day, and to meet up on Morta (where Heather and Gopto were returning so that she could visit the Collective and Gopto could share his experiences) in a week or so. Still, it was difficult for them to be apart, and not just because they were the only humans for untold billions of miles.

Heather went to Neja's home and met with her family. It was, as Neja's "echo" had predicted on The Plain, an extremely awkward experience for everyone. Heather was *not* Neja, and yet, very quickly the family decided that Heather was also very definitely part of their family. She was what was left of Neja, and while no one would ever truly know how much of Neja now existed as part of Heather, clearly *some* of her was there, and that was enough for them. For her part, Heather was overjoyed to be considered part of their family.

Heather made it a point to live a part of her life in a way that would love, honor and respect Neja's memory. It helped, of course, that the two of them had so many core things in common (like a love of science), but she did the little things too. While she was visiting her family there, Heather made it a point to go running on the beach that Neja had told her about on The Plain. She went to some of Neja's favorite places, visited friends and did things that she knew Neja would have done. And, of course, Heather visited Taynar's family, and helped them through the grief of losing their beloved son.

It was, understandably, a very strange time for both Heather and Andy. As the news of their existence and their story spread, they were very much like celebrities everywhere they went. Fortunately, as a species, the Japel were very respectful of individual privacy, and there were very clear boundaries that allowed them to go about their lives in relative peace when they so desired. Heather was especially grateful for these boundaries as they allowed her take care of the promises she made to Neja without feeling as though she was part of a media circus.

Meanwhile, Andy had begun what was basically a tour of the planet, learning about Japel culture, sharing what he could about Earth and, again, doing his best to follow the instructions that he had been given. But as the weeks became months and the things he was asked to do as Ghalla became fewer, it became harder and harder for Andy to feel like he was still a Second Lieutenant in the United States Air Force. There were days when he missed Earth. He thought about his parents and wondered what they had been told, how they were, and if he'd ever see them again, but he also knew that he was now living a completely unique existence, one where the rules of life as he had known them simply didn't exist anymore. The freedom to do *anything* gave him an overpowering desire to see and learn everything he could ... about *everything*. And it was that desire that had brought him to this moment, sitting at his working table, looking up at the tops of the trees beneath the emerald sky, feeling a sense of wonder and contentment that he hadn't known was possible.

"Andy!" one of the Japel shouted from about 30 feet away. Andy looked over and saw his friend Haben pointing to someone. It was Heather. As she walked towards him, he smiled broadly. "Klanna Heather!" he said, "Nikto hi."

"Klanna Andy," Heather replied, looking impressed, "your Japel is improving."

"Yes, well, it hasn't been easy," Andy said with mock exasperation, "thanks to you and Gopto, a significant number of the female Japel on both planets can speak perfect English, so it's harder to practice."

"Hey Andy," a voice said walking past them. It was Jeenar, another of his new Japel friends.

Andy looked at Heather and gestured towards Jeenar as if to say, "see!" Heather smiled and rolled her eyes a little. "Hey Jeenar," Andy replied.

"Are you playing Kapton with us after dinner this evening?" Jeenar asked.

"I'm certainly going to try," Andy said. Then he looked at Heather and quietly added, "I'm *totally* getting hustled."

Heather laughed. "I'll bet," she said. "If it helps, I was terrible at that game." The two of them had both long gotten used to and now ignored the confusion inside Heather's head when it came to which memories were Heather's and which ones were Neja's.

"So how are you?" Andy asked, "I haven't seen you in like a week."

"Yeah, I'm sorry. I've been spending a lot of time with the Collective," she answered, sounding genuinely sorry to have been gone for so long.

There was a silence between them for several moments. Andy suddenly felt awkward and wanted to keep the conversation going. "So," he said, "when you spend all of that time with the Collective, do you do that just, you know, outside ... or, you know, in your ... womb with a view?"

Heather laughed out loud. "OK, that was funny," she said, "how long did you work on that one?"

Andy smiled and looked down, "a little while."

"Well, if you're actually interested and not just *jealous*," Heather said with a wry smile, Andy gave her a look of mock shock, "the connection to the Collective is always much clearer with direct contact and the longer I'm gone the more it makes sense so ... inside if you must know." There was another pause. Heather smiled and said, "what?"

They both knew it was a little uncomfortable to talk about. Andy was, in fact, a bit jealous of Heather's relationship with Gopto, but he wasn't sure if their relationship was a boyfriend/girlfriend type of thing and therefore one where he was certain he couldn't ever compete, or if it wasn't like that at all ... and he didn't really know how to ask. "Well," he said, kind of fumbling over his words, "doesn't that ... I mean ... isn't it ... you know, a little weird?"

Heather was pretty sure that she knew what was going on in Andy's head. He liked her and he was worried. "You know you're genuinely cute when you're like this," she thought. She looked at him honestly and said, "Yeah, of course, it's definitely a little weird." And then she got worried about whether or not he understood. "Is that a problem?"

"No!" Andy said quickly, "no, no ... it's just..." Andy wasn't sure how to say it, but figured he should just try to ask. "Look, I, I ... are you guys?"

Heather's heart melted. She looked him square in the eyes and said, "No. No we're not. It's hard to explain, and ... and complicated and ... weird." Now it was Heather's turn to go out on a limb. "But if ... you know, if you're interested? ... You have to be OK with that."

Andy smiled and nodded, "yeah, well, I am ... interested ... so..."

Heather smiled back. "Well good," she said, "me too." And then suddenly both of them felt a bit self-conscious and that the conversation was getting a bit heavy for the moment, so Heather took a quick breath in and said brightly, "so, you know, I've been sharing and learning. How about you?"

Andy took the cue and lightened up as well. "Well," he said, "the Japel Council figured that I should take some time to learn about Morta too, so they put me on a shuttle and arranged for me to come over here for a few weeks. It's been pretty interesting." He paused, then added, "plus, you know, we said we'd meet over here, and this gave me the chance to be ... closer to where you were too." Andy was immediately annoyed with himself for adding that thought out loud. Clearly, she had just tried to lighten things up and he'd made it heavy again. He started to apologize. "Ummm."

Heather immediately let him off the hook, "it's OK. I missed you too. Look, I've never been here either. We'll figure this out ... or we won't, which is kind of why I wanted to see you this morning."

Andy was worried. "What's up?" he asked.

Heather was worried too. She had no idea how Andy was going to react to the news she had. "Well," she started, "Gopto and I have had a lot of time to talk to each other and to talk with others in the Collective and, umm, well, as crazy as this might sound, we want to go back ... out there."

Andy said incredulously, "to Earth?!"

Heather gave him an odd look, "no! Well, I mean, yes, someday, but no, not right away. I mean, *out there*," she said.

"Really?" Andy said, instantly intrigued by the possibility.

"Yeah," Heather said. "As it happens, because I have Neja's memories, knowledge and experience, the Space Corps is willing to give me all of her qualifications and certifications."

"And me?" Andy asked.

"Well," Heather said, "you'd need to do a month or so of training on the support systems for the crew requirement, but, there is room for another researcher on the ship..."

"Huh," Andy said. His mind was trying to imagine sights and experiences that were, by definition, beyond his imagination. He also thought that it might be dangerous, but if that was true, then for sure he didn't want Heather to go without him. And then he thought about how he got to that particular moment in his life, literally on another planet. "What was it that started all of this?" he rhetorically thought to himself. It was the same thing that was driving him now, that desire to learn and know ... and *explore*. It was *curiosity*.

Heather had no idea what was going on in Andy's head but she couldn't take it anymore and decided to go for broke, "oh come on!" she said, almost pleading with him. "How big of a set up do you need? There's you and me and Gopto and a spaceship and ... a *galaxy*! Come on!" she said, and she reached out and grabbed both his hands. "Come with me," she said earnestly.

As her hands touched his, Andy felt a charge, a warmth and comfort flood completely through him. The truth was that he'd been in love with her from the very first moment he'd even looked at her. There was literally nothing else to do. He leaned in and kissed her, and with great relief, he felt her kissing him right back.

After a long moment, they separated. Andy looked directly at her and thought, "That's it. I'm hooked forever."

Heather looked right back at him and thought, "Yes, yes you are ... and so am I."

Suddenly Andy's face changed. He squinted a little, looked at her skeptically and said, "Do I have to call you Captain?"

Heather smiled, then stared right back at him, and with a completely straight face said, "absolutely."

MAP OF BONITO LAKE

Imagery ©2015 USDA Farm Service Agency
Map Data ©2015 Google

Note: The dam is on the far right (east) side of the photo. The crash site is on the southeast shore, just west of the dam where the trees begin. I recommend using Google maps online for the best view.

BONUS! PREVIEW OF ADA

I very much hope you enjoyed reading my first full novel, Gopto. In Chapter 22, I refer to the fact that UNCLE has been "seeding" humanity with technological innovations. They are doing this to help push the human race forward faster than it otherwise would go but not so fast that it causes unacceptable problems. It's a delicate balance filled with both promise and peril. In my next novel, ADA, we will explore the benefits, difficulties and issues that surround the most significant undertaking in UNCLE's history; the attempt to introduce artificial intelligence into human culture. Below is a preview of that novel. I hope you will enjoy it even more than you have enjoyed reading Gopto (and if you enjoyed Gopto, many of these characters will be back in book number three). Look for the second book in this series some time in 2016. Thank you!

-Duane N. Burghard

ADA

Prologue

Time: Monday, June 7, 2032
Location: Moscone Center, San Francisco, CA

Eden CEO Todd Baker had a natural aversion to chaos, even the organized kind that was currently underway. But he had also long learned to conceal even his most strongly felt reactions and emotions, so he appeared calm and expressionless as at least a dozen people moved rapidly around him backstage in frantic last second preparations. The music playing out in the convention hall was, as his MARCOM (Marketing and Communications) staff had directed, low in tone, selected specifically to heighten the already highly elevated levels of anticipation in the room.

Over the last several months, Eden's marketing department had done a masterful job at carefully leaking just the right bits of information about today's announcement. As a result, the media, developers and fans present were all in a near frenzy for the presentation to begin. Baker had been through this routine many times before of course, but today was different. Today, for the first time in many years, Eden was truly poised to change the world again.

Eden had been the largest technology company on the planet for years, and had long since completely transformed the computing, communications and entertainment industries. But as the 2020s had rolled on, society's endless and voracious appetite for the next big thing had once again reached a critical mass, and so today the world was watching. Could Eden "do it again" or were their best days finally behind them?

Baker knew the answer of course. Today's announcement was literally going to shock the world and he knew it. If the next hour went right, the company would be part of every newscast and Infofeed in the world for days. For years the company had, as quietly as possible, been carefully buying up the assets needed for what they hoped would be the next global revolution in technology.

They acquired expertise in robotics, biomechanics and animatronics, along with the associated parts and suppliers. And then there was the software. Literally billions of lines of code, easily the largest and most complex software undertaking in the history of man. Not surprisingly, the hardware and software engineering costs were also far larger than any other project in history (and had ended up being considerably more than anyone had initially realized). But it was now moments away from all being worth it.

"Ladies and gentlemen," a muffled voice boomed from out in the convention center, "please take your seats, the presentation will begin momentarily." Baker took a last look at his digital notecards, then he quietly walked over to the subject of the day's announcement. He looked at it carefully one last time. He half smiled, then, quietly and stoically, he turned and walked back over to his mark. The frenetic activity backstage had stopped and all eyes were on him. The voices in the convention hall were starting to quiet down; it was time. He turned to the backstage director and nodded slightly. The director nodded back and said into his communicator, "ready all, we are live in five, four, three … …" Baker counted two and one in his head. The music and lights rapidly faded in the Hall and it immediately exploded in *thunderous* anticipatory applause. The spotlight faded up on the floor just in front of him and he stepped out onto the stage.

As he appeared the applause got even louder. There was even some audible cheering. Baker smiled and raised his hand towards the crowd to wave. He didn't dislike these moments, but it was also true that if they were gone tomorrow and he never saw another crowd of cheering people again for the rest of his life, it wouldn't bother him at all. But for now he stood, allowing the applause and nodding in appreciation. Finally, he raised both hands (which was the cue for the director to activate his mic) and said, "thank you!" as enthusiastically as he could. For all of his incredible intelligence, the fact was that Baker had never been very emotionally expressive and had to work hard to appear genuine to others. The applause continued, so he raised his hands again, this time to indicate his desire to start, "thank you … please, let's get started." The audience sat and quieted down almost as rapidly as they had started up.

"Thank you all for that wonderful welcome, and welcome to what we believe will be the most important event in Eden history," he began. Again, there was applause, but this time only for a moment; the audience knew its role as well. "Just think about the scope of that statement," Baker continued, "in its history, Eden has already revolutionized so many parts of our lives, and yet we believe that what we will show you today will blow all of that away."

Baker then launched into a brief set of "rah rah" highlights of the company's impressive past, going over achievements that he and every member of the audience already knew backwards and forwards. Through this part of the presentation he could almost set his brain on a kind of autopilot. As he spoke, part of his mind did take a moment to marvel at the impressive looking, three dimensional holograms which hovered above and in front of him to support his talking points. While hardly a new technology in 2032, the holograms were a LONG way from the old days of having a screen with slides.

"But that is where we've been," Baker continued, "not where we are going. Technology has done so much to improve our lives, and at Eden we're so very proud to have been such a big part of that for so many years, but there's one area that's remained stubbornly beyond the reach of our abilities. Until Now. And that area ... is robotics ... and more specifically, androids."

The crowd murmured and Baker couldn't help but crack the smallest of half smiles on the side of his mouth.

"Robots have, of course, been around for years now," Baker began, "and we've been able to do a lot with them. As many of you know, Eden saw the potential of this technology a long time ago. In fact, we began strategically investing in it more than ten years ago now. Our goal has been to bring robotics into more practical, consumer applications. One of the key problems facing the industry early on was known as the Robot Navigation Problem. Simply put, what you and I do naturally in just walking around in a room was a very hard thing to teach a robot to do. The problem wasn't solved until an engineer at a Japanese company called Yokosume made a breakthrough back in 2018, and as many of you know, Eden acquired that company just two years later. Of course, even with that problem solved, the vast majority of robots, including the ones that were being made to more resemble us, were still clunky and heavy. They could only perform limited, specific tasks and they were, of course, prohibitively expensive; certainly not anything you could have or would have wanted to have in your home. Significant advances were still needed in engineering, materials and of course, software."

"But even if I were here today to tell you that we had solved ALL of those problems," Baker continued, "even bigger problems would remain. Creating an artificial brain that can interact with us in a dynamic way has been a goal of science for decades. And while significant progress has been made in this area too in the last several years, those successes have required enormous computing power and could only be housed in facilities that rival the old, giant computer server rooms of the late 20th Century. Collapsing that power down into something even remotely portable, well that just couldn't be done."

Baker paused, allowing himself to genuinely enjoy the moment. "Until now."

"Ladies and gentlemen," he quickly continued, "I am here today to introduce you to the most incredible advance in robotic technology in human history. We call her ADA. The letters of her name stand for Artificial Domestic Assistant, but if you look online, you'll find that the name Ada meant noble in ancient Europe, and beautiful in ancient Hebrew. And at Eden, not surprisingly, we think she's both. Would you like to meet her?"

The crowd applauded politely on cue, but as the curtain drew back and Ada walked out on stage, the applause turned to gasps and then wild, raucous, explosive, cheering. It was instantly obvious to everyone in the room that they were present for a *world*-changing event. This wasn't a product announcement; this was nothing short of human history being made. Ada was very obviously, and by FAR, the most lifelike robot ever made. It was 5 feet, 9 inches tall, with dark gray hair and blue eyes. It had clearly been designed to be neither particularly attractive nor unattractive physically and it eerily resembled an average woman in her early fifties (this was of course intentional, Ada had been designed specifically to resemble Baker's late Aunt Marilyn, who had helped to raise him when he was young). But what was truly amazing was that Ada was walking on stage with almost no hint of artificiality. Ada walked several steps up into the spotlight, stopped, bowed her head slightly for a moment, and then looked around the room. As the applause continued, she raised her left hand and waved slightly, then gently folded her hands together in front of her. For his part, Baker had stepped back and was carefully scanning the room (and knowing that, for the moment, literally no one in the room was looking at him). Never before had it been so obvious, so instantly, that a company had changed the world. Before the event, he had directed that a display be placed in the back of the room, visible only to anyone on stage, to monitor the number of petabytes being transmitted out of the room on the various wireless networks present. Within moments, the number on the back wall began to explode. At first it was thousands, then tens of thousands, then over a hundred thousand, and on and on. Baker knew that, within a matter of minutes, millions and millions more people around the world would be following the event. Untold billions of dollars in free advertising was just starting. Moments later, the display next to the "bandwidth ticker" which displayed the current Eden stock price on the global exchange, jumped a staggering 22% in one move (moving Baker up an impressive 7 spots on the list of the world's richest people).

On cue, Ada looked over towards Baker and gestured towards him, which only sent the crowd in a new frenzy of applause. Baker looked back at Ada and gestured back to her, and then looked out to the crowd and said, "amazing isn't it?! Absolutely amazing!" The applause continued, and he allowed it for a moment, and then put both of his hands up again to signal to the crowd that he was ready to continue, but this time the cheering did not stop, and Baker was not yet in the mood to force the issue. Finally, there was a bit of a lull and Baker pounced on the reduction in noise and said, "thank you! Thank you all very much. I know that every Eden engineer in this room, as well as all of the other people on the ADA project who couldn't be here today and who worked tirelessly on this project, in some cases for over ten *years* now, really appreciates your reaction and applause."

Finally the applause stopped and the audience sat back in their seats. "Now," he thought, "now we're really going to blow them away."

"Ada," he said, "that was some reaction you just received."

"Yes, it was very nice," Ada replied. There were audible gasps in the room when she spoke.

'How are you?" Baker asked.

"I'm doing very well thank you," Ada replied, with only the very slightest hint of artificiality in her speech, and really that was only because her diction and pronunciation was so perfect. "It was very nice to be welcomed so warmly by the people here," Ada said. The crowd was awash with hushed and whispered "wows" as she spoke.

"Ada, I'd like for us to talk a bit about you for a few moments, if that's alright," Baker continued.

"Certainly," Ada replied, "I'm sure the audience is very curious to know more about me. What would you like to know?"

"Well first, let's talk about your appearance. You look very much like, well like us," Baker said.

"Thank you," replied Ada, "a lot of people at Eden worked very hard for a long time to make me look as much like you as possible."

"How did they do it?" he asked.

"Well my skin is actually a biosynthetic compound that was created by a company called Biomi and is specifically designed to look, feel and act just like your skin," she replied. "I use it to help regulate my body temperature in the same way that you do. I can sweat, just like you do, if my internal systems get too warm. And if my skin is compromised, I will even bleed a non-toxic chemical that's used in several systems." There were a few quiet whistles and audible laughs out in the crowd. "My skin is wrapped around a skeletal structure that's made of a lightweight, composite compound," Ada continued, "but unlike your bones, mine contain hollow chambers that contain all components needed to make me, well, me." Her movements looked almost completely natural.

"Your voice is the most lifelike artificial voice I've ever heard," Baker said.

"Thank you, but it really should be shouldn't it?" replied Ada. "Eden has been at the front of the digital voice technology field for many many years now. I think it would be unusual if I didn't sound very much like you."

"How many languages do you speak?" Baker asked.

"I will ship initially speaking just 32 languages fluently, but many more are coming soon," Ada replied. "And of course, within those languages, a significant number of dialects."

"Dialects?" Baker asked.

Ada replied in a voice that was every bit as perfect as her previous voice, only now she had a decidedly southern accent, "why yes Mr. Baker. Though you wouldn't know it from the way you speak now, you yourself are from Alabama are you not?"

"I am," said Baker, over a murmur of amazed chuckles and more "wows" from the audience.

"Well," Ada continued, "it turns out that people are often more comfortable interacting with others who speak in a way that's similar to the way they talk."

"That's amazing, and it makes sense," said Baker.

Ada's voice changed again, this time her voice sounded like a proper English governess, "Indeed it does sir." The crowd was a mixture of small laughs, a few claps and more whispers. "And as you can see," she continued, "it isn't just the tone or accent, but the patterns of speech themselves; pronunciation, vocabulary, everything." The crowd broke into open applause. Ada, who had turned slightly towards Baker, turned the upper part of her body a bit back towards the audience, smiled, and nodded her head once, adding more laughs and applause.

"Well you sound very much like us, and your appearance is obviously incredibly close to ours," Baker said, "but what about what's on the inside?"

Returning to what would be known as her default voice (aka "Nebraska"), Ada replied, "on the inside we are both very similar and quite different," Ada replied.

"What do you mean?" Baker asked, taking just a moment to mentally remember where they were in the script. He also stole a glance at the audience, which he noted with satisfaction was now back in stunned silence and focused intently on everything happening on stage

"Well, of course, physically we are quite different. Below your skin, you are a very complex biological machine made up of lots of different kinds of cells. My insides contain some biological components, most of which are there to make me appear more like you, but I am otherwise a very complex, biomechanical machine with literally hundreds of microprocessors, miles and miles of fiber optic circuitry and of course, lots of storage space for all the software necessary for me to function."

"I see," said Baker. Ada took an audibly deeper breath. "Ada, are you, are you breathing?"

"Yes," said Ada.

"Is that also just to make us more comfortable with you?" he asked.

"You mean am I imitating the behavior? Not exactly," Ada replied, "it would be more accurate to say that I am using my vent system to regulate the operating temperature of some of my internal systems, which is also one of the things that you do when you breathe."

"That's remarkable," said Baker, "I see what you mean when you say that we're very similar but very different. Let's talk more about your programming. What can you do?" Baker asked.

"Well, I can be programmed to do a number of things," Ada answered, "but I was built by Eden to be your home assistant."

"You mean to cook meals, do dishes, do the laundry, that sort of thing?" Baker asked, trying to put the right emphasis on the question to make it sound like there must be more.

"Well, yes, I can do all of those things," Ada replied, "but I can do much more. I am designed to help manage your home life. While you are gone I can manage your voice and data communications, maintenance the home including things like repairs, or increasing energy efficiency, I can go to the grocery store for you, pick up your children at school, take your vehicle in for service."

"You can drive?" Baker asked incredulously.

"Well," Ada answered, "for the moment, I can only drive on digitally coded roads. And technically, of course, the vehicle is driving itself. I am simply programming the vehicle with points of origin and destination. However, Eden is currently hard at work, lobbying governments to allow me to have an actual driver's license, which I'm really looking forward to," Ada said as the crowd laughed lightly.

Baker knew it was close to the time to really blow them away. "So you're saying that you're kind of a housekeeper, nanny, secretary, home repairman, property manager, cook, cleaning lady, errand runner and more ... all rolled into one?"

"Yes," said Ada. "And, of course, over time, the engineers at Eden, as well as many of the software developers in this room, will learn to write more programs for me, and then I will be able to do even more things."

"Are there limits to what you can be programmed to do?" Baker asked.

"If you're asking if I could ever be a danger to you," Ada replied, "yes, there are important limits. I obviously represent a quantum leap in the marriage of robotics and artificial intelligence, but despite how alive I may seem, I assure you that I am still very much a machine. Over time I will learn to do more and more. I will get better and better at anticipating and caring for your needs. I will improve at dynamically responding to my environment. But even after I do all of that, I will still be doing nothing more than executing a program. And most importantly, I am hard wired with the famous three laws invented by Sir Isaac Asimov."

"Well you certainly are a quantum leap forward in both robotics and artificial intelligence," Baker said, now wrapping up the presentation interview, "is there anything else you have to add?"

"Yes. I would like to say thank you to the more than 10,000 individuals who invested over 300 million man hours of work over the last several years to make me and this day possible," Ada replied.

"Well, I know that, right now, every one of those people is as excited as I am to see and hear you here on this stage today. We're so glad you could be here. Thank you Ada," Baker said.

"Thank you sir," Ada said, and with that, she smiled, waved to the crowd, turned, and walked back to the curtain, which opened just as she got there and just enough for her to walk through, and then closed.

The crowd went wild. Baker smiled. It was something he rarely allowed himself to do publicly anymore. He stood there for several moments, allowing the audience to release all of the energy they'd built up during the presentation, and then he made his first attempt to speak over the crowd. "Thank you!" he nearly shouted. The cheers seemed to get louder. Baker suddenly remembered to check the tickers on the back wall of the auditorium. The bandwidth monitor had gone so high it displayed only "E-10" indicating an error, and the stock price was now up a staggering 35% on the day alone and was still climbing.

Finally, he tried to wrestle back control of the room again. "Thank you! Wasn't that just amazing?!" he said loudly. The crowd cheered loudly again, but only briefly this time as they understood it was time to go on. There was quiet again. "Just think about the incredible potential that Ada represents to our society," he began. "Think about how much easier our lives are about to become, the problems that we'll be able to turn our attention towards fixing, the art and literature that we'll have time to create and participate in. This is truly the dawn of a new day for humanity."

Baker paused for a moment. He knew that there were only two questions left on the minds of everyone in the room: when and how much. "I know that, now that you've seen Ada, you have only two questions; when will it ship and how much will it cost. Well I have some good news for you. We are already in mass production of the Ada and you will be able to start placing your pre-orders ... TODAY!"

The crowd broke into loud but measured applause. By 2032 everyone knew that ordering and shipping were two very different things, and Baker still hadn't said a word about price. For his part, Baker held back for a moment to let the suspense build, and then he said, "and Ada will ship before the end of this year!" The applause for a moment grew slightly louder and then died off as the entire world fell silent. They wanted to know one thing: how much?

Baker stopped, and for one of the very few times in his life, went completely off script and spoke from his heart. "You know," he began, "there really are very few moments when the world changes like this, and I was just thinking about how fortunate I am to be here with you right now, having this moment with all of you." It was a rare moment of complete sincerity and honesty that ended as abruptly as it began. Baker regained his composure and went back to the script. "As I'm sure you can imagine," he began, "developing Ada has consumed thousands of man years of effort and, to be completely honest, even I don't know exactly how many billions of dollars. I know it was a lot. But what Ada is and does and represents for all of us is too important to only make it available to the wealthiest of people, so we've worked really hard on lowering the costs of production ... and after taking into account the additional services and products that people will buy to support their Ada, we have come up with a number that we think is going to absolutely blow you away. As of today, you can order Ada for a staggeringly low price ... of just $9,999."

As the words left his mouth the room went completely insane. Eden "fanboys" in the room with decibel meters later reported that the volume in the room momentarily exceeded 110 decibels, temporarily deafening pretty much everyone in the hall. It was in fact too loud for a visiting Professor from Stanford University who had been standing in the very back of the hall watching. He turned and pushed on the door and walked out. His graduate assistant followed immediately.

"Wow, that's really something isn't it Doctor Powell?" the assistant said.

"Yes," Mike Powell said quietly, "yes it is."

As they walked towards the main doors out of the building the assistant added, "I mean, just think about the logistics needed to coordinate all that stuff, it's incredible."

"Mmm," Doctor Powell agreed. And then, with a little half smile on his face he thought to himself, "you have no idea."

Baker found it hard to conceal his surprise at the literal *force* of the explosion from the audience. He had a few more closing remarks he had planned to make, but the crowd was in such a frenzy that he decided to just let them go. So he waved forcefully to the crowd and mostly unsuccessfully tried to shout, "thank you! Thank you very much for coming! Have a great day!" The music began to play and Baker walked to the edge of the stage and behind the curtain. The cheering didn't stop for several minutes.

Over the next several days and weeks, Eden did indeed receive literally billions of dollars in free advertisement. And the story nearly melted down every news server on the planet. Within just a few hours after Baker walked off stage, over half of all the people on Earth had seen at least some part of the announcement.

There were, of course, critics. Some fell into the "haters" category, but many more had a significant number of legitimate ethics questions surrounding what Ada meant to the world. Many of the interviews that Eden executives did in the following days ended up sounding more like a college philosophy class than a business brief about a product release. For his part, Baker was careful to sound understanding but also dismissive of these concerns. He also constantly expressed his confidence in the company and in the controls that the Eden software engineers had built in to handle any issue. He assured ethicists that the Ada was not sentient in any way, assuaging their concerns about enslaving some sort of new artificial life form. He talked about how Eden was carefully controlling what jobs it could do in order to calm labor unions, and he repeatedly assured the general public that the programming prevented any danger to them. Mostly, of course, Baker had confidence in his army of lawyers to pursue any individual or group who tried to take an Ada "off the grid." By 2032, a staggeringly high nearly two percent of all lawyers on the planet worked in some way for Eden or one of its subsidiaries. For its part, the public and the media were reassured, and while historians would later be highly critical of the public's willingness to simply accept that everything would happen exactly as Eden had promised, the simple fact was that Eden had done it again; they had created a product that the public wanted so badly that it willingly ignored the most basic truisms about the introduction of transformational technologies into the market.

True to their word, Eden shipped the first Ada before the end of the year. The very first unit shipped to a technology manager from the San Francisco Bay Area on October 29th, 2032. And production ramped up *quickly*. By Christmas, almost 250,000 Ada units had shipped worldwide. Within 5 years there were millions and millions of Ada units in service all over the world. But as Ada became more successful, more popular and more widespread, the level of control that Eden was able to exert over them began to diminish. Within months, groups of hackers sprang up and began to write unauthorized software for Ada. Eden had a large community of authorized Ada developers of course, but Eden had the final word on whether or not any piece of software written would be officially authorized and, more relevantly, allowed to be sold via the Ada Online Store (which was, of course, the only legally allowed place to sell software for Ada). As the number of rejections grew, the number of disaffected and angry programmers grew with it. At first, these bits of unauthorized code made changes that were subtle and simple and fit into the "harmless mischief" category. One of the first really popular hacks included a minor behavior modification that allowed Ada to curse. Within weeks, millions of teenagers around the world were laughing hysterically as their parents told Ada to do something for them and Ada responded with a very dismissive "fuck you".

And then there were the hardware changes. Ada's hardware (specifically the exterior casing or body) was reverse engineered with surprising speed and, while initially expensive, black market dealers in Ada body parts were doing a significant volume of very profitable business within two years. It wasn't long before reasonably talented technicians could change Ada's skin color, eyes, etc., allowing Ada to take on the appearance of dozens of ethnicities. But the vast majority of these modifications, not surprisingly, were centered around making Ada intentionally more physically attractive and, in most cases, younger. Finally, and somewhat inevitably, the adult entertainment industry found their way into the game. The early attempts to build a truly anatomically correct Ada (of both sexes) were generally regarded as less than acceptably realistic, but they were also among the most lucrative for black market dealers to sell, and they improved quickly.

Any threat to their complete and total control over *every* aspect of *any* of their products made Eden's executives furious, but the ones which Eden saw as inappropriate or perverted were especially galling. Eden's legal team attacked where and when they could with unprecedented legal efforts. For his part, Baker was rumored to have gone into a completely uncharacteristic, ranting fit (one far more characteristic of his long ago predecessor) when he learned that Ada, the product which he by then viewed as his greatest accomplishment and which had further been made in the image and likeness of his beloved Aunt, was being converted by some into a sex toy.

The fundamental problem facing Eden, however, was that a lot of the black market programs and parts were proving to be very popular, far more than popular enough to keep their creators in business. Further, as with similar technologies in the past, successfully prosecuting the rapidly growing number of black market developers proved to be far more difficult and costly than Eden had anticipated. In early 2035, the company tried an unusual tactic to control the growing problem; they attempted to make the customers liable for damages if their Ada had any unauthorized hardware or software modifications. This idea was quickly challenged in Court and in late May of the same year (two months after the EU Court had already ruled against Eden in a similar case) the United States Supreme Court (in a 6-3 decision) ruled that owners could not be held financially liable for any modifications made to their Ada units. However, the Court *did* uphold Eden's right to remove any and all unauthorized hardware and software from any Ada that was brought into any of its ASPs (Authorized Service Providers) for service. The Court further ruled that Eden had the right to destroy the hardware (though, if they did so, they also had to replace it with a standard part for free) without reimbursing the customer for the cost of the unauthorized piece(s). But this decision backfired as well. Almost overnight, a network of unauthorized service providers sprang up to help customers simply swap out parts before bringing their Ada in for service. It also became difficult, time consuming and expensive for Eden to police their own ASPs. Many of them began taking money on the side for removing and restoring software. Others became back door dealers in the black market parts they were confiscating ...

although Eden quickly solved this problem by implementing an exchange program for the replacements. This constantly escalating, back and forth conflict between Eden and the most basic of free market dynamics went on and on, but in the end, the inescapable reality was that the bigger and more popular Ada became, the bigger, more complex and more difficult it became to maintain the kind of control that Eden insisted upon having over their products.

By mid 2036, the black market software modifications for Ada were getting extremely complex. At that point, Ada's personality subroutines were being so significantly modified that, in rare cases, with the right combination of hardware and software modifications, some Ada units were (at least casually) completely unrecognizable as what they were.

But through it all, for the most part, Eden maintained an impressive amount of control. And there was no question that, with Ada, the company had once again, completely changed the world. As the years went by, some people even suggested that the day the Ada was introduced was one of the most important moments in all of human history. There were others who disagreed with that statement. They argued that Ada wasn't the great moment in history some people claimed ... at least, not until a late spring morning in 2037, in a North Chicago suburb......

AUTHOR'S REMARKS

For those readers who enjoy special, "behind the scenes" and "special features" sorts of things, here are some additional, personal notes on Gopto that I hope you will find interesting. (Warning! you should absolutely NOT read this section until AFTER you have read the book).

The weekend before I finished the first "final draft" version of Gopto, I was in my office and, while searching through my computer's hard drive for something else, I accidentally stumbled on my very first draft of this story. It was dated January, 2011, which means that, technically speaking, Gopto took just over four years to write. However, it would be far more accurate to say that, while I was constantly turning the story over in my head for years, the majority of it was actually written in February and March of 2015. In looking back at that first draft, one of the most interesting things to me isn't how different the final version is, but rather how many of those original ideas actually found their way, in some form, into the final book.

The majority of the characters in all of my books are (with highly varying degrees of accuracy), essentially, amalgams of people I know. So if you are a friend of mine and you think you recognize some piece of yourself in one of the characters, you might be right. A notable exception in Gopto is Andy Newton, who is based mostly on me and is, at least to some degree, the character I speak through. Ironically, in that first draft I just referred to, Andy was originally a "throw away" character who was supposed to show up for a moment and then go. As the story developed, however, Andy quickly became a central part of the flow, and ultimately he helped me solve a number of *really* big problems I had with how to keep the story moving. In a way, Andy basically hung around my mental doorway and kept showing up until I figured out that he was actually one of the main characters.

Jim Landrum is loosely based on my friend and NROTC classmate, Mike Vansickle. Mike was killed during Operation Desert Storm (the character's last name comes from another good friend of mine who recently passed). When I heard that Mike had been killed, I immediately thought of President John F. Kennedy's reaction to the death of Major Rudolph Anderson during the Cuban Missile Crisis (President Kennedy is reported to have lamented that it is always the brave and the best who die). Mike was a natural leader. He was smart. Everyone liked him and he seemed to genuinely like everyone. No one was more respected and admired in our unit. A lot of Jim's character is basically an affectionate embellishment, my guess and wish for how my friend would have turned out had he had the chance to live.

Mike Powell is loosely based on my childhood friend John Powell. I hope he will be flattered by how I thought he would turn out when we were young. Even "cameo" characters are based on real people ... in fact one (and only one) is a real person. For the record there really was a LCDR Mike Todd (Chapter 4). The now retired Captain Todd was a *brilliant* Public Affairs Officer (and, for a brief time on a TAD assignment, my boss). I hope that he finds his character's role in this book consistent with his definition of an ideal PAO (say as little as possible, and then quietly recede, preferably unnoticed, into the background).

I'm also a big believer in strong female characters. I have been blessed throughout my life to have been surrounded by amazing, wonderful, beautiful, talented, and most especially, smart women. Colonel Jane Wisener, in particular, is based on a woman who was, without question, the best boss I ever had as a Naval Officer (she was also the only female, and the only civilian, I ever worked for). Her name is Judy Condra. Judy was smart, incredibly talented, and an *extraordinary* teacher. She could be either as tough as nails or as sweet as honey depending on the situation. She cared deeply for all of the men and women who served under her, and we, in turn, would have walked through fire for her. If she ever gets the chance to read this book, I hope she will feel some small part of the respect, admiration and gratitude that I and countless others still have for her.

Beyond the characters, I'm a big fan of at least some level of plausibility in the books I read (and now write), even in the obvious "suspend your disbelief" field of science fiction. As a result, it was important to me that many of the elements of the book have their basis in fact. The "setup" for the crash of the alien ship, for example, is based on a number of real life situations. I did a significant amount of research on the International Space Station before writing the prologue (which was originally two whole chapters of stuff that *I* considered fascinating, but many of my test readers found sleep inducing ... so, out it went). The SARJ on the ISS has, in fact, had the type of problem I describe. Losing tools out into space has also happened before (the incident I refer to in the prologue with the bag of tools actually happened on a shuttle mission). And, as I think everyone knows, the issue of space junk in orbit is a very rapidly growing crisis and extremely dangerous. But perhaps the most challenging part of the book in terms of plausibility involved timing. Be assured that I agonized over the exact amount of time each series of events would take. Organizing the characters and situations in such a way that the end of the story was plausible (in terms of timing) took far more planning than any other part of writing the book. This need of mine for the timing to be right is also several chapters overlap in terms of time, (it is necessary to jump around a little and show you things that are happening simultaneously).

The choice of Bonito Lake as a landing site was a mix of convenience and necessity. First, I chose the general area because I am a huge fan of the desert southwest, but especially New Mexico (and my current home town of Tucson, Arizona). The original crash site was going to be southwest of Carrizozo, New Mexico, in a spot much closer to the Oscura auxiliary landing strip.

But then I took a road trip through the area in late 2013 (so I could personally see it) and what I saw forced me to rethink that decision. In late 2014, after actively looking around for the right location for almost a year, I stumbled onto Bonito Lake and, after playing around with Google Earth for a just a few minutes, I knew that I had found the crash site.

My decision to make the base commander at Holloman the primary antagonist in the story was most emphatically *not* based on any personal experience. As a former United States Navy Officer, I have great respect for all of our men and women in uniform, and that absolutely does include *all* of the fine people serving at Holloman. The bottom line was that I needed the bad guy to be in the military, to have resources, and to be nearby.

BioSec Inc., of course, does not exist, nor does UNCLE (at least to the best of my knowledge anyway). In my mind, the BioSec campus is located immediately north of Alamogordo, up highway 70 a bit towards La Luz (this location makes the timeline I refer to above the most plausible). There was actually a backstory involving how Mike Powell knew about BioSec that I ultimately scratched from the book entirely. The idea was that he knew about it because he had done some work there a couple of years back (which may or may not have been related to an UNCLE project) ... at one point I even toyed with the idea that he knew Heather because of her ill thought out and ill fated relationship with a married coworker that I refer to in the book. As I tried to weave that into the story, however, it became a distraction, so I killed it. I also nixed an entire character and subplot involving a frustrated reporter. His story was ultimately just one too many things going on, but I liked the character and he may yet make it into a future book in this series. In any case, the mission and scope of UNCLE evolved significantly while I was writing the book. I actually began writing my next novel, ADA (the preview for which you've just read, look for the book to be released sometime in 2016), about a year before finishing Gopto. Originally, the stories had nothing to do with each other, but as I logically explored what the mission of UNCLE should include, suddenly the very simple and logical way that I have now weaved UNCLE into ADA became obvious and fun. If you have enjoyed the characters and possibilities I present regarding UNCLE in this book, then you should really like my third novel, which I'm currently hoping to have done by the summer of 2017. That story will integrate the storylines of these first two books and bring UNCLE back into the spotlight.

Finally, music is an integral part of my creative process. I spent many years of my life creating relational database management systems for businesses. And if there is one thing that I found to be universally true in the gazillion hours I spent programming, it is that there is no better aide in the world for that process than the timeless and incredible music of Jeff Lynne. For me, trying to work creatively without music is like trying to live without breathing. Of course, I'd never written a novel before, so I didn't know what music would go "with" such a process. When thinking about what music I should be listening to while writing Gopto, I wanted to find a piece of music that "sounded" to me like this book. I needed a piece of music that would get me and keep me in the mood, that would transport my mind into the world I was creating. I needed music that would give me the feeling of Gopto. I had no idea who Klaus Schulze was before I heard his music, and I can't even tell you how it was that I found it that first time, but the moment I heard the "Kontinuum" album, I knew that I had found what I was looking for. So if you're looking for a piece of music to play quietly in the background while reading this book to create the kind of mental atmosphere I was in while writing it, that's the music to go get (thank you Klaus! ... and if we ever get to make a movie of this book, I'll be in touch!).

-Duane N. Burghard

ABOUT THE AUTHOR

Duane N. Burghard is a former United States Navy Officer and two-time nominee to the United States House of Representatives. He has also started over 15 businesses and is a self-proclaimed "recovering serial entrepreneur." A highly effective and entertaining writer and public speaker, Mr. Burghard is the author of numerous essays on a wide variety of topics (many of which can be found at duaneburghard.blogspot.com). GOPTO is his first novel. He currently lives with his family in Tucson, Arizona.